THE
LEMON
CHICKEN
JONES

LES ROBERTS

THE LEMON CHICKEN JONES

A Saxon Mystery

St. Martin's Press New York

All characters in this book are fictional, and any
resemblance to persons living or dead is purely coincidental.

Design by Basha Zapatka

Library of Congress Cataloging-in-Publication Data

Roberts, Les.
    The Lemon Chicken Jones / Les Roberts.
        p.   cm.
    "A Thomas Dunne book."
    ISBN 0-312-10490-1 (hardcover)
    1. Saxon (Fictitious character)—Fiction.   2. Private
investigators—California—Fiction.   I. Title.
PS3568.023894L46   1994
813'.54—dc20   93-34886
                                                    CIP

First edition: January 1994

10 9 8 7 6 5 4 3 2 1

For Shea with love

THE CHINESE PEOPLE have a particular god for every occasion, a system that predates our current age of specialization by several thousand years. There's the Kitchen God, for instance, the Sea God, the God of Business, the God of Love and Romance, and lots of others whose names and functions elude me right now. It's a much more efficient arrangement than monotheism, when you think about it. We who worship one deity have a run of bad luck and we believe that God is punishing us because we've done something to make him angry. The Chinese, on the other hand, simply assume it is only the Kitchen God who is pissed off when the soufflé falls, and there's no reason to think that their business will fail, their ship will sink, or that they'll be unable to sustain an erection. They just eat out for a while until it passes.

I mention this because it would disturb me mightily to think that one Supreme Being looked down on me and made a special point of cooking up all the trouble I got into when Nappy Kane came into my life. I'd rather believe it was just one of many gods who was annoyed at me, and that all the others were smiling on me benevolently and watching over my soufflés. It's more comforting.

You remember Nappy Kane if you're old enough to have watched *The Ed Sullivan Show* or hung around Las Vegas in the sixties and were able to tear yourself away from the tables to see the kind of main room show where the customers wore suits and ties and shiny satin dresses and the entertainers kept their tops on. Kane and his partner and straight man, crooner Jerry Cahill, were hailed for a while as a latter-day Abbott and Costello—the slim straight man and the funny little fat guy. The truth is, they were never anywhere near that good, but they had their moments, and back when headliners didn't need a million-dollar light show and gigantic set pieces sliding on and off the stage and a chorus of thirty people behind them, Kane and Cahill got top dollar in the big clubs.

Even my assistant, Jo Zeidler, remembered Nappy, although she wasn't the least bit impressed when he called to make the appointment. But then Jo hates show business, largely because her husband Marshall has been busting his chops for years trying to get a toe in the door as a screenwriter and waiting tables in a Westwood restaurant until his big break comes along. It'll be awhile, I'm afraid—the screenplays Marsh Zeidler writes make *Barton Fink* look like *Mr. Mom.*

Andy Warhol once said everyone should be famous for fifteen minutes. Nappy Kane's fame had lasted longer than that, through the fifties and sixties. But now Ed Sullivan is dead, as is the TV variety show, and the comics who currently headline in Vegas all wear jeans and sailcloth jackets over T-shirts and make jokes about drugs and cunnilingus. Nappy Kane, with his one-liners on mothers-in-law and nagging wives and women drivers, is a dinosaur.

Personally I never found him funny. There was always

something abrasive and hostile about him. He looked funny enough, I suppose, with a face like a basset hound's, and reddish sideburns that were too long even back when everybody wore them down below their earlobes and walked around with a sneer humming "Hunka Hunka Burnin' Love." Topping them was a ridiculous blue-black rug that he might have mail-ordered from Wal-Mart along with his phony-looking dentures. In the center of all this was a prominent and unfortunately bulbous proboscis. If noses were diamonds, Nappy Kane would never have had to work a day in his life. No wonder he used to get laughs.

But there was always a nasty edge to Nappy's humor that led me to believe he was a misanthropic little son of a bitch. Now, nearly thirty years later, sitting in my office, filling the air with rancid smoke from a cigar the size of a sixteen-ounce beer can and looking at me through red-tinted glasses with his little pig eyes and a face obviously daubed with theatrical greasepaint to hide the signs of aging, my first impression was reinforced; Nappy Kane was not funny. The hangdog look on his face and the slump of his chubby shoulders made it seem a black cloud hovered over his head, ready to rain heavily on him at any minute.

Scrunched down in the chair across from my desk, he looked around and blinked as though a genie had put him there and he couldn't figure out why. Finally after about ten minutes of stalling and rattling off jokes about what the Jewish woman said to the butcher, he decided to tell me what he was doing in my office in the first place.

"This is embarrassing," he said.

No surprise there. Half my clients start out by telling me it's embarrassing to have to hire a private investigator.

That's because they've done something either very nasty or very stupid, else they wouldn't need one.

"Ease yourself," I told him. "Have some coffee and talk to me."

"What's the hurry? You got a cab waiting?" He stuck his cigar between two pudgy fingers and waved it at me, and I ducked a few gobs of spit as they flew across the desk. "I'll talk to you, don't rush me. I just want to make sure I'm doing the right thing."

I took a slug of my own coffee and sat back to wait. Nappy's personal manager, Alexander Halliday, had asked me to see him as a favor, which amused me because I'd only met Halliday once in my life and we weren't exactly on a favor basis. But a large chunk of my clientele comes from the entertainment world, mainly because when I'm not working as an investigator I do some acting myself, some TV, an occasional movie, and once in a while a commercial. Word gets around in the industry to people who know people who know other people, so when someone like Alex Halliday wants to send some business my way, I'd be a damn fool not to look into it. Hollywood is like a small town—a glitzy, egotistical, bullshit-scented small town.

So Alex Halliday knew my rep, and I sure as hell knew Nappy's: he was a scrounging cheapskate who hadn't picked up a bar tab in twenty years, who'd never bought anything at retail in his life, and who owed money to everybody in town—his bookie, his tailor, his writers. Even Alex Halliday.

"Can you be discreet?" Nappy Kane said. "I wouldn't want this all over the front page of *Variety*, y'know."

I tried not to laugh. At this stage of his moribund career Nappy would sell his own mother to white slavers to be on the front page of *Variety*, or any other paper in the world.

He'd made a modest fortune during the good days, but when he and Jerry Cahill broke up their act several years earlier, things hadn't gone well for him, and he was as cold as a Spago martini. In the current parlance of Hollywood, he was toast.

"An investigator wouldn't stay in business ten minutes if he couldn't be discreet, Mr. Kane."

"Nappy. Call me Nappy, everybody does. What do I know from investigators?" he said, making it a very dirty word. "I know laughs. I know jokes. This . . . " He shrugged as he looked around my office like it was a sewer in Beirut. That hurt my feelings. Saxon Investigations is nothing fancy, but it's not exactly Skid Row, either. "Look, I came here because Alex suggested it, but I don't like it. It makes me feel like a sleaze."

I ignored the gratuitous swipe. "I know it's never pleasant to hire an investigator, but it's probably going to help you in the long run," I told him. "Just think of me as your dentist."

One hand flickered up to cover his bad bridgework. "Whattaya mean by that?"

"What?"

"The dentist business. Is that supposed to be a crack? You start trading cracks with me, I'll bury you. Don't think I can't. Milton, Rickles, Fat Jack, they all tried to shpritz with me and lived to regret it. Now I gotta take cracks from a guy wearing a little five-dollar number he bought at Tie City?"

He put his fat cigar back between his fat lips, but it had gone out, so he relit it with a knockoff Dunhill lighter you could buy off a blanket on a New York street for ten bucks. And my tie so happened to be a twenty-five-dollar Geoffrey Beene, which shows you what Nappy Kane knew.

5

He glowered at me through the blue smoke. "I'm not sure you're the right guy to handle this for me."

"I'd be happy to recommend someone else."

"I came to you. I hear things about you, pretty good things. The book on you around town," he said between puffs, "is that you're good, you're tough, you're honest, but that you can't keep your dick in your pants."

That was about enough for me, client or no client. "And the book on you," I said, "is that you're a schnorrer who doesn't pay his bills and hasn't picked up a bar tab since Christ was a corporal. So we both fuck people—only you don't take your clothes off to do it."

His face turned dark red under the greasepaint, and his neck and chest, which were revealed by the open collar of his sports shirt, along with the fat gold chain at his throat. He put both hands on the arms of the chair as if to get up and leave. Then he sat back, and the defeated slump of his shoulders gave me a little stab of guilt. He was in trouble and he'd come to me for help, and the least I could do was make it as comfortable for him as I could, even though I didn't like him very much. If I only took on clients I like, I'd be living in a cave someplace in Arizona, weaving placemats out of tumbleweeds to sell to the tourists.

"Nappy," I said, trying one last time to save it, "let's not get off on the wrong foot here. I can't do anything for you if you don't tell me what the problem is. Just spill it, and afterward I'll let you know if I think I can help. Either way, it doesn't leave this office."

He chewed on his cigar for a while and gazed at his heavy gold Rolex watch, looked at my framed business license on the wall, stared out the window, studied his manicured fingernails as if he could read the future in them. Anywhere but at me. Finally he leaned forward and bit the bullet.

"My wife left me," he said, almost like it was an admission of some sordid sexual compulsion he was ashamed of.

I waited.

"We hadn't even been married a year. Go figure."

I waited some more.

"I just came home one day from doin' two nights in Tucson—four shows, all sold out except the early Friday one." He paused. "I was fantastic. Anyway, I do the late show, I fly home, and she's gone. All her clothes are gone. Jewelry too. And of course, her car."

"Make and model?"

"It was a white Acura Legend." He held his hands up near his ears, palms facing me. "Don't ask me the license number."

"And that's it? That's the last you heard from her?"

"End of story. Bingo-bango, no note, no message, no kiss-my-ass, nothing. And she cleaned out our joint checking account. Seven thousand bucks and change. But who's counting?" He sighed. "I didn't even know there was a problem. I mean, we got along great." He looked away. "I thought we did."

"You didn't have an argument of any kind?"

"Nothing, I swear, may God strike me dead. She drove me to the airport and kissed me good-bye, and that was the last I saw of her."

"When was this?"

He put his cigar in my ashtray, where it rested at an angle and sent a thin line of smoke up to the ceiling. "Six weeks ago. Not a word from her for six weeks. I don't even know where she is. Then I got served with divorce papers."

"Did you bring them with you?"

He opened up the worn leather brief bag he'd brought and shoved a manila envelope across my desk. "Read 'em and weep," he said.

I opened it and scanned the documents quickly. They'd been drawn up by an attorney in West Los Angeles named Yale Rugoff, and they didn't tell me much except that one Doll Kravitz had filed for dissolution of marriage from Napoleon Kravitz. Nappy had apparently never bothered to change his name legally.

California is a no-fault divorce state, so there was no complaint of mental cruelty or irreconcilable differences. Just a petition for the dissolution of the marriage.

"Your wife's name is Doll?"

"Yeah. Wind her up and she——" He stopped and looked away. It was probably the first time he'd ever aborted a joke in his life. "She's Chinese, Doll. From China. From Hong Kong, really."

"Have you met with her lawyer yet?"

"Next week. Don't bother talking to him; he won't tell me where she is, either."

"Are you sure she just left? Do you think maybe something has happened to her?"

Again he looked away. "I dunno," he said miserably.

I put the divorce papers back into the envelope. "I'm sorry about this, Nappy. I'll do anything you want."

He made a funny noise at the back of his nose, as if he was clearing his sinuses. "Reminds me of the guy walks up to a hooker, she says 'I'll do anything you want for fifty bucks.' He says, 'Okay, here's the fifty—paint my house.' "

He waited for his laugh. He's still waiting, I guess. He was quick with the jokes, that was his way of life. But I could see they masked a lot of confusion and insecurity. And fear too.

I said, "What is it you want me to do?"

"Find her," he said finally, a sad clown.

"Do you want her to come back to you?"

He shrugged.

"I probably can find her, but I can't drag her back by the hair if she doesn't want to come. You have to know that going in."

"I just wanta talk to her. I don't know what's the deal with her. I wanta know *why* she took off. I don't understand what happened to me here."

I took another hit of coffee, but it had gotten cold. I drink too much coffee anyway. "I get three hundred a day plus expenses, one week payable in advance."

He paled a little under the greasepaint. "That's no problem," he said, although he almost choked saying it.

"If it takes less than a week I'll return the unused balance," I assured him, and the deep breath he took told me that that made him feel a little better.

"Does she have family?"

He shook his head. "She's from Hong Kong. I brought her over here." He grinned sheepishly. "She was a mail order bride."

"You're kidding!" It came out before I could stop it, but the information set me back on my heels. That a wealthy, semicelebrity like Nappy Kane would have to marry a woman he'd never met was hard to believe.

He picked up his cigar and puffed at it noisily, waving the smoke away from his face, and unfortunately right toward mine. "You gotta understand about me. I was married once before, back in the sixties. She was a dealer at the Sands in Vegas. It didn't last very long, because she was a money-grubbing bitch, like most American women. A Jewish girl. I should've known better.

"Hey!" he said, and took his handkerchief out of the breast pocket of his blazer. "You know what Jewish girls always say after oral sex?" He took a mouthful of his coffee and said, "I love you," letting the coffee dribble out through his lips and down his chin to where he held the handkerchief.

There's nothing sadder than a comic who doesn't get an expected yock. Awkwardly he wiped off his chin and stuffed the handkerchief back into his inside jacket pocket. "Anyway, I'd been single since then. But I always had a real thing for Chinese girls. They make me crazy, no kidding. During the Vietnam thing I went over a couple of times to entertain the troops, y' know? Me and Jerry. And they're all so beautiful and quiet and mellow, those girls. I mean, they treat their men like they were gods or something. And I used to think, wouldn't it be great to be married to somebody like that?"

"And you thought about it for twenty years?"

He opened his arms wide, the smoke swirling. "I'm a cautious guy, what can I tell you?"

I clicked a ballpoint pen into working order and pulled a yellow legal pad in front of me. "Start with how you met her."

"This is really humiliating," he said. He dug into the brief bag and fumbled around for a while, finally coming up with a four-page brochure.

I took it. It was headed ASIAN NIGHTS and featured about sixty black-and-white photographs of mostly young and pretty Asian women, along with brief descriptions of each: *Blossom (21) Taiwan. 5'2", 115 lbs. Loyal, caring, loving. Likes bowling and cooking. Gloria (25) Korea. 5'4". Enjoys sports and bicycle riding. Hopes to meet a man with a warm, loving heart.*

Another sheet of paper with no photos enjoined the reader to subscribe to the service, which promised letters from "sincere, marriage-minded Oriental ladies" from nearly every free country in the Far East, ladies who didn't care who you were, what you looked like, how old you were, or how much money you made, and who "respect and admire American men." At the bottom of the page was an application blank, and on the reverse side was a price list: deluxe membership, regular membership, a pamphlet on where to find "an Oriental dream wife," and various combination packages. The whole tone of the brochure was condescendingly racist, as though these women were simple-minded peasant children who could be bought with a smile and a Hershey bar.

The kicker down at the bottom was that the more you paid, the more letters you got from women. Asian Nights had a post office box in San Angelo, California.

"This isn't very much information to go on about a woman you're going to marry."

"Yeah, when you send them money they give you a lot more details, and letters the women wrote, and you start corresponding with the ones you're interested in."

"That's how you did it?"

He looked down at his lap, obviously mortified to tell the story. "I wrote to three of them, one from Malaysia, one from Korea, and Doll. She thought my letters were funny. They were," he added defensively. "The way to a woman's heart is to make 'em laugh. So I quit writing to the other two."

I studied the pictures in the brochure. The women were all smiling. Maybe they'd heard Nappy's act. "Where did you hear about Asian Nights?"

"Saw an ad in a magazine," he mumbled. I could imagine what kind of magazine.

"You think only a loser would have to pick a wife through the mail," he said, and it wasn't a question.

"What I think isn't important."

"It's not like I never met her before we got married. I mean, we spent three weeks together first. It wasn't so different from a lot of people I know, except for the way we first got together."

I waved the brochure at him and his eyes followed it like a concertmaster's follows the conductor's baton. "Is one of these women Doll?"

He shook his head no.

"Where is San Angelo? I never heard of it."

"I dunno. I just mailed them a check and they sent me back a bunch of letters and pictures."

"Can I keep this brochure?"

His face fell, and he looked every bit of his sixty-plus years, makeup or no. "I don't need it anymore."

I took a blank file folder from my drawer, labeled the tab NAPPY KANE, and slipped the brochure inside. "Do you have a picture of your wife? One you can leave with me?"

He dived into the brief bag once more and came up with three photographs. One, matted in a cardboard folder, was obviously their wedding picture, Nappy wearing a dark suit and a yarmulke, Doll in a green satin dress adorned with a huge orchid corsage. She lived up to her name, with a pretty round face framed by a Prince Valiant haircut. She looked about twenty-four.

The second was a snapshot, taken on the terrace of a high rise overlooking the Pacific. Doll was in tight blue jeans and a white sweater, and the wind was tossing her hair. In that one she looked like a high school girl. It was hard to tell with nothing to measure by, but she seemed very short and petite.

The third photo was a black-and-white glossy eight-by-ten head shot, obviously taken professionally in a studio. Doll was heavily made up, her lips glossy and her eyes dreamy and sexy. It looked like the kind of picture you see displayed outside dollar-a-dance joints.

I looked up at Nappy, and he said, "That's the picture that Asian Nights first sent me. She's a knockout, huh?"

I nodded. "I'll make copies of these and return them."

He looked nervous. "Don't lose 'em, all right?"

"Who were her friends, Nappy? People she spent time with, girlfriends?"

"She didn't really have any of her own. I mean, her friends were my friends, the people I know."

"Like your former partner?"

He turned from basset hound to pit bull. "Jerry? Miserable wop son of a bitch, he should die with a hard-on!"

"You're not in contact with him, then?"

"We got nothing to say to each other."

"I didn't know you broke up the act with hard feelings."

He bit down on his cigar as if it were a Tootsie Roll. "Lots of 'em. Goddamn cooze-hound, that's what he was. I got sick of him moving in on me every time I got interested in some broad, or she got interested in me. That's all he ever thinks about. Jerry Cahill has been down longer than the *Andrea Doria.*"

"You broke up over a woman?"

He twiddled his thumbs over his stomach. "A lot of women. A lot of years, a lot of women."

"Your wife?"

He jumped as if I'd touched a boil. "Forget it, okay? They

13

don't even know each other. Jerry and I were quits before I ever met Doll."

"Okay, forget Jerry," I said, although I had no intention of doing so. "Does Doll have a problem with the English language?"

He looked at me as if I were a moron. "Hong Kong is a British colony," he said, "at least for the next couple of years. She talks English better than me."

"What did she do with herself, with her time? Who did she see?"

"Nobody. She never went anywhere on her own except to the store. That's the way she was; she devoted her whole life to me. That was the beauty part." His eyes teared up, and he snuffled and blinked, hoping I wouldn't notice.

"What about when you were out of town working?"

He shrugged. "I don't know."

"Girlfriends?"

"Not really. Once in a while she used to have lunch with Rebecca Cho. She's an actress, she's on a soap. Doll knew her in Hong Kong, I think."

I asked him for the spelling of Rebecca Cho's name and scribbled a few more notes. "Can you get me copies of your telephone bills for the last six months?"

"Why?"

"I'd like to know who she was calling, especially when you were out of town."

He puffed up like a corn fritter dropped into hot peanut oil. "You think she was seeing somebody? Listen, if you think that, you're fulla shit!"

"I'm not assuming anything. But she left without a word and took everything with her; she had to go somewhere."

His head bobbed in full agreement. "Everybody's gotta be

somewhere. Look, I don't have those phone records. I don't pay bills, I have 'em sent to my business manager."

"And who's he?"

"John Garafalo Associates in Beverly Hills."

I gulped at that one. John Garafalo was an old-timer, like most of his high-profile movie and television clients, and it had long been rumored around town that he got his start back in the early sixties as an accountant for some very heavy people in Vegas. The rumor was unsubstantiated, but in Hollywood, where everything is written on the wind, a rumor is nearly as good as something graven in stone.

"Look," Nappy said, "you don't have to call him up or anything. I'll take care of it." He gnawed at his lower lip. "You really think that's necessary, the phone bills?"

"If we find out who she called, we might get some idea where she went."

All the air went out of him again, and his chin dropped onto his chest. "Yeah, all right," he said.

I took a standard contract form from my file cabinet and filled it in with his address and phone number—his *private* number, he took great pains to tell me—spelling out the exact terms of our agreement. He signed it with a flourish, as though giving me an autograph.

"So whattaya think?" he said.

"I don't know yet. Are you telling me everything?"

"Meaning?"

I sighed. "The more I have to go on, the faster I can get this done for you. If you don't level with me, it isn't going to work, and we can tear this contract up right here."

I could tell he was fighting a little private war within himself, deciding whether he should reveal something he'd rather keep secret. He patted at his face, his eyes searching out every corner of the room as though looking for a hidden passage through which he could make his escape. Finally he said, "There is one other thing you probably oughta know."

He seemed to grow smaller in the chair, aging in front of me like the Man from Half-Moon Street. "About three months ago . . ."

My pen hovered over the legal pad. "What?"

"Well, listen, I'm a lot older than her. It only made sense that I'd probably go first, you know? I . . ." He'd started to sweat, and he wiped a hand across his brow, smudging the greasepaint and almost dislodging the bad toupee. "I put everything I had in her name. The condo, the stocks and bonds, even the car I'm driving. Everything."

I put down the pen. "Oh, Nappy," I said.

"A stupid yutz, huh?" He looked pained and lost all of a sudden, and his hand went to his throat, unconsciously stroking the pouch of skin there.

"Nappy, you've been scammed. Royally."

"You don't understand," he protested. "I'm an old cocker, all right? And I wasn't much to look at when I was thirty, you wanta know the truth. I'm not exactly a hot ticket in the business anymore, either. So it isn't so easy finding someone you can love. When you do, you hang on to her any way you can."

"And you figured you could do that by turning over the keys to the vault?"

By way of reply, he ground his cigar out in my ashtray. He really didn't have to answer me; we hold some truths to be self-evident.

"Was that her idea or yours?"

He stuck out a pouty lower lip and cast his eyes down again. Obnoxious as he was, and as badly as his cigar was stinking up my office, I felt sorry for him. "Okay, Nappy," I said. "We'll take a run at it."

He stood up, shook my hand, thanked me, and started to leave.

"Nappy?"

"Speaking."

"You forgot to write me a check."

After he left and I'd made out a deposit slip for his advance, I sat for a few minutes looking at the faces of the smiling Asian girls in the brochure. It had all the earmarks of a classic scam, proving once again that no matter how rich and famous you become and no matter how old you are, somebody out there has your number.

I got up and went out into the anteroom to give Jo the check to take to the bank and the photos of Doll Kane to have copied.

Nappy Kane was still there, hanging over Jo's desk, waving his cigar in the air.

"So anyways," he was saying, "this Jewish guy goes into a bar, and on the stool next to him there's this luscious-lookin' broad . . ."

Jo looked over at me. Her eyes were rolling like a pair of dice on a Las Vegas crap table.

2

YALE RUGOFF, A sweaty, overweight lawyer somewhere in his middle thirties, was losing his hair and his waistline at approximately the same rate. He wore the blue pants and vest of a discount store suit and his tie knotted ever so slightly askew under his multiple chins, to convey that this was a very hardworking and busy man. On the phone he'd agreed to give me only five minutes, which I suppose was meant to further that impression.

But he wasn't fooling me. He was strictly a low-rent guy. His office was in a stucco building on Santa Monica Boulevard near the West Los Angeles–Santa Monica border, the kind of structure they'd thrown up in the postwar building frenzy of the late forties and tried to pass off as authentic Spanish. His desk was metal, his appointment calendar had come from the drugstore, and the law diploma on his wall was from a college in Missouri I'd never heard of. He had the look of the nebbishy kid everyone else used to beat up on in junior high school.

There are certain professionals, some attorneys and doctors and college professors and business executives, who are so impressed with their own importance and convinced of their own superiority that they treat you like pond scum because you aren't in their little select fraternity, making you simply want to swat them like mosquitoes. And even though he had neither the appearance nor the personal presence to pull that attitude off, Yale Rugoff almost buzzed. He spoke like he had a mouthful of spit.

"I don't even have to talk to you, y'know," he reminded me before I sat down. "I'm just extending a courtesy."

Put in my place, I could but nod.

"Now let me understand; you represent Nappy Kravitz? Nappy Kane, excuse me."

"I'm a private investigator," I said. "I don't represent him, I work for him. I'm trying to ascertain the whereabouts of Mrs. Kane."

"And what business is that of yours?"

"Let's not waste each other's time, counselor. I don't care at all, personally. But Mr. Kane does, and he's paying me to find out. I'm told that when he asked you, you withheld the information."

"And you figure that even though I wouldn't tell him, I'd tell you?" He gave the kind of phony laugh you use when you're talking to your boring uncle at your sister's wedding. "You still believe in the Easter Bunny too?"

"No, Mr. Rugoff—but I won't tolerate a discouraging word about the Tooth Fairy. I was hoping you and I could reach some sort of understanding."

The laugh dried up and blew away like the last leaf of autumn. "You want to know where Mrs. Kane is and I'm not going to tell you. You understand that, or shall I use smaller words?"

He was too fat to intimidate me. "I think the man has a right to know where his wife is, don't you?"

"Not legally, no."

"Morally, then?" He started to say something but I raised a hand to stop him. "Sorry, I forgot where I was."

He gave me a wounded look. "You going to do lawyer jokes? Kane did, when I talked to him on the telephone. That old one about the snake and the skid marks. Do you believe that?" He leaned back in his chair and laced his fingers together behind his head. There were round wet stains under his arms. "He doesn't have the right to know anything his wife doesn't want him to, and that includes her whereabouts. Women aren't chattel anymore, they aren't their husbands' property. Don't you know that? This is the nineties."

I snapped my fingers. "Right, the nineties. I read about it in the paper."

He smiled, having made his point. "There you go, then."

"Nappy Kane's a very sad man, Mr. Rugoff. He loves his wife and misses her. She just left his bed and board with no notice—not even any cause, as far as he's concerned."

"Oh, there's a cause, all right," Yale Rugoff said, stretching his hands high above his head and grunting comfortably. "There's always a cause. I'm not only a divorce lawyer, but as an undergraduate I majored in psychology. So it's my business to know about people, about relationships. And if there's one thing I've learned, it's that no one can ever know what goes on behind the closed doors of somebody else's bedroom." He pointed a pudgy finger at me. "I'm speaking in generalities here, not specifics."

"Am I to understand that Mrs. Kane is *never* going to talk to her husband?"

"Never is a pretty big word, Mr. Saxon. Suffice it to say that I represent Mrs. Kane, and any communication between them will be funneled through this office."

"Suffice it to say? And you're sensitive about lawyer jokes!"

Even he smiled at that one. He decided to switch tactics—now it was going to be just between us guys. "Can I get a break here? Look, don't give me a hard time; my mom had her heart set on me going to law school."

"That explains it," I said. "So are you telling me that Mrs. Kane is your principal client?"

He hesitated for the flicker of a hummingbird's wing. "I represent Mrs. Kane's interests."

That wasn't what I'd asked him, and I filed the discrepancy away in my little book of memories. "Mr. Rugoff, are you aware that all the Kane assets—assets that Mr. Kane had before he ever met his wife—have been put in Mrs. Kane's name?"

Licking the canary feathers off his lips, he allowed me a small, pitying smile. "That's what I've been told. Of course we'll do a thorough search before we go to court to ascertain what belongs to who. We don't want to be unfair—"

"An attorney, unfair? Perish the thought."

He squinted at me in a misguided attempt to look tough. "Be careful," he warned me. He pulled the Sav-On-Drugs appointment book toward him and flipped a page. "I'll be meeting with Mr. Kane at noon next Wednesday," he said. "Or with his attorney; as he wishes. He's welcome to ask anything he wants at that time."

"And will you answer him?"

"I'll do whatever Mrs. Kane wants," he said. "Till then, I think you and I have finished our business, don't you?" And he closed the appointment book with a thud, for emphasis.

I stood up, effectively dismissed. "One more question?" I glanced at my watch. "I still have twenty seconds."

He rocked forward in his chair. "You have exactly what I want to give you, Saxon, and at the moment that is exactly bupkes!"

I shrugged. "Okay," I said. "I'll just have Mr. Kane's business manager contact you and ask you instead. John Garafalo?"

I couldn't swear to it, but I think his sweaty face got a little sweatier. He gnawed on the inside of his bottom lip, and he must have dislodged a tiny piece of skin, because he chewed for a second or two. "Okay, one more question," he grudged. "But no more lawyer jokes, okay?"

"Have you ever heard of Asian Nights?"

An extra crease appeared between his chins as he lowered them onto his chest and thought for a minute. Then he raised his eyebrows in a misfired attempt to look innocent. "Sure I have. Scheherazade and Sinbad the Sailor?"

"Minored in literature, did you, Mr. Rugoff?"

In Los Angeles, August brings deadly air, worse than at any other time of year. Inversion layers lock the smog in as though someone had lowered a giant lid onto the Los Angeles basin. You smell it, taste it, feel it sting your eyeballs, and see it in the air. Yellow-brown—the color of things you don't even want to think about. The smoke from the Rodney King riots of 1992 was hardly noticeable what with the crap we have to breathe every day.

Especially in Burbank, where the studios of Triangle Broadcasting are located. The sea breeze that tanned and impossibly beautiful surfers ride in from the west blows all the air pollution in the county across the city and into the curve of the Santa Monica Mountains, where it is trapped in Burbank at the southeastern end of the San Fernando Valley. Burbank people aren't really as sad as they look—their eyes are simply tearing from the smog.

I know a lot of people at Triangle because I've acted in several TV shows over there. I was also neck-deep in a murder involving some of their top executives a few years back. Most of the people from that case are gone now, moved on to other jobs at other networks and film studios.

But Jay Dean, who is in middle management and has for twenty-two years survived the musical chairs game that networks play, is a particular buddy of mine, and after ascertaining that Rebecca Cho was one of the stars of *Love Conquers All,* a Triangle soap opera, I'd called him to get me a drive-on pass to admit me to the parking lot. Otherwise I would have had to stand in line with the tourists from Iowa who think seeing a television show being produced in the studio and watching somebody win lovely parting gifts on a no-brainer game show is pretty hot stuff.

Jay was waiting for me at the entrance to studio C, puffing on the briar pipe that years ago had taken up permanent residence between his teeth. He had on a tweed jacket over a white shirt and a drab tie. He's managed to keep the same job at Triangle all these years by dressing down, never calling attention to himself, never making a decision, and never expressing an opinion unless he's sure it coincides with those of the big shots at the far end of Executive Row, where the offices all had private johns and showers. Jay's ass hasn't been uncovered since they took him out of training pants.

"Whatever you're doing isn't going to blow up in my face, is it, guy?" he said, shaking hands. He called people "guy" a lot. "You're not going to spring it on me that Rebecca Cho smuggles heroin or leaks state secrets to Iraq?"

"I just want to ask her about a friend of hers, Jay. It's one of those domestic disputes. I can't tell you any more, but it's not going to turn into a network scandal, if that's what you're worried about."

He crossed himself and we went into the studio, ignoring the flashing red light telling the world they were shooting. You can do that when you come from Executive Row, even if you use the same john as the peasants.

The set on which they were videotaping *Love Conquers All* was surprisingly cheesy to the naked eye, although when viewed on the large color monitor just out of the light it looked like the penthouse terrace it was supposed to be. Three actors in poses of tension were cheating their bodies to get as much of their faces as possible on camera: a dark-haired young man with a fashionable five o'clock shadow and a thin leather jacket with no shirt under it, a busty blonde in a floor-length satin robe with not much of anything under it, and an exquisite, willowy Chinese woman I took to be Rebecca Cho.

"Christian, you must tell Quinn," Cho was saying to the man in a low, husky voice with a slight, intriguing accent. "You can't let him marry Kelsey thinking Lacey is really his baby."

The blonde said, "When he finds out she's really Kirk's daughter it'll kill him."

"Quinn is my brother!" the man said through clenched teeth. "How can I hurt him like that?"

"It'll hurt a lot worse if he finds out after the wedding," Rebecca Cho told him.

"Leticia is bound to hear about it," the blonde said. "And

when she does, there goes Quinn's contract with Heathcott Industries. He'll be ruined."

"It's your responsibility, Christian," Rebecca Cho said. "If he marries Kelsey, *it will be on your conscience.*"

She turned and walked through the French doors at the rear of the set. The two remaining actors looked soulfully at each other, then the blonde hurled herself into the man's arms.

"Oh, Christian—hold me!" she begged.

The camera zoomed in for a tight close-up of their kiss. Open mouths but no tongues, not even in a tight close-up.

After about twenty seconds, an electronically augmented male voice boomed out across the studio, "That's got it, kids." It sounded like the word of God—if God had a Jersey accent. "Let's do lunch. Back at one thirty."

The two actors broke their passionate clinch, suddenly ignoring each other, and walked toward the studio door as if they'd never even met, scooping up their scripts from a metal table. Apparently love *didn't* conquer all.

Rebecca Cho came out from behind the set and walked toward us. Close up she looked older, maybe in her mid-thirties, but still very beautiful. Her jade green dress emphasized her sultry good looks; her shiny black hair was pulled back into a fashionable knot.

Jay Dean introduced us. He'd called her on the set earlier that morning and told her I was coming.

"I'm happy to meet you, Mr. Saxon," she said. "How may I help you?"

Stagehands and electricians were swarming all over the set, looking busy. Except for the ones drinking coffee and playing pinochle. I said, "Is there someplace we can talk privately for just a few minutes?"

"Why don't you come down to the dressing room? I have to change for lunch. If I spill anything on this dress before the next scene they'll have my head."

"You don't need me anymore, do you?" Jay said. "I've got a meeting in fifteen minutes."

A meeting. It figured. If they ever decide meetings are illegal, the entertainment industry would shut down tighter than a kosher butcher shop on Yom Kippur Eve. I thanked Jay and followed Rebecca Cho out of the studio and down a long corridor. Her heels clicked loudly on the linoleum. The doors on either side all had gold stars on them, and slots holding cards on which were printed two names.

"I'm sorry I don't have a lot of time," she said over her shoulder, "but I have a scene to learn, so . . ."

"Five minutes is all I'll need," I said. I was beginning to think I might have to compartmentalize my whole life into five-minute segments, since no one seemed to want me around for longer than that.

She stopped at the door that bore her name and that of Mindy Minor and opened it just a crack.

"Min?" she called out. "Are you decent?"

"Nobody ever accused me of *that* before," a woman's voice said from inside. "Do we have company?"

Rebecca pushed the door open. A pug-nosed redhead was sprawled on the sofa inside, a paperbound script in one hand, a lipstick-stained plastic coffee cup in the other. I assumed she was Mindy Minor. She was wearing gray sweatpants and a chocolate and orange Cleveland Browns sweatshirt that made her hair look even redder. Another midwestern kid who'd chased her dream to Hollywood.

When she saw me she swung her legs over the edge of the

sofa and sat up. "Oooh," she said. "They're making stage-door Johnnies better than they used to."

I introduced myself as Rebecca disappeared into the bathroom with a change of clothes.

"Don't tell me you're a fan of this piece of shit?" Mindy said, holding up her script. "You look like you'd have better things to occupy your time than *Love Conquers All*."

"So do you."

She stood up, closing the script. "It's a living. I work two days a week and they pay me enough to feed my habit."

"What habit is that?"

"Eating," she said. "I'm one of the lucky ones. I could be wearing an ugly uniform and asking people if they want fries with their burger. Instead I'm Sue Ellen Heathcott, quintessential spoiled-brat kid sister on *Love Conquers All*, and every time I cash my paycheck I can delude myself for a while longer that I'm doing something meaningful with my career."

"I know—I do some acting myself."

"I'll just bet you do," she said. "Are you a friend of Bec's?"

"Not exactly."

She had twinkly brown eyes and she turned them on me full force. "Then what exactly?"

"Business."

"You don't moonlight as an insurance salesman, do you? I couldn't stand it, a cute guy like you talking about term life."

I hate being called cute, but the way she was looking at me, she could have used any adjective she liked. "Nothing like that," I said.

"Mysterious too." She smiled. "I like that in a man."

27

"You like everything in a man," Rebecca Cho said, coming out of the bathroom in designer jeans that left little to the imagination and a soft beige cashmere sweater that left a lot. She carried her costume on a hanger. "Min, could you give us a couple of minutes alone?"

Mindy looked at her watch. "The proverbial nooner, huh? Right on time." She took up a brown eyebrow pencil and scrawled a phone number on a corner of the back cover of the script, ripped it off, and stuck it in my jacket pocket. "Give me a call sometime, and I'll tell you what's going to happen on the show next month."

"I'm dying to hear about it."

"Mindy," Rebecca said, an edge of exasperation creeping into her soft low voice.

"I'm going, I'm going," Mindy Minor said. "But if I get ptomaine poisoning from the meat loaf in the commissary, it's on your head." She turned to me, eyes twinkling at a million candle power. "Call me, okay?" She walked out of the dressing room with a toss of her red hair.

Rebecca carefully hung her dress up on a metal rack in the corner. "Sorry. Min's a sweetheart, but sometimes her brat kid sister act wears a little thin." She seated herself at one end of the sofa. "Now," she said.

I took one of the straight chairs from in front of the makeup table and sat down. "Rebecca, I'm a private investigator."

She looked startled. Apparently Jay Dean had just asked her to spend a few minutes with an acquaintance of his without telling her who I was. I showed her my license, which she examined carefully before handing back.

"I don't think I've ever met a private detective before," she said. "Is this an official visit?"

"It's a business visit," I said. "I understand that Doll Kane is a friend of yours."

She blinked once. "Yes?"

"Do you happen to know where she is?"

"Me? No, why should I?" She picked at a flake of polish on one long fingernail. "We're not so close that I monitor her movements, Mr. Saxon. She's only been in this country a short while, and I'm the only other Chinese person she knows that doesn't work in a restaurant. She needs someone to talk to who shares her background. It was natural that we become friends."

"Where did you meet her?"

She had to think about it. "Her husband was doing some game show here, and she came to see the taping. We ran into each other in the ladies' room and started talking."

It's a puzzling thing in our society that everyone wants to downplay the real differences between men and women, when it's obvious that they are practically two different species. I can't imagine any innocent scenario that would prompt two unacquainted males to strike up a conversation in a public john, much less a friendship.

"So you're originally from Hong Kong too?"

Rebecca fixed me with a hard stare; I was amazed how well she did it. Of course, she was an actress, and could summon up any look she wanted. "Can I know what this is all about?"

"It seems," I said, "that Doll has disappeared."

Concern creased the space between her eyebrows. "I don't like the sound of that."

"Don't be frightened. She's left her husband and filed for divorce, but he has no idea where she went. He's very worried, as you can imagine, and he's asked me to help find her."

She sat down on the sofa. "Why come to me?"

"When I asked Mr. Kane for the names of her women friends, yours was the only one he came up with."

She shook her head slowly. "That's very sad, isn't it, that he couldn't think of anyone else? It says a lot about the way she was living, the way he treated her. She was like a toy he'd take out and play with and then stick back on the shelf. He had no idea of her needs or desires—they just weren't important to him. Well, I'm sorry, but I don't know where she is either."

"When's the last time you saw her?"

"I can't remember. A month ago, maybe two. Our pattern was to have lunch maybe once a month, but I've been really busy." She patted her script on the arm of the sofa. "Julie Huang—that's my character on the show—Julie has been very heavy in the story line lately, and when I'm not here at the studio I'm home learning my lines."

"Have you heard from her at all?"

"We spoke on the phone two weeks ago. About."

"She didn't say she was separated from her husband?"

"That's not something I'd forget."

"Did Doll ever tell you anything about her marriage? Did she ever say anything about not being happy?"

She compressed her lips into two straight lines, giving her for a moment the unsettling appearance of a pen-and-ink drawing. "What's your definition of happy? Her husband was nearly forty years her senior, Mr. Saxon. That kind of marriage has its inherent problems for a young, healthy girl."

"Did she ever mention wanting to leave him?"

"Not to me."

"What about other men? Was she seeing anyone?"

Cho laughed. "Doll was an old-fashioned Chinese woman."

"Chinese women don't play around on their husbands?"

"Sometimes they do, I suppose, but they certainly don't talk about it."

"Loss of face?"

Something happened to the muscles beneath her skin, tightening it unpleasantly. "That's dangerously close to an ethnic slur, Mr. Saxon."

"It wasn't meant that way. I'm just trying to figure out why she left without a word, and where she might have gone."

"If it was her wish that no one know her whereabouts, you certainly won't get any help from me. Doll is my friend, and you aren't, so you can see where my priorities lie." She rose, her script rolled up in her hand as if she were going to swat the dog for peeing on the carpet. "I really must ask you to leave now. I have lines to learn."

I gave her a business card: SAXON INVESTIGATIONS, printed in raised blue lettering on a discreet gray background. "If you hear from Doll again and you find out where she is, will you get in touch with me?"

She stuck the card into the pocket of her jeans, though there was barely room in there for it. "Not if she doesn't want me to," she said.

I went up to Jay Dean's office to ask for another favor, and then went back downstairs to the publicity office and cashed it in by picking up a press bio on Rebecca Cho. I also got the one on Mindy Minor, just for the hell of it.

I mean, I was there anyway.

3

WEST OF THE San Diego Freeway and past Brentwood
with its trendy restaurants and gourmet food shops, San
Vicente Boulevard turns into a wide, tree-shaded avenue
where each morning hundreds of early morning joggers
trample flat the grass on the median strip with their Reeboks
and Nikes. Why anyone would want to exercise vigorously
and breathe deeply in the middle of one of Los Angeles's
most heavily traveled streets is beyond me. Maybe they think
filling their lungs with exhaust fumes is good for them; people who'll eat kelp and drink carrot juice will believe anything.

The houses lining either side of San Vincente are often as
big as those in Bel Air but aren't perceived as being quite so
fashionable and so are assessed at about a million dollars less.
Most of the residents are not in show business but do normal,
nine-to-five things with their lives, so at two in the afternoon
there wasn't much traffic. I lazily followed along behind a
red Porsche with a personalized plate that read HIATUS. Either the driver's TV show was on vacation or he was announcing to the world that he suffered from a hernia.

I found Jerry Cahill's house easily.

It was at the top of a small rise on the north side of the

street, a pleasant-looking gray stucco built some time in the early fifties and surrounded by willow trees and jacaranda bushes and tropical palms transplanted from somewhere else. A few dry, burned patches on the front lawn were mute testimony to the killer drought that gripped California for the past several years. The whole southern part of the state is an ecological time bomb; between the lack of water, unbreathable air, ridiculously overcrowded freeways, ugly racial tensions, and the coming earthquake—the long-predicted "big one"—I wonder why any of us live here. Masochism, perhaps, or mass denial, or the eternal optimism that tonight oil wells will suddenly gush skyward in our backyards or that a career-making phone call is sure to come from our agent tomorrow.

I'd called Cahill and identified myself as a private investigator who wanted a few minutes of his time, without telling him what I was investigating, but he'd agreed to see me, probably because not that many people called him up anymore, for anything.

There's nothing sadder than a show business has-been. At least a washed-up athlete understands that it's because he's grown old and can't do what he did when he was twenty. But for an actor or singer or comic there is the bitter knowledge that they've simply gone out of fashion and nobody wants or remembers them anymore. How many people that were celebrities in the sixties and seventies, whether trendy comics or top-ten recording artists or sitcom stars, have you seen working within the last few years? Some of them have gone back to wherever it is they came from or taken jobs selling real estate in Sherman Oaks. The smart ones—all three of them—saved their money.

Jerry Cahill, né Catalano, was the same age as his former

partner, but he wore the years better. He was about my height, a tick under six feet, and he'd lost little of the dark curly hair, now flecked with silver, that had been his trademark as a ministar in the era of handsome Italian boy singers in the Las Vegas and Reno lounges, before he'd teamed up with Nappy Kane to feed him the straight lines and sing a few ballads in between yocks. "Can't Take My Eyes Off of You" had been one of his biggies, I recalled, but even on his best day Jerry Cahill wouldn't have made anyone forget Frankie Valli and the Four Seasons.

Now, with layers of fat around his neck and jaws and waist and wearing a black velour pullover with no shirt under it so that the gray hair on his chest poked out over the neckline and an Italian horn on a thick gold chain, which glinted in the grizzled nest, Jerry Cahill resembled nothing more than a Brooklyn restauranteur who'd taken early retirement.

We sat on white wicker furniture drinking vodka on the rocks in a glassed-in garden room at the back of the house, overlooking a yard richly planted but not well cared for. The tropical shrubs and palms, drooping bottlebrush, a scraggly lawn, and a hedgerow with what looked like terminal root rot were all browning from thirst. All over every wall in the house were framed photos of a much-younger Jerry Cahill with people like Milton Berle, Jerry Vale, Mitzi Gaynor, Wayne Newton, Vikki Carr, and Steve and Eydie—the usual Las Vegas show room contingent. Surprisingly, there was one of Jerry with his arm thrown around George McGovern's neck.

Notable by their absence were any pictures of Nappy Kane.

"Nappy and I aren't exactly pals anymore," Jerry said, sipping his drink. "He dumped me, y'know, just when things were going great. Man's a big goddamn baby, that's all. He and I never really got along, even when we were on top. We're just different kinds of people. We came from the same kind of background—I'm a guinea from South Philly and he's a Brooklyn Jewboy—so we should of understood each other better, but somehow we never really did."

"But you were partners for nine years?"

"Yeah, but we never hung out. It's okay, I guess, it even worked better for the act. Gave us an edge. But you know comedy teams. They all hate each other—Abbott and Costello, Martin and Lewis, all of them. I resented his getting all the attention because he was the funny one, and he didn't like it that I got all the broads because I was handsome and had hair. We were on a collision course for quite a while, and it got pretty tense there toward the end."

He rattled his ice cubes, put the glass to his lips and sucked one into his mouth, munching it noisily. "But that's part of life, right? Differences. We could've worked it out if we'd wanted to. If Nappy wasn't such a loser. We owned the world, and then he hadda get thin-skinned and blow everything."

"It was Nappy's idea to break up Kane and Cahill?"

"Damn right it was," he said. "You don't think I'd kill the golden goose, do you?"

I didn't bother telling him he'd screwed up the metaphor.

The wicker creaked as he eased back in his chair. "Back in 'seventy-one, it must of been, we went over to the Far East to entertain the troops during the war. You know, I did a few songs, we did our shtick, we had a couple girl dancers in skimpy costumes, a six-piece combo. Something for the boys. I mean, we didn't have any Miss Universe or Les

Brown and His Band of Renown or anything, but it wasn't a bad little show."

"Vietnam?"

"We never went to 'Nam," he said. "Too dangerous. We didn't wanta get shot at, even if Maggie did."

"Maggie?"

"Martha Raye," he explained. "She spent more time in Vietnam than General Westmoreland."

"Oh."

"So we stayed out of the combat zone, but we went to the R and R centers, the staging areas. Taiwan, Hong Kong, like that. And Nappy got crazy about those cute little girls over there. Like a kid with a new toy, y'know. You'd think he'd spent his whole life in a cave or something. I mean, Nappy was never very good with the chicks—the way he looked and all. If he wasn't a star, he couldn't of gotten laid in a women's prison with a pocketful of pardons. But those little Chinese girls just blew him away."

He leaned forward again, warming to his subject. "After we come back he always went for the slopes."

"Asians," I said.

"Huh?"

" 'Slope' is kind of an insulting word, isn't it?"

He put his hand into the neck of his pullover and scratched an armpit. "Who can keep track anymore of what everyone wants to be called? It changes week to week, y'know." He finished his drink and got up to make himself another one from a rolling cart in the corner, forgetting to suck in his gut. He was drinking vodka, Absolut, and this time he didn't add any ice. He drank half of it while he was standing there and then refilled his glass.

"So from that time on Nappy only chased the sl—the

Asian ones." He leaned on the word so I'd know he was being politically correct. "Even when he bought a hooker, she was Chinese or Japanese or Filipino."

I didn't tell him that the correct term was Filipina. "Did he go to prostitutes a lot?"

"If you looked like him, you would too. Hey, listen, everybody's gotta do their own thing. Me, I never hadda pay for it in my life. But Nappy, that's another story altogether. It was no skin off my ass, what did I care?" He sat down again, heavily. His face was gradually taking on a dark alcohol flush.

"So," he said, back on track, "it's 1985, we're playing the main room of the Flamingo, and Nappy gets silly about some little chickie dancing at the MGM Grand. Korean, I think this one was." He frowned. "I don't remember her name. Susie something. Susie Wong, maybe?" He brayed an unpleasant laugh. "Anyway, he takes her out a few times, she gets a night off, and he brings her to see our act, and—hey, what can I say? Could I help it she liked me better?"

I knew what was coming.

"So I nailed her." He was almost preening, a man in late middle age gloating over his past sexual conquests and getting sloshed at three o'clock in the afternoon. "I'm only human, for Christ's sake. She was a knockout. Normally I like the big blondes with the legs that go all the way up, but this one was grade A finest kind."

"And Nappy found out about it."

"Jesus, he pitched a fit. Even took a swing at me in our dressing room, the shit-for-brains. I used to box when I was a kid, Police Athletic League and that, so I knocked him flat on his ass. It was touch and go if his nosebleed was gonna stop in time for us to do the midnight show." He chuckled.

"And when a nose that size starts to bleed it makes the Johnstown Flood look like a trickle."

"And that's what broke up a million-dollar-a-year act?"

He gulped so much vodka it made his eyes tear. "Right then—ten thirty at night—he got on the phone with his lawyer to dissolve the partnership. We even hadda cancel all our future bookings—Reno, Tahoe, Miami, The Front Row in Cleveland, and the Music Fair in Jersey. We were doing good back then." He screwed up his mouth, and I could see beneath the fat and the wrinkles the traces of the tough Italian kid from South Philly. "I sued the little son of a bitch for all that money, all that lost income. And I won too."

He sat quietly for a moment, remembering the days when he was a star and people would line up around the block to kiss his ass. Then he said, "Now I sing at industrial conventions or on an occasional nostalgia package show, and Nappy hangs around the Friars Club playing gin with Milton and those guys. Two careers in the shitter, and for what?"

"You tell me," I said.

"I wish I could, pally. Look, I've got no complaints. I know my limitations. As a singer, I couldn't carry Sinatra's jock. But for a guy with a minimum of talent, I had a pretty good run—better than most. I'm no kid anymore, and sooner or later the career probably would have died a natural death anyway. But hey, the house is paid for, I lease a new Caddy every three years, and I work enough to keep me in Absolut. It's not bad. But it still doesn't keep me from hating Nappy Kane's guts."

"So you haven't seen much of him since the breakup?"

"I'd walk across the freeway through rush-hour traffic to avoid him. We're what Walter Winchell used to call 'don'tinvites.' " He waved his glass at me. "I run into him once in a while, by accident, maybe someplace like Nicky Blair's, but we usually don't even talk. We nod, but we don't talk. Maybe because we got nothing to say to each other."

"Do you know his wife?"

He sat silent and motionless for about five seconds, staring out the window at the browning garden; he could have been posing for Mount Rushmore. "I've met her once or twice at big parties," he said, all at once guarded. "Why?"

"Did you try to 'nail' her too?"

He glared at me and then looked away again; then macho pride loosened his tongue. "Damn tootin' I did. I'd hit on Hulk Hogan if he was with Nappy—I hate the son of a bitch. Paybacks are rough." He considered it for a while, nodding grimly, relishing the thought. Then he said, "Nothing ever came of it, though. She's a quiet one. Kind of standoffish. Either that or Nappy warned her not to talk to me."

"Did you know she'd left him?"

"I heard it through the grapevine," he sang, and did a seated version of the Motown shuffle. It was pretty grotesque.

"Have any idea where she might be?"

He stopped boogeying and set the drink down on the table, hard enough to send some of it sloshing over the edge onto his hand. "How should I know?" he asked, licking it off. Waste not, want not.

"I don't know. That's why I'm asking."

"You got the guts of a burglar, coming in here and accusing me—"

"I'm just asking a question."

"Ask it somewhere else," he said, pushing himself to his feet with effort. He was starting to slur his words a little, and his *s*'s were acquiring *h*'s. "I'm tired of talking about Nappy Kane. Ruined my life, the stupid dick!" He looked out the window, where an orange cat shadow-boxed with a hovering butterfly. "If she ran out on him, it serves the little bastard right. He don't deserve being married to a nice woman like that."

I stood up too. "You ever been married, Jerry?"

Without taking his eyes from the window, he said slowly, "A long time ago. Lasted a couple of years, and then I threw her the hell out of here." Then he turned to face me squarely, his fists on his hips. "You know what that bitch called me?"

I shook my head.

His tone was that of a man about to speak the unspeakable. "She called me a—a *lounge act!*" he said.

Jerry Cahill's house wasn't that far from mine if you drew a straight line on a map. Unfortunately I can't get home on a straight line and so fussed and sweated through a half hour's drive in the late afternoon rush hour. Of course, it's always rush hour in Los Angeles, even at two o'clock in the morning, but between four and seven P.M. heading toward the beach in an automobile is an exquisite kind of torture. Most of the way I found myself stuck behind an old Chevy bearing two bumper stickers; one said I LOVE TIJUANA, with a red heart in place of *love*, and the other proclaimed I LOVE JESUS. I would have thought that the two were mutually exclusive.

I rent a house in Venice, which is a beachside community just south of Santa Monica. Its fame derives mostly from Ocean Front Walk, with its bicyclists and roller skaters and itinerant jugglers and musicians, its street vendors in their open tents selling everything from LIFE'S A BEACH T-shirts to sunglasses to cheap electronic audio equipment from Taiwan to some interesting pharmaceuticals, and its one remarkably good bookstore, Small World Books and Mystery Annex. The outdoor cafés that dot Ocean Front Walk are relentlessly awful unless you're into grease, but if you enjoy people watching, there's no better place in Southern California. When viewed at a distance, from the water's edge, Ocean Front Walk is colorful, quaint, and bustling. It's not until you get up close that you realize how tawdry it is and that the people, even the young ones in their scanty bathing suits, firm flesh well displayed, are all burn-outs. Even the "straights," citizens who live elsewhere and lead perfectly respectable lives, come to Venice for a Sunday outing at the shore and take on a certain sleaziness.

And there are the canals. They were built early in the century in hopes of turning the community, named for the Italian city on the Adriatic, into a tourist paradise. But it didn't catch on, and now Venice is home to a few families and a lot of fairly disreputable folk who spend their days and nights in pursuit of mind-altering substances, sex, and a tan. My house is on one of the canals, the Howland, and of a warm evening, sitting outside and watching the ducks is infinitely preferable to anything the TV networks have come up with.

The only reason I own a television set at all is my son, Marvel. He pronounces it to rhyme with "do tell," with the accent on the second syllable. He's eighteen years old, as near as we can figure; we celebrate his birthday on the same July day mine falls on because we don't know when his real one is. He's an African-American, handsome as O. J. Simpson and nearly as athletic, with a quick true wit

Nappy Kane would have killed for. I met him while I was on the Triangle Broadcasting case and adopted him a few years later, which took both of us by surprise, since my careers as an actor and as a private investigator seem to require as few ties as possible.

I've never regretted it. Marvel and I have a lot of fun together, since we share a lot of the same interests, namely sports, food, and the opposite sex. And if once in a while he plays his boom box at a level that threatens my hearing or leaves his shoes around for me to trip on or eats me out of house and home, what he's brought to the party has more than made up for it. He's one of the kindest and most caring kids I've ever met, and considering his background that's an amazing thing. Any time you feel like you're having a bad time of it, let me sit you down and tell you a little about Marvel before he came into my life. It'll make you feel lucky.

When I got home from Jerry Cahill's, Marvel wasn't watching TV, nor was he out by the garage shooting hoops. He was sitting at the dining room table with a pencil in his hand and a frown of concentration on his coffee-colored face, college catalogues spread out in front of him. He'd passed his high school finals two weeks ago and was considering where he wanted to go to continue his education. We figured we'd start small, with a community college in the city, and after a year or two he could decide whether he wanted to go on and what he wanted to do with the rest of his life. For a kid who couldn't even read five years before he'd learned very quickly and was now pretty much a straight-B student except in math, a subject that always defeated me too.

Do I sound like a proud father?

"Hey, Jefferson!" That was Marvel's own particular spin

on the old hipster's greeting, "Hey, Jackson!" He figured Jefferson was as good a president as Jackson, and it was different enough, just slightly off center, to appeal to him. Marvel is his own man and never does things the way anyone else does them.

"When's dinner?" he said.

"I just walked in the door!"

"I'm hungry."

"I can see you're wasting away to a stick." I riffled through the mail. A few bills, a lot of junky ads, an invitation to invest in a new mutual fund, and a letter from an old girlfriend, Kim, a petroleum engineer whose relationship with me had ended with brave smiles and stiff upper lips when she'd decided to spend two years down in Guatemala looking for oil.

All the bright ones leave eventually, the ones with fire and brains who always have something to talk about; it's the flakes, the airheads, and the Twinkies that hang on, call up on a Sunday morning "just to see how you're doing," bring over plates of tollhouse cookies and a small pot of African violets in the middle of a ball game, and send hopeful, treacly Thinking of You greeting cards years after the dance has ended. They were all nice enough people, but in any relationship you eventually have to get vertical and attempt a conversation, and that's where the trouble starts. I suppose that says something about me, but I choose not to deal with it.

I pulled a John Courage out of the refrigerator and read Kim's letter, smiling as she extolled the delights of living in a tent and shaking scorpions out of her boots each morning. I guess the old song is right—"for every girl who passes by I shout, 'Hey, maybe . . . ' " But with Kim I'd really thought there was going to be something at the end of the road. Unfortunately, we wouldn't go down it together.

"How 'bout Chinese?"

I looked up from the letter. Marvel was leaning over the counter that separates the kitchen from the dining room.

"How 'bout you whip up some lemon chicken? I got me a real jones for lemon chicken, or some other kind of Chinese."

"Jones" is street slang for an addiction. It pleases Marvel to talk like a jive-ass most of the time, although when he wants to, he can sound like James Mason. And he's more than a little manipulative when it comes to getting what he wants.

"Just like that, huh? I don't have any chicken in the house, and I don't have any lemons, either."

"Aw. Gee, I guess we'll have to eat out then."

"Think you're smart, don't you?"

"I *know* I am," Marvel said. "We talkin' about degree here."

I glanced up at the clock on the wall. It was a little after five. "Let me make a call first," I said. I took out my little pocket address book, pulled out the antenna on my cordless phone, and tapped out Nappy Kane's number.

"Yell-o!" he chirped.

I winced. My father always says yell-o! when he answers the phone, and it bugged hell out of me when I was a kid. The old man and I have finally reached some sort of rapprochement after half a lifetime of estrangement, but it still drives me ballistic whenever anyone says yell-o!

"Nappy," I said, fighting back my annoyance, "did you get those telephone bills for me?"

"What telephone bills?" He was trying to sound vague and not doing a very good job of it.

"The ones I wanted from your business manager."

"Oh, those," he said.

There was such a long pause that for a moment I thought I'd been disconnected.

"Nappy?"

"Speaking."

"The phone bills?"

"Oh. Uh, there's a little problem about that."

"What?"

"John Garafalo doesn't want to release them."

"Release them? They're yours. They belong to you."

"Uh, well, we don't really need them anyway, do we?"

I held the bottle of John Courage to the side of my face. The house isn't air-conditioned; being so close to the ocean, we rarely need it. But I was working up a sweat with Nappy Kane and the frosty brown glass felt good against my cheek. "I wouldn't have asked you for them if I didn't need them."

"Whattaya want from me, blood?" he shrieked. No one screams like that on the phone unless they are severely unbalanced or very frightened. I held the receiver away from my ear. I've managed to save my hearing thus far by strict avoidance of loud rock and roll—no mean feat when you live with a teenager—and I didn't plan on losing it because some hysterical out-of-work comic felt the need to shout into the telephone.

"Nappy, you want me to find your wife or not?"

He caught his breath, and when he spoke again it was with low, intense desperation, as if he was making a supreme effort not to cry. "Jesus, yes. She's the best thing that ever happened to me. She's what I been looking for all my life. You gotta find her for me. You just gotta!"

Marvel, it seemed, wasn't the only one with a jones for things Chinese. I said, "Then you have to help me out."

"Anything," he pledged.

"Get me those phone bills."

"Enough with the phone bills already!" He was yelling again, only now it seemed anger was increasing the decibels. "Garafalo don't wanta give me the phone bills. So call me pisher!"

"Nappy . . ."

"Don't bust my chops, all right? You just figure out some other way to find her. You're the detective. What the hell am I paying you for?"

As he slammed down the phone, I wondered the same thing myself.

4

IT MUST BE nice being rich enough to need a business manager. For those who are, it's almost like having a mother. Your BM keeps you on an allowance, pays all your bills for you and invests whatever is left over, holds your hand when your Disney stock dips a point and a half, puts you into tax shelters, and once in a while makes you the part-owner of a cattle ranch or a gypsum mine or a winery in Sonoma County that's bound to lose money, giving you a nice write-off and making things a little more comfortable for the cattlemen, who are also the business manager's clients. Every so often they pocket considerably more than their allotted percentage, but most business managers are honest enough. Everyone who's anyone in the entertainment industry has a business manager, and a damn good thing too, because most actors aren't capable of any financial undertaking more complicated than putting quarters into a condom dispenser.

I got to the offices of John Garafalo Associates at about eleven o'clock the next morning. They were housed in a big sand-colored building on the corner of Wilshire Boulevard and Peck Drive, a very substantial Beverly Hills address, if things like that mean something to you, and if you live in this town they do. They were only on the fourth floor, a disap- pointment, since I'd expected the penthouse, but they took up the entire floor, so in the display-of-conspicuous-wealth- and-power department, that almost made up for it. The office was decorated with discreet good taste; nothing in it smacked of Garafalo's purported wise-guy connections.

I told the gorgeous brunette at the reception desk that I'd like to speak to Mr. Garafalo.

She flipped open a daily log, bound in leather as if it were the Domesday Book, and ran a blood-red false fingernail down the columns. Watching her try to type with those acrylics would have been a morning's entertainment. "Mr. Garafalo can't see anyone without an appointment," she finally announced.

"I'm a private investigator," I said. "Please tell him I'd like to speak to him about Nappy Kane."

"Will you have a seat, please?" she said, and pointed me toward a bank of chairs along one wall. The magazines on the coffee table, *Fortune* and *Business Week* and *Time,* were all current, unlike the ones in my dentist's office, which date from the Reagan administration. I was impressed, but of course that was the general idea.

The receptionist picked up the receiver from the Monop- oly board–size console on her desk, pushed a few buttons, and turned her head away from me to speak into it softly. Then she hung up and said, "Mr. Garafalo can see you for a few minutes. This way, please."

Her nylons whispered a siren song as I followed her down the hushed corridor to Garafalo's inner sanctum. It was that kind of an office, and she was that kind of a receptionist. Through open doors along the hallway youngish men and women, dressed in Beverly Hills upwardly mobile office chic,

48

could be seen talking on the telephone or playing with their calculators, or both.

Garafalo himself had the gray pallor of a man who has spent his life crunching numbers. Somewhere in his late fifties, slim and stoop-shouldered, he combed his thinning dark hair across his head to camouflage his white scalp. His nose was prominent between cheeks once ravaged by acne and left deeply pitted. The rimless glasses were too small for his face; he would have looked better in heavier frames.

He would also have looked better if he'd been happier to see me—one of the drawbacks of my profession is that people rarely are. As it was, despite the fact that there were two brocade chairs in front of his desk, we conducted our brief interview standing up.

I showed him the photostat of my PI license, which he examined without much interest, and after giving it back he crossed his arms across his chest defensively and asked what he could do for me in a way that let me know in no uncertain terms that he really didn't want to do a damn thing.

"I've been retained by Nappy Kane," I told him.

He nodded sagely. "To do what?"

"I can't tell you," I said. "But it would be easier if I could get hold of the telephone bills Nappy asked you for."

He recoiled as if I'd requested classified files in connection with the proposed invasion of another oil-rich emirate in the Persian Gulf. "I'm afraid I can't do that."

"Why not?"

"I'm not going to blithely turn over financial records to you just because you ask me," he said. "It doesn't work that way. Clients put their trust in us because we're good at what we do, and because we're discreet. We have to maintain confidentiality. That's our job." He'd obviously worked hard to get rid of his New York accent, but not quite hard enough. A few dentalized *t*'s crackled in his speech like rifle shots.

"Mr. Kane tells me you refused to give them to him either. And they do belong to him, not to you. That strikes me as a bit unreasonable, Mr. Garafalo."

"I don't give a flying Wallenda how it strikes you," he said, his mouth turning mean. "Who the hell d'you think you are?"

"Somebody who's supposedly on the same side as you, although you'd never know it."

"What side is that?"

"Nappy Kane's."

"Well, you watch your tone with me, mister. I'll decide what's unreasonable and what's not. You understand that?"

Looking at Garafalo I was sure that his so-called "mob connections" were not those bonds of blood and fealty you see in Al Pacino movies. He'd merely been an accountant for them back in New York. Nonetheless, like most of them, he deluded himself into toughness. He probably had visions of himself picking up the phone and ordering a hit on me if I talked out of turn, and though my experience with the Outfit is practically nil, I know they don't go around icing people for being rude to an accountant.

Nevertheless, I cast down my eyes and nodded my head. I'd get more out of him if he wasn't mad at me.

Once I'd shown the proper respect, he spoke to me with infinite patience, as though he were consciously trying not to use any multisyllable words. "All of Nappy's records—and there are a lot of them, he's been with me for more than twenty-five years—are being packed up and will be shipped to his home as soon as possible. We can't go poking through all those cartons looking for a few random scraps of paper—

50

it would take forever. Until the documents are ready to be released, it isn't going to speed up the process any by sending over the hired help."

I ignored the dig. "All his records are being sent to him? Why?"

"We have no use for them anymore."

"You mean he's no longer a client?"

The embryo of a smile played at his mouth as he peered through his thick glasses. The lenses enlarged his eyes, giving him a hyperthyroid appearance. "He didn't tell you?" He chuckled, and it came out pretty nasty. "He's such a putz. Yes, we severed our business association about two weeks ago."

"Why?"

"You'll have to ask him that. I don't discuss clients' business with outsiders, whether the clients are past or present."

"Twenty-five years is a long time. Did he fire you, or did you fire him?"

"You'll have to ask him that too."

I sighed. "All right, I will. But wouldn't it be more friendly if you just told me and saved me the trouble?"

He cocked his head to one side like a dog that's just heard a peculiar sound. "Let's just say there wasn't too much more we could do for him."

"You mean, now that the marriage is splitting up and Mrs. Kane owns just about everything except his shorts."

The bright sunlight from the windows flashed off his glasses as he moved his head, making them opaque. "You're very well informed," he said.

"That's *my* job."

"Nappy Kane, like so many people in the industry, has absolutely no sense when it comes to money," he said, spreading his hands wide. "That's why he turned his affairs over to me. But he didn't ask my advice when he put everything in his wife's name. If he had, I would have told him he was crazy. In fact I told him anyway, but he didn't listen." A sorrowful look crossed his face for a moment; the foibles of humankind obviously gave him pain. "Love has a way of clouding the more practical issues, doesn't it?"

"So you dumped him? After twenty-five years?"

"I had no other choice. Loyalty is a lovely virtue, but I have to be realistic. It takes almost as long to service a pauper as it does a potentate. When Nappy signed away the family farm, it left Doll with everything he owned and him with nothing. And five percent of nothing is nothing, if I know my rudimentary math. I'm running a business here. In the name of efficiency I have to prioritize my time. It's only fair to my other clients." His fingers went to the knot of his tie and dithered there.

"And would those other clients happen to include Mrs. Doll Kane, Mr. Garafalo?"

His pasty face got even pastier. "That's none of your business, Mr. Saxon."

I was hungry, so I stopped into the Hamburger Hamlet on Beverly Drive. It sounds like a burger joint, but it's really one of a chain of medium-priced restaurants, and the food is pretty upscale. Their menu features "lobster bisque famous for this," with no punctuation, and "onion soup fondue one of the best," as well as a variety of sandwiches, salads, and omelettes, and something I've never tried that the bill of fare archly calls "those potatoes."

You'd be amazed at how many different ways you can

order a burger. I chose the one with blue cheese and bacon, and washed it down with a vanilla Coke. There are few places left in the world that make vanilla Cokes; they evoke my Chicago boyhood, when drugstores had soda fountains and a Coke with a squirt of vanilla or cherry syrup that sank to the bottom and could be sucked out of the last remaining ice chips cost only a dime.

Poor Nappy Kane, with his bad toupee and his baleful basset face. He flushes his career away over his obsession with Asian women, and when he finally finds one to love, not only does she run out on him, taking everything he owns with her, but then his longtime business manager drops him, probably replacing him on his client roster with his soon-to-be-ex-wife. A double betrayal. No wonder he drags that black rain cloud around with him all the time.

I opened my briefcase and took out the TBC press biography of Rebecca Cho. Marvel had been so anxious to feed his lemon chicken jones at the Chinese restaurant on Santa Monica Boulevard that I hadn't had the chance to look it over the night before. There was a studio portrait, a head shot that made her look exotic, and a one-page printout.

> Rebecca Cho—Bec to her pals—brings a wealth
> of experience to the demanding role of Julie on
> LOVE CONQUERS ALL. A native of Hong
> Kong, she migrated to Los Angeles six years ago
> and immediately caught the eyes of the casting
> directors of such shows as M*A*S*H, CHINA
> BEACH, and JAKE AND THE FAT MAN
> before finding a home at Triangle on their
> long-running daytime drama.

In addition to her LOVE chores, Rebecca makes frequent guest-starring appearances on nighttime dramas, and acts whenever she can in local theatre productions around Los Angeles.

Rebecca's first love is cabaret singing, and she's chirped at most of the elegant boites on the West Side and on Ventura Boulevard in the Valley.

Her favorite actor is Bob De Niro and her favorite car is anything with a convertible top. She jogs at least four days a week, loves to cook, and tells us she's pretty handy around the house with a hammer or a screwdriver. She has to be, she says, because she's single, and still looking for that special fella. Rebecca has twice been nominated for an Emmy for her work on LOVE CONQUERS ALL, but she says her greatest ambition is to someday win an Academy Award.

Bob De Niro? Where, I wondered, do they find the people that write these things? "Elegant boites"? I haven't encountered that phrase since I cancelled my subscription to *The New Yorker* fifteen years ago. "Looking for that special fella"? I doubted Rebecca Cho was doing so, and that she ever said any such thing. And all that business about jogging and loving to cook sounded just like the come-ons in the Asian Nights brochure.

The scary thing is that all the Hollywood flacks who crank that crap out daily are writing novels in their spare time.

I opened my notebook and jotted down *R. Cho—sings?* Maybe she'd be more amenable to conversation when pursuing her "first love." I'd make a point to find out what club she was working and go check it out. As I put her bio back into my briefcase I noticed Mindy Minor's beneath it. The photo was of Mindy smiling broadly, the kind of girl you marry and have children with, but the press release was written in the same florid prose style. I smiled to myself, which caused two leathery-skinned Beverly Hills matrons wearing tennis whites and munching on avocado omelettes to look at me strangely.

I drove over to the offices of Pacific Bell, the local telephone company. Pac Bell has its problems these days; they recently added a brand-new area code, the third within the city limits, and with it came a lot of confusion, outraged customers, and a snafu that could only occur in a city whose population grows at such an alarming rate that every ten years or so there aren't enough telephone numbers to go around.

Bettyann Karpfinger is one of the supervisors or managers or something. I'm not exactly sure what she does, but she has an honest-to-God office with her name on the door, and when she spends too much time at the coffee machine the bosses don't glare pointedly at their watches, so I guess she must be pretty important.

Bettyann's son Roger, who has the kind of dazzling and unfathomable mind that can make a computer do just about anything except the lambada, had gone through the last four years of school with Marvel, and they'd become best friends. I'd met Betty at an open-house night when we were listening to the school psychologist talking in euphemisms like "intellectually challenged" and "difficulties with social intercourse among peers," which translates that some poor kid is not only stupid but he gets into fights a lot, and our eyes just happened to meet as we both got the giggles. She's divorced and has a huge belly laugh, which booms forth at all the same things I find funny, is a 197-average bowler, a dedicated umpire baiter at Little League games, and works as hard at being a parent as anyone I've ever known. She's also adamant that the *p* in Karpfinger is silent.

We've done a few joint outings with the boys at Dodger Stadium, rented some videos and sent out for pizza a couple of times, but somehow Bettyann and I never got any further than that. Maybe because we didn't want to jeopardize Roger and Marvel's friendship. Or our own.

"What a terrific surprise!" she said when I stuck my head around the door of her office.

Her nose crinkles up when she smiles. She's not beautiful, but she's terminally cute, especially when she does that with her nose. She has terrific dimples too. And cheekbones. I have a thing for cheekbones.

I sat down on a vinyl-covered metal chair I was sure had been designed for efficiency: no one would want to stay in it for more than ten minutes. "Actually, I need a phone company kind of favor."

She frowned. "Oh-oh."

"I'm working on a case. My client's wife walked out on him and he doesn't know where she is. I'm trying to locate her."

Resting an elbow on top of her desk, she put her chin in her cupped hand. "You've got to be kidding," she said. "You know we can't give that kind of information out, not since that actress got murdered a few years ago."

"Bettyann, I'm not going to kill anybody."

"But I don't know that your client isn't. I'm sorry, I really can't. Please don't make it an issue, okay?"

"How about this, then? Without telling me her address or even her number, could you just give me a yes or a no as to whether she's ordered telephone service in the last few weeks?" I saw that she was about to shake her head so I rushed on. "You won't be violating anyone's confidentiality, you won't be telling me how I can reach her. I just want to know if she's still in Los Angeles. Please?"

She mulled it over. "It's my ass if they find out."

"I'm not going to tell anyone," I assured her. "Besides, it's a nice ass."

She picked up a pencil and tapped her front teeth with the eraser. "If I didn't like Marvel so much, I'd kick you the hell out of here," she said after a moment, pulling a scratch pad over. "What's the name?"

"Kane," I said. "Or maybe Kravitz. First name Doll."

"Doll? What kind of a name is that?"

"She's Chinese. Her husband used one of those mail order introduction services to import her from Hong Kong."

She scribbled it down. "Within the last six weeks?"

"Make it eight, just to be on the safe side."

"Thank God for computers, huh?" She tossed me a mimeographed employee newsletter. "Here. This'll take a few minutes."

She left me reading about the plans for the upcoming Independence Day employee cookout in Griffith Park. It sounded like fun, if you're into charred hot dogs and seventeen different varieties of potato salad and tossing water balloons and running in three-legged races.

Bettyann came back fifteen minutes later, empty-handed. "No Doll Kane, no Doll Kravitz."

"Damn! That means she's either left town or she's moved in with somebody else."

"Maybe she doesn't have a phone."

"Not likely."

She cocked her head, thinking. "Could she have gone back to Hong Kong?"

"The whole point of marrying a perfect stranger for most of those women is that they can come to the States to stay. Besides, she's now a very rich woman. She owns a condo, cars, stocks; she wouldn't leave the country. At least, not till after the divorce is final."

"Did it ever occur to you that someone might have taken her against her will?"

"I doubt it. She filed for divorce six weeks after she left. Whatever might have happened since then I don't know."

"There is another possibility," Bettyann said. "Big smart detective like you, I'm surprised you didn't think of it."

"What's that?"

She sat back down behind her desk, smiling with undue satisfaction. "She just left her husband, right? Maybe she reverted to her maiden name. What is it?"

I had to admit that I hadn't the foggiest idea. I picked up the phone on her desk and dialed Nappy Kane again. He wasn't in, so I tried the Friars Club. The Friars is an old and respected organization for show people, strictly stag and pretty raunchy sometimes—their dinner tributes, or "roasts," are legendary for their scatological content. I've been to one or two myself, as a guest—I'm not much into joining clubs—and have to admit they were very special and screamingly funny evenings.

The Friars operator said he'd page Nappy and put me on hold. The music that played in my ear as I waited was big-band stuff, probably Harry James, apropos for the average

age of the members. After a few minutes Nappy came on the line.

"Yell-o!" he said. Naturally.

I told him what I wanted.

"Why do you need to know her maiden name?"

"It might help me find her." I didn't tell him about my visit with John Garafalo.

"I don't see how her maiden name's going to help."

"Nappy, it'd make my job a hell of a lot easier if you didn't make me justify everything I ask of you."

"Listen," he said, "you interrupt a gin game to ask me a damn dumb question—"

"How'd you like to get yourself another investigator? Who'll ask half the questions and charge twice the money?"

"Don't get excited," he said.

"I'll try not to."

After a pause he said, "It's Cheung."

"Spell it."

He did. "I still don't see why you need to know that."

"Nappy, let's make a deal. You don't tell me how to do my job and I won't try to punch up your jokes. Okay?"

"Saxon," he said after a pause, "you're starting to get on my nerves."

Bettyann disappeared again to run a check on Doll Cheung, and since I'd already read the newsletter from cover to cover I didn't have anything to do. Private investigating in the movies is exciting and glamorous, but in real life it's a lot of sitting around waiting for something to happen.

"I checked all the way back through the middle of March," Bettyann told me when she came back, "and nobody named Doll Cheung, or anything Cheung, applied for new service in our calling area. I'm sorry. I wish I could have helped."

Even negative information was something of a help, since it eliminated several possibilities. I invited Bettyann to bring Roger over that evening for a couple of ordered-in pizzas and the viewing of a video, perhaps something with pizzazz and a lot of excitement for the boys, just to show my appreciation and gratitude.

"Stuff your pizzas!" she said. "This was a big favor. For this, you're going to cook."

People seem determined to get me into the kitchen these days. I'm a damn good cook, but most of the time I don't because it's too much trouble. However, I owed her. "You drive a hard bargain," I said. "I'll cook Italian. Seven o'clock?"

She shook her head ruefully, but her eyes were dancing. "I hate myself for selling out so cheap."

5

ROGER KARPFINGER IS a solidly built kid, about four inches shorter than Marvel, with a blond buzz cut and a well-developed set of muscles he tones each morning with his own weights, blowing hell out of the stereotype of the nerdy computer genius. After four years of going through school together, he and Marvel knew each other so well they finished each other's sentences. There was a third member of their little hunting pack, a serious-minded Mexican-American kid named Amador Felipe, who was hell-bent on being a brain surgeon and had been welcomed into UCLA's premed program with open arms. The three of them palling around together in a mall or at the beach—a blue-eyed blond, a Latino, and a rangy young black—looked like a bad sitcom.

But Ami worked evenings at a local Burger King and couldn't make it for dinner that night, so it wound up just the four of us sitting on the floor around the coffee table in my living room. I didn't have the time to fuss too much, so I did a pasta casserole with four different cheeses, mushrooms, and diced olives, topped off with cream and a dollop of cognac. I fixed some hot Italian sausages on the side, which I simmered in red wine and onions, plus a big green salad with jicama and cucumbers and a homemade vinaigrette. I don't bother making desserts—I leave that to the Betty Crocker crowd—but I did serve ice cream, chocolate for Marvel and some sort of praline swirl for the rest of us. The whole meal was enough to clog anyone's arteries for a month, but Marvel and Roger are too young to worry about their cholesterol count, and I figured the bottle of dark purple Chianti classico Bettyann and I split would serve as a sort of arterial Roto-Rooter.

Conversation eventually got around to Nappy Kane. I don't talk about my work at home, even though Marvel is a lot more fascinated with my investigating business than he is with my acting career. But because Bettyann had kind of a rooting interest, having put her job in jeopardy trying to get information for me, the subject was bound to come up.

I started at the beginning for the benefit of Roger and Marvel, who had never heard of Nappy; they weren't around during his glory years, and since he was never on MTV or the Comedy Channel or Arsenio Hall, he might as well have been a silent movie star. Bettyann remembered Cahill and Kane from television when she was a kid, but she couldn't begin to visualize how Nappy looked today, old and defeated and ridiculous.

"How could anyone that rich be stupid enough to put everything in his wife's name?" she said, munching on a half pecan she'd discovered in the ice cream. "God, when my husband walked out on me he barely left enough for the rent."

Roger had been half lying on the floor, propped up on an elbow, but he sat bolt upright in a modified lotus position and stuck out his chin. "Is this gonna be dump-on-Dad time again?"

"Nobody's dumping," Bettyann said with a trace of heat.

"Sounded like it to me."

"But let's not be afraid to look at the truth, okay?"

I jumped in quickly to stave off what was obviously an ongoing argument in the Karpfinger household. "Nappy's a tired old man," I said. "He thought it was a grand, romantic gesture to sign everything over to her—and that it was the only way he could keep her. If anything happened to him he didn't think she could handle probate and things; he did it out of the goodness of his heart, because he never believed she'd leave him."

"When you're married you never really believe that," Bettyann said wistfully.

"But you say this guy's a star," Marvel chimed in. "He's been around. He's too old to fall for that happily-ever-after crap."

"*Was* a star. Now he's a funny-looking old guy in love with a dream."

"And the dream has disappeared," Bettyann concluded.

I nodded. "Into thin air."

"And took the family jewels with her," Roger added.

Marvel gurgled down the remains of a can of Pepsi and crushed it in his hand, looking around for approval as though it had been made of galvanized steel. "Maybe she split back to those people."

"What people?"

"Those mail order people, where whatsisname—"

"Nappy."

"What kind of name is Nappy? Anyway, maybe she went back to where he found her in the first place. If she's not here and you don' think she's in China, maybe that's where she is."

Roger punched Marvel on the arm. "Excellent," he said. "That's excellent, Marvel. Sure she'd go running to them if she wanted to hide from her old man. They'd be the only people she knows." He turned to me, spilling over with eagerness and the enthusiasm of the very young. "Where are they? Maybe I can tap into their computer."

"That's illegal, Roger."

"Well, excuse Roger all to hell," Marvel said, rolling his eyes skyward. Marvel often finds succor from the strain of living with me by looking to the ceiling.

"Wait a minute!" Bettyann was almost as excited as her son. "I'll just bet Marvel is right. Sure, that's where she went. How can we check it out?"

I uncoiled myself from the floor and went upstairs to the small den I'd set up under the eaves in what used to be a storage area. When I'd lived alone in an apartment in Pacific Palisades, I'd worked wherever I felt like it, in the living room, in the kitchen, even in a hot soak in Epsom salts with a flute of champagne on the edge of the tub. But since Marvel came into the picture and we'd moved to Venice, I'd had to make adjustments.

I rummaged through my briefcase for the Asian Nights brochure, and brought it back downstairs. The boys were all over the photos at once, picking out the prettiest faces and the best figures, too young to know they were being sexist pigs. Not that they would have cared.

"No street address," I told Bettyann. "Just a post office box."

"They probably don't want to encourage walk-in business," she said, finally getting the brochure away from her son. "San Angelo, huh? I don't even know where that is."

"It's up north," Roger offered. "Around Sacramento

somewhere, by the delta." What Roger Karpfinger doesn't know isn't worth knowing.

"No phone number, either." Bettyann wrote *Asian Nights, San Angelo* on one of the unused paper napkins and stuffed it into the pocket of her jeans. "When I get to the office tomorrow I'll check if they have a listed phone. But I doubt it."

"If not," I said, "I'll take a run up there to see if I can find her."

Marvel turned to look up at me and leveled a graceful finger at the middle of my chest. "Aw'right! When we goin'?"

"We?" I said.

"Yeah."

"Where do you get this 'we' stuff?"

"It was my idea."

"So?"

"So?"

"So thank you," I said.

"So let me come along."

"No way."

"Way!" he said. He'd been watching too much *Saturday Night Live.*

"I don't know what I'll be getting into up there, Marvel. It could get rough."

He grinned a satyr's grin. "You look to me like if it did you could use you some muscle. Too much pasta, ol'timer. You gettin' ol' an' soft."

"I'm not going to put you into a situation where you might get hurt."

His big brown eyes locked on to mine, and I knew I was going to take a hit. That's the look Marvel always gives me

65

before he shoots me down. "No biggie," he said quietly. "I been hurt before."

I reached for my wineglass, a life preserver on my troubled sea. "We'll talk about it later, okay?"

Marvel's face was absolutely still, like an ebony carving you pick up in one of those African craft shops in Westwood Village. Then he got up, said "Shit" very quietly, and went down the hall and into his bedroom. He didn't slam the door.

He didn't have to.

After a while of counting the seconds of our lives, Roger uncoiled himself from the floor. "I'll go talk to him," he said.

I stood and watched him go. To fill up the tense silence he'd left I said, "You want some more wine, Bettyann?"

"There is no more."

"A cognac?"

She shook her head.

"A Pepsi? Milk? How about a glass of water?"

"Sit down," she said.

Here comes another shot over my bow, I thought. I sat down on the sofa and she slid over and sat at my feet, resting an elbow on my knee. "Ever since you put Marvel into the Bishop School and he and Roger became buddies, I've been watching him. Five years ago he was a scared, abused kid who couldn't read, barely talked, and jumped at shadows. He was that way for a long time. I've seen him grow and blossom. It's been incredible. He's reading college catalogues, for God's sake."

"I know," I said thickly. "I'm very proud of him."

"You should be. You should be proud of yourself too, because you've helped him become who he is."

"Is this conversation going to center around what a wonderful human being I am?"

Bettyann wasn't charmed. "Hardly. Because every once in a while, you take off. You've been to Mexico on a case, two weeks in Chicago, six weeks in Minnesota doing a movie, and you leave him with me, or with your secretary and her husband."

"I took him on location to Arizona with me last summer."

"Arizona in August—what a treat!"

"It's what I do, Bettyann. I don't work nine to five at a desk. Sometimes I have to be away."

"I know. And I watch Marvel when you're gone too. On the surface he does his macho number, and most people don't notice that underneath the cool and the hip there's that scared little kid who's secretly afraid he's going to be abandoned on the streets again."

I got up and poured myself a cognac. I needed one. "It can't be helped," I said over my shoulder. "I think I've been a damn good father—you can't lay a guilt trip on me."

"I'm not trying to," she said quickly, scrambling up onto the sofa. "I'm trying to tell you that all this time, there's been a part of your life you haven't let him into. And now that he's eighteen and going away to school in September . . ."

"He'll probably wind up at Santa Monica or El Camino or some other community college for the first two years. He's not going to the University of Istanbul, for God's sake."

"But he's going. He's grown up, and whether he still sleeps here or not, your son is going to turn into a man and move from the center of your life to the edge—just like Roger will in mine. They'll make new friends, lovers, get jobs. They're going to be men starting this fall. It's your last summer to be with him as a kid, whether you like it or not."

67

"If I don't locate Doll Kane in the next few days I'll have to go up to San Angelo and look for her," I said. "I've taken the man's money—what do you want me to do?"

"Would it hurt so much to let him come with you?"

I warmed the balloon of cognac between my hands. "It might hurt him. What if somebody did snatch Doll Kane, or killed her along the way? I'm not going to put him in jeopardy."

"But you don't mind putting your relationship in jeopardy, huh?"

"Meaning?"

She got up on her knees, leaning over the back of the sofa to talk to me. "Look,you took him out of a nightmare—living on the streets and doing God knows what just to survive. And he's grateful, you know that. Believe me, he talks about you like you're some sort of little tin Jesus. You're his hero."

"I'm no hero," I said. "The kid needed a break and I was lucky to be able to give it to him."

"Then give him another one. Look, he came up with a great idea tonight. Even Roger was impressed."

"I would have thought of it eventually."

One eyebrow cocked into an arch of skepticism. "Yeah, right. The point is, I think he wants to give you something back."

"Getting himself hurt is repaying me?"

Bettyann grasped the back of the sofa. "This is a simple runaway wife case! You're looking for a little tiny Chinese woman, not the Medellin drug cartel!" Shaking her head, she took a deep breath and then sighed. "Marvel's never even been to northern California. He hasn't been anywhere since before you knew him, and those were places nobody would want to be. He wants to go. He wants to be a part of what you do. For a minute there he was more excited than I've seen him since he made first string on the Bishop baseball team. Can't you give him this before he goes and does the rest of his life?" She ran a hand through her hair. "Before you lose him."

And that was a direct hit.

I cleaned up the kitchen after Bettyann and Roger left, and then I went into Marvel's room to tell him that if I found it necessary to go to San Angelo to search for Doll Kane, he could come with me. He didn't even bother being unimpressed. Usually when I give him some good news, like that we're going to the Dodger game or when I got him a TV set for his room, he just cocks his head and says something like "Tha's cool."

He wasn't cool this time.

"Aw-RIGHT!" he said, leaping up from where he'd been sitting on his bed and giving me a high five that almost knocked me off my feet. "When we goin'?"

"*If* we're going," I said, "we'll drive up Sunday. It's against my better judgment, but if it gets rough, you'll do what I tell you to."

He made a fist and jerked it toward his body. "Yessss!" he said.

I made a mental note to do something very nice for Bettyann.

The Pacific Shores Towers was, true to its name, right across the street from the camera obscura on the grassy palisades overlooking the ocean in Santa Monica. It was a high rise of dirty white brick, all rounded corners and wide picture windows. The traffic running by it on Ocean Avenue, both vehicular and pedestrian, is hellacious during beach season and not much better any other time, a big price to pay for living with a view of the sea. Most of its residents were over seventy, tucked safely out of the way of their wealthy children who lived in fashionable Brentwood or Fox Hills. They spent their days sitting on benches in the park, looking out at the horizon with sad, empty eyes and fondling the rosary beads of their memories.

God's waiting room.

Why Nappy Kane had chosen this as home I couldn't imagine. It was far away from the Hillcrest Country Club and the Friars and Nicky Blair's on the Sunset Strip, all the places that old actors haunt, and despite its view it wasn't too fashionable, being in the wrong neighborhood. If you have enough money to live anywhere you choose, Santa Monica is hardly anyone's idea of paradise. Film industry people who want to live by the ocean usually choose the Malibu Colony, six miles farther up the coast and protected from the great unwashed by armed guards and security gates and inaccessible roads. For a very young woman like Doll Kane, living in the Pacific Shores Towers must have seemed like being entombed.

It was fairly early, not yet eleven, and the sun hadn't reached its zenith, so the coastal temperature was still about ten degrees cooler than inland. By one o'clock in the afternoon not even the sea breezes cool off Los Angeles in summer.

When Nappy opened the door he was wearing a short-sleeved blue and white striped shirt and wrinkled blue corduroy pants. He hadn't yet put his makeup on, and he looked every second of his age. His toupee was slightly askew, and I could see dried flakes of glue at its edges.

70

"Come on in," he said cheerily. "Take a load off. You want something to drink? A coffee? Something stronger?"

"No thanks," I said.

"You're still mad at me. Look, I'm sorry I lost it on the phone. I didn't mean to yell at you. I'm an excitable guy—that's what makes me so lovable."

"I've been yelled at before," I said. "I'll live."

"Then have some coffee."

"I really don't want any coffee, Nappy."

"Are we pals again, then?"

"You're in my will."

"That's funny," he said, nodding in appreciation. "*That's funny!*" Comedians and comedy writers never laugh, especially not at other people's jokes; they simply say, "That's funny." Coming from Nappy, it was an accolade of the highest order. "Come on out on the terrace," he said. "We'll talk."

I followed him through the open sliding glass door with some trepidation. I have a galloping case of chronic acrophobia, and although flying in a large plane doesn't bother me unless I think about it, I'm not crazy about tall buildings and balconies with only a railing keeping me from hurtling through space. The apartment was on the seventh floor, however, which wasn't too bad. I pulled the aluminum deck chair as far from the railing as I could before I sat down.

Nappy wasn't bothered by the height. He stood at the railing, taking a deep breath of the salty breeze mixed with the exhaust fumes from the street. "Some view, huh?" he said.

It was if one could ignore the traffic and the elderly people in the park and the drug pushers and the joggers and the homeless living on the park benches, their belongings in stolen shopping carts beside them. I recognized the terrace as the setting of the photograph of Doll he'd given me.

"You live around here too, don't you?" he said.

"Venice."

"No kidding? Hey, if you lean out a little you can see Venice from here." And he did so, making me grip the arms of my chair with suddenly sweating hands. "What is it some guy said? 'See Venice and die?' "

"I've seen Venice. And I'm still here."

"That's funny," he said, sitting down opposite me, his hands on his hams. "So. Have you gotten a line on Doll?"

"Maybe," I said.

He frowned slightly, his plucked eyebrows knitting together over his prominent nose. "What is that, maybe?"

"Nappy, does she have credit cards?"

"Sure," he said. "Who doesn't?"

About eighty million Americans, I thought but didn't say so. "You haven't canceled them?"

"No."

"Why the hell not?"

He looked really pained. "I couldn't do that to her."

"She walked out on you and left you flat broke."

"Nevertheless," he said. "I love her."

"Do you have the numbers of her credit cards?"

"What do you need them for?"

"Nappy, you have to make up your mind whether you want her found or if we're just dancing around. And I don't dance."

"Okayokayokay! I got 'em inside." He disappeared into the apartment and came back a few minutes later with a sheaf of bills in his fist. "A MasterCard," he chanted, pointing to each one with a pudgy finger. "Two Visas, a Discover card, Mobil, Shell, Unocal, Saks, Bullock's, Robinson's, and a gold American Express card." He seemed inordinately proud that he'd been astute enough to keep the information on file. "Why do you need credit cards?"

"I haven't been able to locate Mrs. Kane anywhere in Los Angeles," I said. "If she's used one of her credit cards somewhere else, then we'll know where she is. Or at least where she's been."

"How do you do that?" he said.

I explained it to him, shuffling through the bills. Nappy, like so many name-brand performers who are pampered and protected and have people to do for them everything the rest of us have to take care of ourselves, was as innocent in the ways of the world as a puppy. He probably couldn't balance his checkbook, change a washer, or fry an egg.

I went into his den off the living room, pine-paneled like a rumpus room in the suburbs, with a polished junior executive desk sporting a personal computer, a built-in bookcase full of tomes on humor and autobiographies of other comedians, and a file cabinet in the corner. Like his ex-partner, Nappy had plastered every available surface with pictures of himself and various celebrities. The star power on this wall was several kilowatts higher than at Cahill's. Ted Kennedy was up there, and Shirley MacLaine and George Burns and Johnny Carson.

"Looka this," he said, making sure I saw his prize. "That's me with Frank at the Sands." The photo was framed more lavishly than the others and had its own place on the wall, with nothing else around it. It was illuminated by a baby spotlight. It was almost like a shrine to the Virgin Mary. And if you have to ask Frank who? you're probably too young for me to talk to.

For the next three hours I sat at his desk, calling the credit card companies and department stores, trying to ascertain whether Doll Kane had used plastic since she deserted her husband. I didn't get much besides a sore ear, but what else I got was a gem.

I walked out into the living room. He was watching an old Hope and Crosby *Road* picture on tape; they seemed to be mushing through Alaska. "Nappy, what day did you come back from Phoenix?"

"Tucson," he corrected. Wrestling his wallet out of his hip pocket, he extracted a card with a nearly microscopic calendar printed on it, the kind you get from the guy who writes your car insurance. He took his glasses out of his shirt pocket and held them in front of his face like a magnifying glass. After calculating for a moment, he said, "The seventeenth. May the seventeenth. It was a Sunday."

"Your wife has only used her credit cards twice. Once on May sixteenth, to fill up at a Shell station near Coalinga, California."

"That sounds like eating pussy," he said. I think I was supposed to laugh. "Where in the hell is Coalinga?"

"A little town in the middle of the San Joaquin Valley just off Interstate Five."

"I never played there," he said. For guys like Nappy Kane, if they've never played a town, it doesn't exist.

"And the other was that same day," I said. "To rent a room at the Marriott in Sacramento."

"Sacramento? What the hell is that supposed to mean?"

One of the things it meant, I supposed, was that Marvel was going to get his trip up north.

6

By the time I got back it was close to three o'clock. Marvel was out somewhere—at eighteen he was completely independent, and Bettyann's warning that he was growing up and away made it seem that much more keen. I hadn't eaten yet, so I made myself a sandwich of hard Sicilian salami with Jack Daniels mustard on pumpernickel, cracked open a John Courage, and sat at my kitchen counter to eat and read the paper, which I hadn't had time to do that morning.

I skipped the news about the economy, which was too depressing to read about, thanking my lucky stars that I wasn't working for an auto company or a large corporation in the middle of a belt-tightening retrenchment. I passed over the sports page with little more than a cursory glance, because the Dodgers, despite a top-heavy payroll full of marquee players, were struggling, and I didn't need to examine the gory details. The entertainment section seemed the only thing left, and the Los Angeles *Times* has a penchant for breathlessly reporting the mysterious doings in the boardrooms of the big studios, major networks, and megapowerful agencies as if the guy on the street who sprung a quarter for a paper gives much of a damn.

So since it was Friday I checked to see what movies were opening. I found nothing exciting, the summer blockbusters being aimed at twelve-year-olds, and idly glanced down the list of other entertainments being offered around town.

But I noted with interest a small item on the TV page announcing that Rebecca Cho, star of *Love Conquers All,* was singing tonight and tomorrow night at the Blue Iris, a club on Melrose Avenue that might be termed in some circles an "elegant boite," and whose name vainly attempted to invoke the title of one of Raymond Chandler's few produced screenplays, *The Blue Dahlia,* which features what is arguably Alan Ladd's best performance. It wasn't exactly my kind of place.

Seeing Rebecca's name in the paper reminded me that her show was on television at that very moment, so I walked into the living room and switched it on.

It was hard to get into the story, but since I'd already seen a preview of what would be on the air in about five weeks, the discussion of the forthcoming nuptials of Quinn and Kelsey and the true secret of little Lacey's parentage, it didn't much matter. The actors, none of whom I had seen before, were all beautiful and photogenic, and if the program's content was banal and mind-deadening, at least the performers were pleasant to look upon.

After a slew of commercials for detergent, disposable diapers, and a product guaranteed to clear up vaginal yeast infection—Jesus, are there no depths that television will not plumb?—the show came back on and there was Mindy Minor, being perky and vibrant and vaguely bratty to a square-jawed executive type and an older woman named Leticia who was, I think, supposed to be her mother.

Mindy was a damn attractive young woman, *young* being

the operative word. Pushing the big four-oh, I don't do well with very young women, mainly because they all think *Casablanca* is trite and full of clichés like "Play it again, Sam."

But she had made a point of telling me to call. Maybe she'd enjoy seeing her costar chirp in an elegant boite. I waited for the next set of commercials—the first one was about a guy who gets off an airplane complaining about his recurrent diarrhea and his wife just happens to have some Pepto-Bismol in her purse—and went into my room, opened the closet door, and retrieved the tattered corner of Mindy's script bearing her phone number from my jacket pocket. I didn't know if she'd be home or at the studio, but I assumed that like most actors she had some sort of answering machine or service or pocket pager. People in show business go berserk if they think they're missing a phone call.

I lucked out. She was home and picked up on the second ring.

"I didn't expect you to call me until next week some time," she said.

"Why not?"

"A lot of guys get off by keeping. a lady wondering."

"I'm not a lot of guys," I said. "I hope I'm not keeping you from watching your show."

She laughed. "It's bad enough I have to go in there and do it. I don't have to watch it too."

"Are you by any chance free this evening? Rebecca Cho is singing in a club on Melrose, and I thought maybe you'd like to catch her act with me. We can grab a bite first."

"You've got your nerve. Do you really think a glamorous and successful actress like me would be free on a Friday night with just a few hours' notice? What time are you picking me up?"

"Eight o'clock."

"I'm counting the minutes."

I hung up, got another beer, and went back into the living room. There were two other actors on the screen, a young couple that I finally discovered were Quinn and Kelsey, who were in bed together, professing undying devotion. Quinn had a very hairy back. The poor schmuck, I thought, he doesn't even know Lacey isn't his baby.

Marvel burst through the front door and rumpled my hair as he walked behind the sofa, knowing how that annoys me. I smoothed it back into place.

"Wha's up?" he said, heading for the refrigerator.

"We're on for San Angelo. We'll get an early start for Sacramento Sunday morning."

He took out a can of Pepsi and regarded me narrowly, leaning against the refrigerator. "Define early."

"Ten o'clock?"

"Oh. Tha's cool, then." Marvel likes to sleep late. He sauntered into the living room and glanced at the TV set, then at me. "What're you watchin'?"

I was suddenly very embarrassed. I looked around for the remote control, but he got to it first and held it out of my reach in a wicked game of keepaway.

"I don't wanna interfere with your favorite show," he said. "You might miss some important development in the story."

I got up and chased him halfway across the room trying to get the remote back. When I got too close he suddenly took a karate stance. "Don't mess with me, man," he warned. "Jus' don' mess!"

I was glad he was kidding. Marvel had taken karate lessons for three years and could probably have dismembered

me without breaking a sweat. Finally he tossed me the remote control and grinned.

"Oh, man," he chortled. "It finally happened. You
watchin' a soap opera! I knew it! You run aroun' with all
those tough guys, you took too many shots to the head and
your brain's finally turned into Quaker Oats."

"Quaker Oats, huh?"

"Quaker Oats," he repeated gravely, and gave me a sym-
pathetic pat on the head, mussing my hair again. "It's the
right thing to do."

Mindy Minor lived on Curson Avenue just north of Hollywood Boulevard near LaBrea, a neighborhood that seems to
be people exclusively with actors who are on the way up but
haven't yet made it. Since she had a steady job and a steady
paycheck she was able to rent a house and so escape the
horrors of the generic Los Angeles apartment—one bedroom, living-dining area, and a postage-stamp terrace. It
wasn't a big house, but there was a tiny pool in the back, lit
with blue and green floodlights, and a small hillside that had
been planted with environmentally correct ivy and ice plant,
protection from the brush fires that race through Southern
California with monotonous predictability each fall. As with
many houses in the foothills, there was no front yard; the
building was right at the edge of the street, and there was no
curb at all.

When she opened the door the warm, soft light in the
room behind her seemed to catch in her hair like tiny fire-
flies. There were three very small freckles at the corner of her
left eye; singly and together they looked extremely kissable.
She took the white carnation I'd brought her with what
seemed like genuine delight. Dressed to go out, she looked

older than the kid-sister role she played on the soap, which made me feel a little better. With my gray hair, if I go out with women too much younger than I am I tend to look like their grandfather.

"This is very sweet," she said, fondling the flower. "I'll put it in water. Or should I wear it behind my ear instead?"

"It'll last longer in water."

She gave me a crooked smile. "Good symbolism."

I followed her into the kitchen and watched her find a pair of scissors and snip off the end of the stem. It was a cozy kitchen, not unlike my own, done all in white with red accents, and it looked well used, as though real people cooked real food and no one ever warmed up a frozen dinner in the microwave.

"I like your place," I said. "It suits you."

"It'll do while the Bel Air mansion's being painted." She stuck the carnation into a peanut butter jar and filled it with water. "That's as close as I come to a vase. Sorry."

"It looks great," I said. And so did she, in a rust-colored suit with a dark green blouse. She would have looked right in the most trendy and elegant restaurant in town but not too dressy for a Burger King.

"I watched your show today."

"I'd thought better of you," she said.

"It isn't *that* bad."

"There are people totally hooked on it; they write us letters every week as if the characters were real people who only live an hour each day and then go back into a box. Some of my mail is threatening, because my character, Sue Ellen Heathcott, is such a bitch."

"Doesn't that scare you?"

She shrugged. "Sometimes. If the letters are really ugly I

turn them over to network security and they supposedly check them out. But I can't walk around looking over my shoulder for a nutburger all the time."

"Is that what you want for dinner? A nutburger?"

"Surprise me," she said.

There are about a million romantic places to eat on the West Side, many of them overlooking the ocean and ideal for a first date. But we were going to hear Rebecca Cho at a club in Hollywood, and Mindy lived in Hollywood, so heading west didn't make too much sense. I surprised her with a little Thai restaurant in a strip mall on a particularly crummy stretch of Hollywood Boulevard, where the ambience is slightly above Denny's and the food is authentic and spicy. Mindy had a great appetite and was adventurous enough to try a prawn dish that looked lethal on the plate but tasted like the nectar of the gods.

She slugged down some Thai iced tea and leaned forward in her chair; I could smell the honey on her breath. "Isn't this about where you ask me to tell you my life story?" she said.

"I know it already."

"You just think you do."

I began reciting, like for a book report. "Born in Duluth, Minnesota, and majored in drama at the state university. Did a few shows on Broadway, including the chorus of *Les Miz,* came to Hollywood in 1991 and landed a second lead on a sitcom at ABC—sorry, I can't remember the name— that lasted exactly four episodes. Worked in Equity Waiver Theatre for a while, made ends meet by being a fragrance model, whatever that is, and last August debuted as the poor little rich kid on *Love Conquers All.*"

Her eyebrows arched. "I'm impressed. Where'd you get all that?"

"Ve haff vays," I said, trying hard to sound like Conrad Veidt.

She bit into a prawn. "You mind if I ask you something? I'm a straightforward kind of person and I usually say what's on my mind."

"Okay; what's on your mind?"

"What are we doing here tonight?"

"Having dinner."

"I mean, why?"

I signaled the waitress to bring me another Amarit beer. They bottle it in Thailand and it really sets off a good spicy Thai meal. "Why does any man ask a woman out to dinner? I could tell you that you're intelligent and fascinating, that I love your acting, and that I want you to help me with my doctoral thesis on recombinant DNA."

"You could," she agreed.

"But I'm pretty straightforward myself, and the fact is, I think your eyes are beautiful, you have the kind of body that makes me crazy, one of the sexiest mouths I've ever seen, and most important, you make me laugh. I want to get to know you better." I stopped as my Amarit arrived and the waitress pattered away. "And giving me your number the other day indicated some sort of interest on your part. So that's what we're doing."

"See?" she said. "Honesty is the best policy." She seemed satisfied for a moment, then popped another question. "What about Rebecca? Are you and she . . . involved? I have to work with her and share a dressing room, and I don't want any tension between us, because she's been on the show longer than me and I'll be the one to get canned. The world is too full of good-looking guys to risk a career, you know? Even for pretty gray hair and hazel eyes like yours."

"They're yellow-green," I said. "There's no such color as hazel."

"They look great in this light."

"Why do you think I chose this restaurant?"

"You didn't answer my question."

"I met Rebecca for the first time about two minutes before I met you. There's nothing going on, believe me."

"And you didn't just ask me out as a way to get closer to her?"

"What do you take me for?" I said.

"I don't know. Maybe another Hollywood user who's good-looking and smooth-talking and about as deep as an oil slick." She was picking at a leftover piece of spring roll with her fingernails. "Nothing personal, but I've been in this damn town too long, and I've been hustled by experts. I was interested—*am* interested. I just don't want to get bounced around."

"Let's just take things slow," I said, "and see how it goes."

"Okay. But I have one more question."

I sighed.

"Why the interest in Bec? I mean, there are a million things we could have done tonight. Why are we going to see her?"

"Well," I said, "I told you I was an actor, right? But there's something I didn't tell you."

She put down her fork and rested her forehead in her hand. "Oh God! You're married."

"No."

"You're living with someone."

"Just my eighteen-year-old son."

"You're gay."

"Mindy . . ."

"You don't have enough money to pay the check."

I started to laugh, and finally she did too.

"All right then—what?"

I pulled out my license and showed it to her.

"A private investigator? Wow!" A vertical crease appeared between her brown eyes, and she looked up at me. "Is Bec in some kind of trouble?"

"Not at all. I'm looking for a runaway wife who happens to be a friend of hers. That's why I came to see her, and that's why I want to hear her sing tonight and maybe get a chance to talk to her again." I put my hand over hers and squeezed gently. "I called you because I wanted to see you. Okay?"

She took a deep breath. "You had me worried there."

The Blue Iris was one of the "in" places in town, for the moment, anyway. There were no carpets on the floor and no pictures on the wall, but there were etched mirrors everywhere you looked, and not surprisingly there was a blue iris on each table in a delicate crystal vase. Everything was polished, glass-topped cocktail tables and shiny brass, with indirect lighting in ebony-colored fixtures, and all of the customers looked as if they had run out and bought their outfits that afternoon. The drink of choice seemed to be some sort of arcane mineral water, but at those prices I was going to get a buzz. I ordered Glenfiddich on the rocks, the closest I could get to my favorite Scotch, Laphroaig. Mindy had white wine. Everybody was as blasé and sophisticated as a William Powell movie, except no one was smoking. Los

Angeles tolerates and even nurtures almost every vice but that one.

We chose a table about four rows back, not wanting to sit up front. There's nothing more disconcerting to an entertainer than to have someone they know right in the front row looking up their nose. There was a cover charge for each set, and a drink minimum; it would have been cheaper to get tickets for *Phantom of the Opera*. I thought that Rebecca Cho better be good.

She was. She made her entrance in a simple black silk sheath that left one golden shoulder bare, making the audience gasp. Her hair was pulled straight back into a bun, and her lipstick was dark, the color of old blood. There was no hint of Las Vegas razzle-dazzle, no bombastic opening, no chatter, hardly a smile at all. She simply stood in the bend of the ebony grand piano holding the microphone in a two-handed lover's caress and sang her ass off.

She opened her set with one of my favorite tunes, "Pieces of Dreams," which most people misidentify as "Little Boy Lost." Her singing voice was soft and throaty, kind of like the young Sarah Vaughan. Her eyes were half closed, but after about sixteen bars she noticed us sitting there and nodded her head imperceptibly. While she was singing you couldn't hear another sound in the Blue Iris; everyone was focused on her. She had the same kind of hypnotic appeal as Barbara Streisand, that kind of controlled passion that tells you she believes what she's singing. It was acting of the highest virtuosity, and it made me wonder why more singers today don't realize vocal tricks and shouting can't compare with genuine emotion.

The set was ten songs long, all of them good ones. No throwaway lounge tunes like "On a Clear Day," no jazz stylings of rock and roll hits. Rebecca Cho's music didn't swing or rock, it swayed gently like Chinese wind chimes on the patio. Her piano player was a late-middle-aged black man who wore his glasses up on top of his head and had a buttery soft touch that fit her voice and style like a silk camisole. No bass player, no drums—just Rebecca and that understated piano and the work of the best songwriters of the century: Mercer, Kern, Rodgers and Hart, Johnny Mandel and Harold Arlen.

Cho was in the middle of her fourth number, a soft, mellow bossa nova called "So Many Stars," when I was shocked to see Yale Rugoff come in and sit in a booth against the wall. He was the only man in the place besides me who wasn't wearing Melrose Avenue chic, opting instead for a traditional blue blazer with an open white shirt. With him was a very young Asian woman who seemed sad and confused, even a little frightened. I stared hard at her but had to admit that she didn't look anything at all like Doll Kane. The moment they sat down Rugoff was all over her, nuzzling her ear, his hand beneath the table working under her skirt. She didn't seem very happy about it but bore his attentions stoically. She couldn't have been more than eighteen years old, if that.

Yale Rugoff was representing Doll Kane in her divorce, but it didn't necessarily follow that he would know Rebecca Cho, who in her own words was not that close a friend of Doll's. Maybe it was a coincidence that he was here tonight to hear her sing, maybe he was just a music lover, but I somehow didn't think so. True coincidences come along about as often as a movie producer who tells the truth.

I turned my chair and moved it closer to Mindy so that my

back was to him. She smiled and put her hand over mine. I liked that.

Rebecca closed with a medley of biting, smoky Kurt Weill tunes that could have cut through window glass: "Surabaya Johnny" and "Pirate Jenny" and "Speak Low." The audience went crazy until she came back and did an encore, Sondheim's "Pretty Women," and then disappeared into the back of the club. The cocktail waitress came over and told us that if we wanted to hang around for the next set they would waive the second cover charge. Magnanimous of them.

"Are we staying?" Mindy asked.

"Do you want to?"

"I'd rather go someplace and neck."

"Sounds like a plan to me," I said. "Let's just wait long enough to say hello."

In a few minutes Rebecca came out again wearing the black dress's matching jacket. She stopped at our table.

"Well, you're the last people I expected to see tonight, much less together," she said. "Thank you for coming."

"You're truly spectacular, Rebecca," I told her, "and so is your musical taste. I wouldn't have missed this for anything."

She inclined her head in modest acceptance. "I'm here every other weekend for the next two months, so you have to come back." She cocked an eyebrow and smiled. "I'm glad you two found each other."

"You haven't heard from Doll Kane, by any chance?" I asked her.

She withdrew her smile as if she'd mistakenly proffered a fifty-dollar tip when a single was what she'd intended. "Is that why you're here? You're wasting your time—and mine.

If Doll wants to contact her husband, she will. If not, I'm won't do anything to cause her grief or inconvenience. I thought I made that clear."

I started to say something else but she turned away from me and looked around the room, nodding at someone behind us. "You'll have to excuse me now. I have other people to talk to, and there's only half an hour between sets."

She drifted off, and Mindy leaned back in her chair and folded her arms across her breasts. "Get what you came for?"

"Cynicism is unbecoming in the young," I said. I swiveled around in my seat and watched Rebecca stop for twenty-second chats with several admiring fans, but it was obvious her real destination was Yale Rugoff's booth. When she got there they touched cheeks, then put their heads together and whispered. Their frequent glances toward me tipped me that I was topic A, rather than her music.

"Is Bec going to be mad at me because of this?" Mindy said.

"I don't know," I told her. "I don't know exactly where she fits into all this."

"All what? I'm really in the dark here."

"It doesn't matter." I stood up and went to hold her chair. "Shall we?"

As we started for the door I heard my name being called. Yale Rugoff crooked a finger at me, the kind of imperious gesture that grates on me like fingernails on a blackboard. I went toward him, slowly enough to let him know that it was my own idea.

"You're getting to be a real pain in the ass," he said without getting up. "I've got a good mind to slap you with a restraining order."

"You don't have a good mind at all. This is a public place, and I got here before you did. You'd better go back to law school, Mr. Rugoff. Sounds like you must have been absent a couple of days."

"All right, that's it," he said. Rebecca put a hand on his arm, but he shook it off and slid out of the booth to stand nose to nose with me. The young woman with him just looked frightened, and very much out of her depth.

"This is your last warning, asshole," he growled, the sour odor of house Chablis on his breath. "Stay the hell out of things that are none of your business. I see your face again, you're going to be damn sorry."

Putting a finger into his soft belly, I pushed just hard enough to back him away from me a bit. "Mr. Rugoff," I said evenly, "you're way too fat to be calling people names."

I felt a hand on my elbow.

To be more precise, I felt a vise on my elbow. I turned around to see a very hard-looking guy trying to cut off the circulation in my arm. His broken nose and the scar tissue around his eyes told me he did this sort of thing often. He had the profile of a pickax.

"Trouble, Mr. Rugoff?" he said. His voice resembled the sound a chain saw makes when it hits metal.

I looked down at his hand on my arm. "Is this a pickup?" I said. "Sorry, but this is my week for women."

The scarred-up eyes narrowed; he looked as though he might be planning to do something about it, but Rugoff said, "Forget it, Neil."

Neil? I'd never before met a knee breaker named Neil. Whatever his name, he was wearing black tasseled loafers, and I moved my foot slightly and ground my heel into the top of his instep. His eyes narrowed even more, and he tightened his grip. I crunched harder. We glared at each other, tough-guy looks, like two kids in a staring contest, only this contest seemed to be about who could stand the most pain.

"I'll bet the bones of your foot break before my elbow does," I said, and rotated my heel. He was getting white around the mouth, and I felt his grip loosening just a bit. Finally he let go, the breath he'd been holding rushing out of him in a tired *whoosh*. I took my heel off his foot. My arm was numb where his fingers had bored in, but I was damned if I was going to give either him or Rugoff the satisfaction of seeing me rub it.

"Thanks for a great show, Rebecca," I said, and nodding briefly to the scared-looking Asian girl in the booth, I piloted Mindy out the door.

"Just like in the movies," she said dryly as we reached the curb. "Why do I suddenly feel like Lauren Bacall?"

I smiled with half my mouth, looking world-weary. "You're good, schweetheart," I said. "You're real good."

As we waited for the valet to bring the car, I wondered why an upscale club like the Blue Iris that catered to an affluent, middle-aged crowd needed on-the-premises muscle.

But maybe Neil didn't work for the club. He had, after all, called Rugoff by name.

7

THERE ARE NIGHTS in Los Angeles—not usually and not many—when the Santana wind from the desert to the east is brisk and high and the air is so clear you can see pinpricks of light twinkling way up in the hills, and you wonder what those people are doing up at that hour of the night. Chances are they're staying up late *with* someone. Driving home alone on such a crystalline evening makes aloneness that much more keen.

Things didn't work out very well with Mindy.

Taking her with me to talk to Rebecca had been a bad idea. She wasn't that upset about the concept, but when things turned sour at the Blue Iris, she did too. It seemed she didn't much like intrigue, confrontations, or bouncers with broken noses. So what started out promising to become a romantic interlude wound up with a handshake—one more evening of emptiness. Driving home, the anonymous lights in the hills mocked in the darkness.

God, I hate dating! You start out with a physical attraction—sorry, but that's how it invariably begins—you have high hopes and fantasies that maybe things will blossom into a mutually satisfying relationship, and then the ball hits a seam in the Astroturf and takes a bad bounce, and you end

91

up wondering why you ever bothered. That's why it's so tough to be single—things go awry more often than not. Even when you buy a cheap toaster, there's some sort of warranty.

So I went home and poured myself a neat Laphroaig, soaked my sore elbow in ice, and nursed a bad case of hurt feelings before dozing off while listening to a Bill Evans CD.

The next morning, Saturday, I spent on the phone with Armand Farber, a San Fernando Valley divorce lawyer I sometimes work for. He knows I dislike doing divorce work, peeking through keyholes and staking out hot-pillow motel rooms on Cahuenga Boulevard, but he occasionally hires me to pore through records and property titles down at the courthouse or to do the same kind of work I'd done tracing Doll Kane's paper trail. If it isn't the most exciting way to spend a day, it's a living.

But to an investigator, everyone he meets is a potential source of information, and I wasn't shy about using my contacts. Farber was mildly annoyed at being disturbed on a day off. A long-divorced man-about-L.A., he lived not too far from me in a spacious condo on the Marina Peninsula and on weekends in summer could usually be found baking himself to a dark bronze on his seaside terrace, a pitcher of bloody Marys at his side and one eye cocked for a comely lass (or comely lasses) strolling the beach. But he agreed to spend a few minutes on the phone with me.

I took it as a bad omen when I asked him what he knew about Yale Rugoff and he laughed.

Farber had gone head-to-head with Rugoff on one or two occasions and wiped the floor with him. The rest was little I hadn't figured out on my own: Rugoff was a low-end shyster whose main area of expertise was family law, especially ridding female clients of husbands who often had tattoos and wore turned-around baseball caps and whose property settlement was usually limited to one six-year-old RV and a beer cooler. With the ethics of a sewer rat, he hung on to his practice by his fingernails and was not above hiring hookers to vamp the husbands of his clients and unscrupulous private detectives to catch them in flagrante delicto.

According to Farber, Rugoff sometimes had sex with the women who retained him.

He'd been reprimanded by the bar association on more than one occasion and, in an incident that had them talking in legal eagle bars for months, had been unceremoniously kicked in the ass by the unemployed steelworker–husband of a client and been sent tumbling down the sweeping marble staircase in the courthouse, his legal briefs flying. Only fear of more razzing from his colleagues had kept him from filing a bodily injury suit.

Yale Rugoff *was* a lawyer joke.

Which made me wonder exactly how someone like Doll Kane, with a wealthy and famous husband, had found her way into his filing cabinet, until Armand Farber informed me that about thirty percent of Rugoff's clients were Asian women obtaining divorces from Caucasian husbands.

Everyone is a specialist.

That interested me, but the more I thought about it the less I could figure out why. It would take me days of sitting in the records room of the superior court ferreting out the names of Rugoff's clients, which I couldn't do until Monday anyway, and in the end it wouldn't buy me much. I wasn't investigating Yale Rugoff's shady practices, inviting as that seemed, but trying to find Doll Kane, and that trail apparently led north, to San Angelo.

"How much extra is this gonna cost me?" Nappy Kane whined when I called and told him I was driving up to the state capital. "Doll pretty much cleaned me out, y'know. I'm not made of money."

"Then just wait until you meet with her lawyer next week and I'll forget it."

He thought it over. "No, go ahead," he said wearily. "I want to find her. I mean, maybe she's in trouble."

"If she is," I told him, "she's in trouble up north."

Marvel and I got started just before ten on Sunday morning. In his white shorts his long legs went on forever, and his blue Dodger cap was jaunty on the back of his head. He was pretty jazzed about going with me. He'd included in his packing a pair of dress slacks, a white shirt, and a lightweight sports jacket in case we went out anyplace nice for dinner. We got into my year-old Chevrolet Corsica and headed up the San Diego Freeway through the San Fernando Valley and its ugly urban sprawl. Then the road turned into Interstate 5, rising into the dry beige high country around Valencia and Six Flags Magic Mountain amusement park and its thrill rides, through the dry brown hills of the Angeles National Forest, past Pyramid Lake and the tiny hamlet of Gorman on the twisty, mountainous road known as the Grapevine. On the downgrade there are several ramps leading upward to nowhere, ending in a barricade of piled sand and gravel, for runaway trucks whose brakes fail—a pretty chilling thought.

It's not a pleasant trip at the best of times, and in the summer the terrain is almost completely without color. The ugly scars of utility roads and water treatment plants slashed across the hillsides where the grass had been baked almost colorless by the heat and sun and the polluted air. But Marvel, born in the flat tidewater country of the South and raised up on the bleak Los Angeles streets, was excited about being in the mountains and even got a kick out of it when his ears popped from the four-thousand-foot altitude going through the Tejon Pass.

After coming down off the Grapevine into the fertile farmland of the San Joaquin Valley, I could have set the car on automatic pilot, because there's hardly a bend in the road until you get to Stockton. The only thing to break the monotony was that for about ninety miles the right-hand side of the road was littered with small red tomatoes that had fallen off the back of an open truck, leaving a trail like Hansel and Gretel in a vegetarian revisionist fairy tale.

North to Sacramento, I-99 is not unlike the interstates that cut through Kansas and Nebraska; you find yourself wondering how many more miles until the next tree. There's nothing to look at except military-straight rows of agricultural crops, Mexican-American farmers in battered pickup trucks, and road signs announcing odd town names like Buttonwillow and Weed Patch.

I've often wondered why a community would want to immortalize weeds in their name. Maybe it's because weeds, along with rats and cockroaches, are biological survivors, while the more beautiful plants, delicate flowers, and small, lovely creatures always wither and die young.

It's the same with people.

I veered off I-5 onto Highway 99 near Bakersfield, which is known for its country music and its lack of anything else to do. It takes about a half hour longer, but at least there are a few towns along the way to break up the mind-numbing repetition of brown grass, brown mountains, and the brown fields of agriculture with their dress-right-dress strips of green.

Marvel was getting hungry, never a surprise, so I pulled in at a café along the highway that was whimsically named the Stop-and-Go. Marvel thought it was pretty funny, and even though I didn't, it was better than one of the franchised fast-food joints that have spread out over the country like the flora of Weed Patch. I wonder if the golden arches and their ilk haven't caused the homogenization of America. They're all the same, whether in California or Ohio or Georgia or Idaho, and bit by bit they're erasing the regional differences that used to make driving cross-country such a richly rewarding experience. Norman Rockwell's vision of America has given way to those of Ray Kroc and Wendy.

We sat at a window booth with a splendid view of the sun-scorched interstate. Our waitress was of a certain age, wearing her hair in a 1955 beehive that made her look like a space alien, with sallow skin and stained teeth and half moons of perspiration under the sleeves of her starched pink uniform. Coffee shops on the side of the highway are often where dreams go to die.

I figured they couldn't do much to ruin a cheese omelette—I was wrong—and Marvel ordered chicken-fried steak with biscuits and gravy. The waitress told him it was their specialty but kindly shared the information that she herself couldn't eat the gravy because it made her burp.

The coffee, however, was splendid.

"So this Chinese woman, this Doll we're lookin' for, is in Sacramento?" Marvel said between bites.

"I know she was through there," I said. "My guess is that she wound up in San Angelo."

"Roger says that's a little bitty town on the river."

"Yep."

"You really think there's gonna be rough stuff in a hick town like that?"

"No I don't. But there's always a possibility." I chewed manfully on my omelette. It was the consistency of Brad Daugherty's basketball shoe.

"Why d'you keep doin' this if it's so dangerous? You like gettin' beat up an' shot at an' shit?"

"It's not that bad. A lot of boring paperwork, usually. Most of the time the worst thing that can happen to a PI is getting hurt in a traffic accident while he's tailing someone."

"So why the big deal about takin' me along?"

"Because sometimes it gets worse than that, and I wanted to keep you out of it."

He leaned back against the patched turquoise Naugahyde of the booth and slid down so he was sitting on his spine, looking at me with what was almost pity. "Man, sometimes you such a dweeb, you know?"

"Now what did I do?"

"Think I can't take care of myself?"

"I'm sure you can," I began, but he interrupted me.

"How the hell you think I survived on the street 'fore you foun' me?"

I tried not to grimace. I didn't like to think about how he had to survive. He'd undergone three years of heavy-duty psychological therapy after I'd filed the adoption papers, but by tacit mutual consent, he and I had never spoken a word about his stint as a male hooker on Santa Monica Boulevard when he was thirteen and fourteen years old, and I didn't think a roadside diner with a Martian-haired waitress hovering nearby was the place to start.

"You think I was a victim," Marvel said, " 'cause I was so

young an' had a pimp that useta gimme shit. An' in a lot of ways tha's right—I was. But man, you don' last a month on the street 'less you tough. Tougher'n the next guy. You do what you got to, an' I done plenty."

He stirred the straw around in his ice-filled Coke, his brow creased, recalling things no teenager should have stored away in his memory bank. Obviously he'd been meaning to have this conversation with me since the night the Karpfingers were over for dinner. "Tha's why it pisses me off, you always tryin' to' protect me an' shit. I'll never tell anybody some of the things I done, specially you, cause you don' wanta know, but I can take care of myself. Better'n you, prob'ly. You s'posed to be the big tough detective, but I bet I been in about fifty times as many fights as you."

It felt like I'd swallowed a tennis ball and it had gotten stuck in my throat, but I tried to keep it light. "The question is, did you win them?"

His eyes drilled into mine. "I'm here, ain't I?"

I pushed my plate away from me. "I'm talking about guys with guns, Marvel."

"What you think they use on the street, man? Pillows?"

"Okay," I said. "You're one tough dude. But according to those papers I signed a few years ago, I'm your father. And one of the things fathers do is try to keep their kids out of harm's way."

"There's nothing so bad can happen to me now that didn't already have a chance t' happen, ol' Dad." He smiled then, and I knew it was all right. "So lighten up a little."

I took out a cigarette, but Marvel frowned at me so I put it back. He's been after me to quit smoking for a long time. "My business can get pretty ugly sometimes," I said.

"No shit! An' here I thought when you came back from

Mexico that time with your face all rearranged, or when you walked funny for a month after your trip to Chicago, or that time you went up against a rattlesnake—"

"It was a cobra," I corrected him.

"An' here I thought those were just exceptions! I guess I musta made an error." Withering sarcasm is one of Marvel's best weapons, and if he ever learns to save it for the coup de grâce instead of spraying it around like shotgun pellets, we're all going to be in trouble. He turned sideways in the booth and leaned against the window. "Sometimes you treat me either like I was six or else a damn fool!"

"Maybe we ought to talk about that."

"We *are* talking about it." He sucked at the rest of his drink, making that horrible sound with his straw. I always thought people stopped doing that when they were twelve.

I suppose kids everywhere have at one time or another rebelled, rejected their parents and the values with which they were raised in order to find out exactly who they are. I did, God knows, and didn't speak to my father for more than half my life. If the parents are lucky, the adolescent eventually grows back into those values instilled in early childhood. But it's a painful time to go through for both grown-up and child, and how skillfully each is able to navigate those rocky shoals of discovery determines how good the relationship will eventually become.

"If you think just because you're eighteen now and bigger and tougher than I am that I'm suddenly going to not give a damn, you don't know me as well as you think you do," I said.

He sighed, poor put-upon fellow, and drummed on the Formica tabletop with his fingers. "Course I want you to give a damn," he said. "I just want you to realize I *am* eighteen and not treat me like some sorta basket case that can't take care of himself."

"You're right," I said.

"Damn right."

"I apologize."

"Apology accepted," he said. He was having a high old time, now he had me on the run.

"From now on, partners," I said.

"Tha's cool."

"Equal to equal."

"All *right!*"

I stood up. "You can pay for lunch. Partner."

We bought a few cold cans of Pepsi before we got back on the interstate to tide us through the rest of the trip. I kept the windows rolled up tight, because not only does the entire valley smell of the manure used to fertilize the fields of alfalfa and walnuts and corn and green vegetables, but there is a dead dog or possum or raccoon decomposing at the side of the road every four hundred feet or so. I have a problem looking at dead things. It's my big phobia—or one of them; high places is the other. And the San Joaquin Valley has to be the Dead Animal Capital of the World.

We arrived in Sacramento just after six o'clock and checked into a TraveLodge near the river for which the city is named, in the picturesquely restored section of town known to the natives as Old Sac. The sidewalks are made of planks, the streets are cobblestone, and the prices are tourist high, but I guess if you want a little slice of history you have to pay for it.

That night we ate dinner on the Sacramento waterfront, on the deck of a reconstructed riverboat known as the *Virgin*

Sturgeon, and Marvel got quite a charge out of it. He knows the Pacific coastline pretty well, but he'd never spent much time around a major river, and the boat traffic fascinated him.

The next morning we headed out again, Marvel craning his neck behind us to get a look at the capitol building as we drove across the Capitol Bridge into Yolo County and then turned south again, hugging the bank of the river. There are times during the rainy season when the curving two-lane known as Old River Road is under several feet of water, and other times when the whipped-cream-thick tule fog makes visibility impossible and renders the drive too dangerous to undertake. But this was a pretty summer day with a high, hot sun, and there were plenty of boaters, bathers, fishermen, and water skiers to look at on our left. To the right was an unbroken stretch of flat farmland, looking fallow for June, which rolled westward to the horizon, some of it planted with dark trees with grotesquely twisted branches. I later found out they bore walnuts.

When we got to the town of Ryde we stopped for directions and a cup of coffee at the Grand Island Inn, an old relic of the thirties in the middle of nowhere that used to be known as the Ryde Hotel, now restored to its former art deco splendor and painted an unlikely pink. The ancient water tower atop the building still said RYDE HOTEL. Mobsters from the Bay Area, lobbyists from Sacramento, and even once in a while a movie star from down Los Angeles way used to conduct their illicit assignations here; certainly no more out-of-the-way place could be imagined. The waitress in the hotel restaurant told us we were about half an hour from our destination.

San Angelo, California, hugged the eastern bank of the

river for about a mile. There were two main streets, boasting a Wendy's, two chain supermarkets, several taverns-cum–fish restaurants, a coffee shop that made the Stop-and-Go look like the dining room of the Bel Air Hotel, and a couple of marine supply shops, along with the other types of commercial establishments one would expect to find in a small town. Many of the buildings, especially those that backed up onto the highway, were made of corrugated tin. For the most part, the people on the streets had the look of the chronically unemployed, and they stood around aimlessly as if waiting for some sort of religious experience, a rapture, to hit them. Most of them were past fifty, a fair number considerably past it.

Also among the inhabitants were a startling number of Asians, although they all seemed to have something to do. One of them was arranging fruit outside an open-air market, one was sweeping the sidewalk in front of an auto supply store, and the rest were walking with apparent purpose.

At the shoreline there was a marina of sorts, where several houseboats were moored, and from the amount of activity on their decks on a Monday morning I assumed that many of them were occupied full time. The live-aboards I could see from the highway were of retirement age, the type of people you often see driving lumbering RVs on the interstate highways of America. In the midst of the marina the familiar red and yellow Shell Oil sign hung from a chain, swinging in the wind.

The motel I picked out, the Rolling Rock, wasn't on the river but about two blocks in from the highway on a side street. At one end of the parking lot was a pint-size swimming pool full of murky green water. A string of floats marking the deep end bobbed on the surface.

The woman at the front desk wore steel-rimmed glasses reminiscent of a Nazi in an old black-and-white war movie; from the glare she gave Marvel while I was registering, she might very well have been one. Or perhaps she was a mutant; one of her most remarkable facial characteristics was a complete lack of lips.

"Check-in time's two P.M.," she said, looking pointedly up at the round-faced electric clock on the wall above the desk.

I glanced over my shoulder at the parking lot outside the window. There were only two cars in evidence. "You don't exactly look as if you're full up," I said. "And your vacancy sign is lit."

She heaved a put-upon sigh. "I'll have to charge you an extra half day, then."

I shrugged, filling out the registration card. "It's only money."

"How many nights will you be staying, Mr. . . . ?" She pulled the registration card around so she could read it. "Mr. Henderson?"

Marvel turned and stared at me and I gave him a big sunny smile that he correctly interpreted as a signal to keep his mouth shut.

"I'm not sure," I said pleasantly. "Two at least."

She looked at Marvel again, sniffed, and told me the room was twenty-seven dollars a night plus tax. Her eyebrows lifted even higher when I put two twenties on the counter.

"No credit card?"

I shook my head.

"Well." She gave a little disapproving cough. "We'll need a fifty-dollar theft-and-damage deposit then too."

"Fifty dollars!"

It's probably difficult to smile when one has no lips, and

when she attempted to it came out nasty. "Take it or leave it," she said.

As we were taking our meager luggage out of the car Marvel said, "I don't think she likes black people."

"You're probably the first one she's ever seen in person," I said. "And you don't look anything like Bill Cosby, so it confused her."

"She seen a lot of Chinese, though," he observed. "Man, it looks like Chinatown out there."

That's when I told him about Locke.

Late in the eighteenth century when they were building the railroad tracks through the Sierras, the Central Pacific had imported boatloads of Chinese laborers on the credit-ticket system—the railroad would advance the price of passage to America, to be paid for out of the laborer's slave wages. When the right-of-way was cleared, the spikes all driven and the tracks laid, some of the immigrants had settled in their own tiny community along the east bank of the Sacramento. The settlement had come to be called Locke, for reasons I couldn't remember, and the current residents are now five and six generations removed from their rail-driving forebears. Some of them opened Chinese restaurants and gift shops along Locke's one commercial street; others commute to Stockton and Sacramento or work in Isleton, home of the International Crawdad Festival. I'd be sorry to miss it. Some obviously had found jobs in nearby San Angelo.

Marvel waited until we got to the door of our room before he asked, "What's with Mr. Henderson?"

"We're undercover," I said. I have business cards made up under several aliases, and Ed Henderson of Alpha Insurance Agency in Santa Monica was the one I'd chosen for our sojourn to San Angelo.

"Undercover? Shee-it!"

I tried not to take his amusement as a personal affront. "I figure that if I just barge in and ask to see Doll Kane, the only thing I'm going to see is the door. You have to be subtle, Marvel."

He shook his head in infinite pity. "See what happens when cousins marry?" he said.

The room was as I'd requested, two queen-size beds with a nightstand between them, and a table and two chairs in case we wanted to play cards. The small bathroom boasted a shower stall that smelled faintly of mold and a sliding window that looked out on the scenic wonders of a rubble-strewn vacant lot. I couldn't complain, though, since from what I could see it was the only motel in town.

Marvel immediately switched on the TV set bolted to the dresser. A pixyish young man was exhorting a family called the Huckabees to name something that comes shrink-wrapped. A vapid-looking blond woman ventured "Hot dogs?" which set the rest of her clan screaming "Good answer! Good answer!"

I walked over and snapped the set into blessed silence. "Give me a break, all right?"

Marvel glowered. "You sure gonna be fun to travel with," he observed.

I opened the drawer in the nightstand and took out the slim telephone directory. It served the communities of Locke, Isleton, Walnut Grove, and Thornton, as well as San Angelo, but I couldn't find a listing for Asian Nights in any of them. Or Asian anything. Or Oriental anything. Some-how I hadn't expected to.

I didn't find any Cheungs, either. Several Chus in Locke, quite a few Chungs, but no Cheungs.

I tossed my briefcase onto the bed, undid the snaps, and opened the lid. The Asian Nights brochure was right on top, next to my holstered Glock 17 pistol, a lightweight number that takes a seventeen-round magazine. I'd bought it for myself for Christmas the year before to replace the old .38 police special I used to carry in its own little holder under the seat of my car. The car, a cute Fiat convertible, got blown up some years ago and the .38 with it, and I'd experimented with several other models before settling on the Glock.

I don't approve of handguns for the general public, which in National Rifle Association circles is going to make me as popular as the Prince of Wales at an IRA picnic. But it's my considered opinion and I'm stuck with it. They're dangerous to have around the house, especially when there are kids in evidence, and mostly useless for civilians; unless you're prepared to go all the way and take a human life with it, some predator is probably going to take it away from you and insert it in your handiest orifice. But in my business, unfortunately, it's often necessary to walk around heeled. I'd been pretty strict about insisting Marvel learn gun safety, even though I kept mine unloaded and locked away in a small safe in my office most of the time. Wild-eyed gun nuts who insist that guns don't kill people are purely full of crap, as even a cursory glance at a newspaper on almost any given day will attest.

"I didn't know you were carryin'," Marvel said, peering over my shoulder.

"The Boy Scouts taught me to be prepared," I said, "but I have every hope that I won't have to take it out of the briefcase. And you keep your hands off it."

I checked the number of the post office box on the Asian Nights brochure. Box 4514, San Angelo. Then I closed the briefcase and slid it under the bed.

"Let's take a walk," I said.

There were really two main streets in San Angelo, both one-way, that ran diagonally and intersected in the middle of town in a kind of rustic Times Square. One, called Dixie Avenue, was reached by exiting from the two-lane highway and driving straight, and the other, San Angelo Avenue, leads onto the highway again. The Rolling Rock Motel was on Dixie, which made a certain amount of sense; you wouldn't want a motel room on your way *out* of town.

The demise of small-town America is the downside of economic progress and technological advancement. Had Norman Rockwell been born sixty years later he would have been a shoe salesman, having nothing to paint. San Angelo seemed a sad place, dying slowly and without dignity from chronic neglect. It seemed to be dusty all over and looked somehow temporary, as though Steven Spielberg had ordered it built last week for a movie. Some buildings had a noticeable cant off the perpendicular and appeared to be waiting for the first strong wind to blow them the rest of the way over. Abandoned shop windows turned blind eyes to the pothole-pocked street. Debris choked the vacant lots that yawned between buildings like the gaps in a minor league hockey player's teeth. There was no movie theater that I could see, and no place to eat dinner or enjoy a cocktail where the regulars weren't likely to beat the crap out of you just for wearing a necktie.

"Where'd you find this little slice of paradise?" Marvel said as we moved along the blighted sidewalks of Dixie Avenue.

"You wanted to come," I reminded him, looking carefully up and down the street.

"I know. But let's have a little fun like the natives do. We can walk down to the grocery store, go into the gourmet food section, an' play with the Velveeta cheese."

"Do what you have to do," I said.

"What're we lookin' for, anyhow?"

"Two things: first, anything approximating Asian Nights, and second, the post office."

"Post office is right over there," Marvel said, pointing to a dilapidated wooden building across the street from the coffee shop, which seemed to have no other name besides EAT. A tiny American flag flapped from a rusty holder mounted on the wall beside the door, and the words U.S. POSTAL SERVICE were lettered in faded gold on the window.

"Thanks," I said, and started across Dixie Avenue.

"Man, the eyes are the first thing to go," he taunted me. "Next the memory; pretty soon you'll be forgettin' where you live."

"If I do," I said, "I'll just listen for the sounds of MTV and follow them home." As we hit the sidewalk in front of the post office I handed him a five-dollar bill. "When we get inside, buy some stamps."

"You gonna mail a letter?"

"No," I said, "but we need a reason to go in there."

"What kind you want? The ones with flags on 'em or the kind that says 'Love'?"

"Surprise me."

An old man wearing the blue uniform shirt of the Postal Service sat on a high stool behind the counter. I think we startled him when we walked in, because he called out,

"Next, please," even though there was no one else in the office.

Marvel went up to the clerk and told him what he wanted, which was to see every twenty-nine-cent issue currently available. The clerk wasn't happy about it, and he appeared to be even less happy about seeing a young black man across the counter, but he opened a folder and took out several sheets of stamps for Marvel's inspection.

I wandered out into the small lobby where the rental mailboxes stood in rows, looking as old-fashioned as the rest of the town, and pretended I was looking at the wanted posters and the notices about missing children. It didn't take me long to find box number 4514. Through the little window I could see it contained five or six envelopes awaiting pickup.

I glanced out the glass door at the diner across the street. It afforded a pretty good view of the postal lobby if we could get a seat near the front window, although my stomach churned at the thought of dining in any restaurant called EAT.

After Marvel finished his complicated transaction at the counter we went outside into the sunshine. Accustomed as we were to the dry desert heat of the Los Angeles Basin, the steamy summer air of the Sacramento Delta was hard to breathe. I guess smog, in its own way, is addictive.

"Where are my stamps?" I said, squinting at Marvel.

He tried to affect that blank look, but his eyes were dancing with merriment. Without comment he handed me a sheet of postage stamps. They bore neither little flags nor the legend LOVE, but the likeness of W. E. B. Du Bois, in celebration of America's Black Heritage.

Humming tunelessly, he grinned from ear to ear all the way to the restaurant.

8

THE FARE AT EAT was every bit as classy as its name. The waitress, who wore a faux brass tag on the tip of one breast announcing she was EM, told us that they were running a special on fried breaded catfish. It was not yet eleven in the morning; even thinking about catfish made me queasy. We ordered breakfast instead.

Bad mistake. The toast was cold, nearly black, and slathered with some sort of spread that made no pretense at being a butter substitute. The eggs were runny, and the coffee tasted like an armpit. Marvel, wielding a broadsword of sarcasm, smacked his lips and sprinkled the conversation with food-critic cracks like "The coffee is a rather presumptuous little domestic, but I'm sure you'll find it amusing." He would probably have sent his compliments to the chef if I hadn't looked out the window and seen a slim young Asian woman walk into the post office lobby and open one of the P.O. boxes with a key. From my vantage point it could have been box 4514.

I gulped down the remainder of my coffee, chewing the grounds, tossed a few crumpled-up bills on the table, and hustled us out of EAT. I felt as if I'd just escaped from Devil's Island.

As we moved down the sidewalk, parallel with but across the street from the Asian woman, several people stopped to stare at us, and I realized how conspicuous we must have been in a town like San Angelo. I slowed down my pace a bit and Marvel shifted gears to match it.

"Marvel, why don't you go on back to the room and watch TV for a while?" I said.

"Oh, sure," he said. "Good-lookin' woman shows up and you try to get rid of me."

"I don't want her to know I'm following her, and you and I look like the road company of *Lethal Weapon.*"

He grinned at the truth of it. "There's nothin' good on TV during the day."

"You never know. Geraldo might be doing a show on people who marry their grandparents."

He made a rude noise.

"Well, why don't you go for a swim, then?"

He brightened at that one, then started to laugh.

"What's so funny?"

"Just thinkin' that if I swim in that old woman's pool, she'll have to drain it." He started off in the direction from which we'd come, then stopped and turned back to me. "You watch your butt, now, ol'timer."

I flicked a quick glance at the retreating figure of the Asian woman across the street. "I'll be too busy watching hers," I said.

The woman, no fool, had chosen the shady side of the street on which to walk, and after a block of trailing her in the sunshine my clothes were sticking to me. When she got to the crossroads, she turned off Dixie on the diagonal and started up San Angelo Avenue. As I followed, I couldn't help notice how the street changed character. San Angelo seemed

111

to be commercially a lot more healthy than Dixie Avenue, if just as seedy. It was full of bars from which loud country and western jukebox music issued even at midday, along with video stores, doughnut shops, real estate offices, and a women's clothing emporium.

She turned into a two-story frame building painted a color that decorators call eggshell or cream and I call dirty off-white. On the main floor was a real estate office, but she went in through another entrance, which probably led to a stairway to the second floor. Next door was another building, long and low and looking like a prefab job from after World War II. Unremarkable, really, except for the square plastic sign that would light up from the inside at night. It made me want to kick myself for my earlier search through the telephone directory. I'd looked up *Asian* and *Oriental*, but I hadn't thought it out quite far enough.

FAR EAST MASSAGE, the sign read.

Inside the walls were covered with inexpensive sheets of paneling, plywood painted and stamped to look like pine. A fluorescent fixture overhead was casting a ghastly light and humming "The Flight of the Bumblebee." Somewhere in the inner recesses a radio played, so faintly that I couldn't make out the tune, and being a bachelor who does his own housecleaning, I was able to recognize the disinfectant odor as that of Pine-Sol. A utilitarian metal desk in the front room held a Rolodex with pink, blue, and white cards, a telephone console, and an intercom resting atop a cheap desk calendar. The calendar showed February. No one seemed to be around.

I eased over to the desk. The Rolodex was open to Delta Refrigeration, and I flipped it to the A's to look for Asian

Nights but came up empty. Then I carefully rolled the cards back to Delta.

I stood there for about a minute, clearing my throat and shuffling my feet, hoping someone would hear me and come out. Finally I just said, "Hello? Anybody here?"

And waited.

After a moment an Asian woman wearing a business suit appeared from a doorway in the rear wall. Her smile was practiced and professional—and stopped short of her eyes, which raked over me like a scanner. She was probably about my age, maybe a few years older, but it was hard to tell because she had on a pair of large aviator glasses with a slight tint to them. "I'm sorry, I didn't hear you come in," she said without a trace of accent. "Good morning."

"Good morning."

"We just opened up for the day so we're not quite organized," she apologized again.

"Well, I'm a morning person."

"I haven't seen you here before, have I?" The question was rhetorical; she knew damn well she hadn't. Despite the smile, the woman emanated the kind of chill you get when too-cold ice cream hits the roof of your mouth and produces a violent pain behind your eye.

"No, I'm just passing through town."

"I see," she said, nodding. "Well, how may I help you?"

I decided that she was no one to trifle with, that I'd be better off asking my questions of someone else. I looked around, playing the bumpkin, and said, "I'd like a . . . massage."

She sat down at the desk, pulled an appointment book out of the top drawer, and flipped it open to where it had been marked with a rubber band. I noticed she was sporting a plain gold wedding ring. "Certainly. A full body massage?" Her eyes challenged.

I shrugged. "I guess."

"All our girls are from Asia," she said.

"Fine."

"That's sixty dollars. For the massage," she added point-edly. "And there is a thirty-minute time limit. After that is twenty dollars extra per half hour."

I pulled out a roll of money—I always carry my currency loose in my pocket—and gave her two twenties and two tens. The cash in her hand seemed to relax her just a bit, like worry beads.

"Tips for the masseuse are discretionary," she said, using a key to unlock the second drawer down and putting my money into a metal cashbox. She relocked the drawer and pushed a button on the intercom, and I could hear a scratchy audio presence in the room where the radio was playing. Now I was able to identify the music—pure, nasal shitkicker stuff about perfidious women and lonesome trains.

"Leng," she said, leaning down to talk into the speaker, "would you come to the front, please?" She flipped off the intercom and sat back in her chair. "I think you'll enjoy Leng. She's very good at what she does."

A little Asian girl came through the door from the back, wearing a knee-length wraparound white smock that was tied at her side. Her permed hair was shoulder length with a little pompadour flip in front, a style favored by Rosie the Riveter in the forties. She couldn't have been more than seventeen years old, and that was giving her the benefit of the doubt. She looked cowed and a little frightened, and after a quick glance she wouldn't meet my eyes.

The woman in the suit said severely, "Will Leng be satisfactory? We don't have a full crew this early, but there is another girl if . . . "

Leng ducked her head a little farther until her chin was resting on her chest.

"No, no, she'll be fine," I said.

The woman nodded, and Leng timidly took my arm and led me through the doorway.

The area beyond appeared to have once been one large storage room that had been cut into two rows of cubicles fashioned of inexpensive movable wallboard. There were no doors, but muslin curtains masked the cubicles from the prying eyes of anyone who might be passing by in the long central corridor. The sound of the radio—Garth Brooks, I think, although my knowledge of country music is limited to Johnny Cash and Willie Nelson—was louder now.

Leng stopped at one of the cubicles and held the curtain aside so I could enter. There was no massage table in evidence but rather what appeared to be a military cot covered with a clean but worn white sheet and a small pillow. On a high table were several folded towels and an array of jars of skin cream. The standing coat tree was an anachronism. The girl pulled the curtain closed and indicated the cot.

"Please," she said.

I moved over to the cot uncertainly.

"Clothes off, please," she said, taking one of the towels and covering the pillow with it. She had trouble pronouncing *L*.

"Can't we just talk for a few minutes?"

She obviously didn't understand much English, but my hesitation seemed to frighten her. "Please?" she said, and it was almost begging.

I began to unbutton my shirt.

She fumbled with the string of fabric that held her smock closed, finally working the knot loose, and shrugged it off. Underneath she wore a cotton bra and white cotton panties, which made her look even more childlike and vulnerable. There were two nickel-sized bruises, one on each side of her left wrist, that looked as though they might have been made by a finger and a thumb. She was only a few inches over five feet, and her body was still chunky with baby fat. She took my shirt and hung it over one of the hooks on the coat tree next to her own smock. "The rest, please?" she said.

Most women don't realize that undressing in front of them is a dicey proposition for a man. If you take your footgear off first, there are the ugliest parts of your body—your bony, funny-looking feet—sticking out of the cuffs of your trousers. And if you're a pants-first kind of guy, you stand there in your underwear with your shoes and socks on at the end of your hairy legs, feeling like the class geek.

I did the shoes and socks first, then unbuckled my belt and stepped out of my chinos.

When I was down to my navy blue briefs, Leng said "Please?" and indicated the cot again.

I gingerly lowered myself onto the cot and rolled over on my stomach in response to her hand signals, my face sideways against the towel on the pillow. I heard her unscrewing one of the jars, and then gasped as the cold goop hit the bare skin of my back.

She spread it around for a minute and then began her massage. She wasn't very good at what she did, despite what the woman in the front room had promised—but then perhaps massage wasn't what she'd been referring to.

"Where are you from, Leng?" I asked as she moved her

hands perfunctorily across my shoulders. She was sort of pushing at me every few inches or so.

"Eh?"

"Where are you from?" I repeated slowly. "Hong Kong?"

"Taipei."

"How long here?"

It took her a moment to translate that, then she said, "Two month." She dipped into the jar for some more cream and smeared it onto the backs of my thighs.

"You have friends here?"

She said, "Um, I don't know." Her hands worked down my legs, rubbing the calf muscles, her touch light, tentative. It was nowhere near a massage. Instead of relaxing me it was making me nervous.

"Leng, do you know about Asian Nights?" I asked.

The rhythm of her hands stopped for just a second, and then resumed more slowly.

"Asian Nights," I said again.

"Um . . . no."

"They help Chinese ladies meet nice American men," I said. "You don't know them?"

She didn't answer but indicated by pushing on me with her hands that she wanted me to turn over. On my back, I watched her scoop up some more of the cream. From the look, feel, and smell of it, it was plain old cold cream. She began smoothing it onto my chest and stomach, not looking at me, her lips pressed together in a straight line as if she were trying not to cry.

"Did they bring you here to America? Asian Nights?"

She just shook her head, flicking a nervous glance at the muslin curtain. More cream now, for my legs, starting at the feet and working her way up.

"Where can I find them, Leng?" She shook her head again, this time almost frantically. "Don't be afraid, Leng," I said. "I'm your friend."

She left her palms on my thighs. "All finish massage," she said. "You want something else now? Forty dollar extra." She moved one pudgy hand up to stroke my crotch through the fabric of my shorts. I think it was supposed to be seductive.

All of a sudden the curtain was yanked open and the woman from the front room stood there looking very angry. "Your time's up, mister," she said. And she didn't say it nicely. Leng seemed to shrink before my eyes. She pressed herself back against the wall, her brown eyes wide open with the whites showing all around the pupils.

In the meantime I just lay there on the cot in my underwear feeling ridiculous. "It hasn't even been ten minutes," I protested.

"Come on, get up!" She marched into the room, swinging her arms. All she needed to complete the picture were jackboots. She took my slacks from off the coat tree and held them out to me. "Put your pants on and go away."

I wondered what I'd done to piss her off, and then it hit me. I glanced over at the table again and noticed behind the rows of jars a small black electronic box with a red light glowing discreetly. The intercom. Most such places have some sort of monitoring system in case a session gets out of hand. The woman at the desk had heard all my questions, and they'd bothered her.

"I didn't mean any harm," I said, struggling into my pants under her cold-eyed gaze.

"I don't know who you are, mister, but you'd better get out of here," she said. Then she turned to Leng and spit out a few guttural syllables in what I took to be Cantonese, and the girl scooted out of the cubicle as if she was on fire.

"Henderson's my name," I said, "Ed Henderson. Look, here's my card . . . " I tried to get my wallet out of my rear pocket to give her one of my fake business cards.

"You can stick your card in your ass," she said.

There's something unsettling about obscenities issuing from the lips of someone who's dressed for a board meeting at IBM.

"Now out! Before I call someone to escort you." She stood with her fists on her hips, ready for a fight, I thought.

I pulled on my shirt and picked up my shoes and socks. "If you'd just let me explain—"

I didn't get the chance, at least not right then, because two men appeared in the doorway behind her. One of them had white hair cut as if around a bowl and the round pink face of a baby. He was in his middle forties, slim and well shaven, in summer-weight pinfeather suit pants one might wear to a chamber of commerce breakfast, a white shirt, red suspenders, and a silly-looking red bow tie. His companion loomed large and cretinous at his shoulder, a giant with shaggy dirty-blond hair and his upper left incisor missing. The remaining teeth were the color of grapefruit juice. He was breathing heavily through his mouth. Earthquake McGoon, from the Li'l Abner comic strip, leapt to mind.

"Helen, Helen," the man in the bow tie chided. "Let's not get excited, shall we? The gentleman's done nothing wrong, and I think he deserves to be listened to, don't you?" Every time he pronounced an *S* he whistled through his teeth— maybe E above high C.

The woman, Helen, stepped aside as he walked into the

cubicle past her and extended his hand to me. "I'm Ash Rustin. Mr. Henderson, is it?"

"Ed Henderson," I said, accepting his handshake. Finally managing to extract one of Ed Henderson's business cards from my wallet, I gave it to him.

He looked at it with interest. "I hope you haven't come all the way up here from Santa Monica to sell us a policy."

"I came up here to find Asian Nights," I said.

He looked thoughtful. "Perhaps we can talk about this in my office. Shall we?" He glanced at my feet. "You might want to put your shoes on—the sidewalk can be very hot this time of day."

I slipped my socks on and wriggled into my shoes, thankful I was wearing loafers. As I started through the curtain I said to Helen, "I hope you're not angry at Leng. She gave me a very good massage."

"Of course not," Ash Rustin said. He turned to Earthquake McGoon and said, "Come back to the office, Frank."

I walked by the big guy, who made no effort to move out of the doorway, and the smell nearly made me gag; his breath was foul with onions, his greasy hair stank, and his body odor was in a class by itself.

As I followed Ash Rustin outside and into the building next door, through the same doorway I'd watched the young Asian woman use after she'd picked up the mail, I felt an adrenaline rush. I'd guessed right, for a change.

On a menu board at the foot of the stairs RUSTIN IMPORTS, LTD. had been spelled out in white plastic stick-on letters, with 2ND FLOOR beneath. The *M* was a little cockeyed.

His office was right at the head of the stairs. It was what you'd expect in an old building in a small town, very unpretentious, although I did notice that the window behind Rustin's desk had a spectacular view of the river. The woman who'd delivered the mail was nowhere in sight.

Rustin didn't sit behind his desk like some Roman procurator about to pass judgment, I'll give him that much. He and I sat together on a cracked-leather sofa next to a bookcase full of boring-looking tomes on trade regulations and immigration law. The malodorous hulk hovered around in the outer office; I couldn't see him from where I sat, but as long as the wind was right you'd know where to find him.

"You'll have to forgive my partner," Ash Rustin drawled. "She's the excitable type. Can't be too careful, you know, when you're dealing with young and vulnerable ladies."

"Your partner?"

He nodded. "My partner and my wife—Helen Ng. We're co-owners of Rustin Imports."

"What do you import?"

He gave a sheepish little lift of his shoulders. "The kind of junk tourists buy in Chinatown. Paper fans, incense burners, cloth slippers. That sort of thing." He harrumphed a little bit and then got serious. "Now then, Mr. Henderson, what's all this about Asian Nights?"

"Is that you? I mean, is this Asian Nights?"

He inclined his head and pursed his lips as though blowing a kiss to a serviceman off to fight a war. "Asian Nights is just one of the businesses I'm associated with."

I allowed a rapturous smile to spread across my face. Being a trained actor sometimes comes in handy in detective work. "Then I've come to the right place!"

He frowned, as if trying to guess what in hell I was talking about. "I saw your ad in a magazine," I went on. "Of course, I'd seen it lots before, but you know, sometimes it takes a person a long time to really get off their butt. Anyway, I've been thinking about it, and this is my vacation week, so I thought I'd run up here and talk to you."

One of his eyebrows arched like a white rainbow.

"I know I should have written first," I said, "but if I had I would've lost my nerve. I'm an impulse person, you know? I figured you'd be in the telephone book, but of course you aren't. So I was wandering around, pretty frustrated about not being able to locate you, and I saw the sign next door and I figured in a town the size of San Angelo, a place called Far East Massage would probably know about you."

His index finger traced the crease in his pinfeather pants. "Asian Nights is a mail order business, Mr. Henderson. That's why we don't give a phone number or a street address. We screen our ladies, and we screen our clients very carefully. What we do here is try to make everybody happy, because we firmly believe that marriage should be for life and takes some serious thought and serious commitment. We don't want people coming in off the street like it was a hardware store."

I ducked my head and tried to look abashed, although I refrained from saying "Aw, shucks."

"But," he said, "I understand that a fellow looking for a beautiful and loving lady to share his life might get a little bit anxious." He leaned back and crossed his ankle over his knee, revealing thin white ankle socks, and peered at me as though trying to see into my head. "Just what did you have in mind?"

I swallowed audibly. "I want to meet a nice lady."

"Uh-huh."

"It's so hard to find an American woman these days who's . . . you know. An old-fashioned girl. Women's lib and all that. And I've always been—attracted to Asian women.

They're very . . . exotic." I had to fight down the impulse to gag as I said it.

"You want to get married, then? Is that it?"

I nodded agreement. "To the right woman, of course."

He nodded. "That goes without saying. But now, this is a business. You've seen our ads, maybe even our brochures—and they cost money. You know what our rates are, don't you?"

"Money's no problem, Mr. Rustin, I assure you."

He pondered for a long while, looking intently at my face to discern whether I was sincere. "Asian Nights has a very high rate of success," he said. "Marriage-wise, that is. Because we bend over backwards to supply our clients with someone whose interests match their own, maybe even their education. And age is no problem, if you were worried about that. Oriental girls like older men, like to benefit from their wisdom and experience, so no need giving that gray hair of yours a thought." He chuckled. "Tell me, Mr. Henderson—"

"Call me Ed. Please."

He beamed. "All right then, Ed. Do you make a nice living from that insurance business of yours? I only ask to make sure any girl of ours you marry won't be stuck in a poverty situation. We have an obligation to them too, y'know."

"I completely understand," I said. "Well, I'm not rich. But I'm the sole owner of the agency, and except for a secretary, I don't have any employees, so we do okay."

The beam went from high to low. "Define 'okay' for me, can you?"

I picked a number out of the air. "Last year we grossed about two hundred and sixty thousand."

Back to high again. "Well, that's outstanding," he said. "Just outstanding." He uncrossed his legs and put his hands on his thighs. "Tell you what, Ed. We're not set up for office visits here, as I've said. But give me a couple of hours and I'll have some pictures and photographs for you to look at, and we can get started right away."

I grinned, hoping I looked like a kid who's just discovered he's on his way to Disneyland. "That'll be great."

"Now, you have a credit card, Ed? We accept checks through the mail because we don't send out your membership material until it clears, but under the circumstances . . . you understand what I'm saying?"

"I don't blame you a bit, Mr. Rustin. I'll bring my Master-Card along this afternoon."

"Good, good," he said, actually rubbing his hands together. "I guarantee you that this will be one of the great adventures of your life. It's going to change things around for you, Ed. Trust me when I tell you. There's nothing like a beautiful little Chinese or Korean or Filipina lady." His smile turned smarmy, he jerked his thumb at his own chest, and said something I still find hard to believe: "Just ask the man who owns one."

9

INTERESTING CHOICE OF words, I thought as I walked back down San Angelo Avenue to the crossroads. I vaguely remembered that when I was a kid, "Ask the man who owns one" had been the slogan of some car company—Buick or Oldsmobile, as I recalled. Hearing it applied to a human being was pretty chilling. The concept of woman as chattel rightfully followed the great auk to extinction many years ago—although perhaps not in Ash Rustin's mind, and not in the way Asian Nights did business.

Poor little Leng, my inept masseuse, obviously was in some sort of bondage to Ash Rustin and the lovely Helen. She certainly had no relish for her job, and her reluctant offer of something else that "costs extra" told me Rustin was running a business a bit more insidious than a good old-fashioned therapeutic massage parlor.

What puzzled me was Doll Kane. She was certainly no one's property; on the contrary, she'd wound up with a good bit of her husband's. Like Scarlett O'Hara, I'd think about that tomorrow.

Today I'd keep my three o'clock appointment with Ash Rustin, hoping his hot-tempered wife and his Neanderthal buddy McGoon wouldn't be around to piss in the soup. I seem to have assuaged some of Rustin's doubts with my forelock-tugging performance; perhaps that afternoon I could gain his confidence and then ask him whether he knew Doll Kane and see what his reaction would be. I hoped I could get that accomplished before I had to fork over nearly six hundred bucks for a deluxe membership and a Chinese wife.

I turned onto Dixie Avenue, the sun baking me to medium well, and went past EAT with a shudder. The grease from my breakfast had congealed in my stomach and was crying for a Tums.

When I got to the motel I walked past my car, which probably felt like a pizza oven inside, and had started to open the door to our room when a short, skinny cop in a khaki uniform and aviator sunglasses came down the walk toward me.

"Your name Henderson?"

The sweat from the hellacious humidity turned cold under my shirt. "That's right," I said.

He swaggered right up to me, closer than was necessary. The tarnished silver-plated name tag on his chest read HAR-BOTTLE. "Chief'd like to see you."

There was no sound coming from inside the room, no television noise, no boom box. The hair on the back of my hands prickled. "Something wrong, Officer?"

"We got us a colored boy over to the station house says he's with you."

Alarm bells were ringing all over the place in my head, so insistently that I bit down hard on my angry response. "Is he all right?" I asked.

Harbottle shrugged. "So far," he said.

* * *

We walked to the police station—it was only a block away. Officer Harbottle was the taciturn type, and answered every one of my frantic questions with "Chief'll tell you." Not *the* chief; just Chief. The way a physician's nurse will always refer to the boss as "Doctor," as in "Has Doctor treated you previously?" or "Doctor is out of the office." Rather the way Tonto used to talk.

I was playing this silly little mental game about nouns without articles as we made our way along the sizzling pavement to keep my mind from conjuring up something terrible that had befallen Marvel. I'd brought him along on this trip against my better judgment and was now being punished by his punishment, whatever it was. If he'd been injured in some sort of freak accident—but Officer Harbottle hadn't mentioned an accident. He'd just said *We've got a colored boy down to the station.*

As Yale Rugoff had pointed out to me, this is the nineties; if someone had deliberately tried to fuck with Marvel, if he'd been harassed or harmed because he was black, I was going to do some serious kicking of ass. Starting with Officer Harbottle.

The San Angelo Police Department was housed in a frame building with faded aluminum siding. Apparently no one in this entire community had ever heard of the Three Little Pigs. It consisted, as far as I could see, of one large room where a wooden divider with a swinging gate separated the public from the three desks used by the minions of the law—the kind of setup you see in old thirties' movies. A reinforced steel door probably led to whatever kind of lockup they maintained here, and I was relieved to see that Marvel was, for the moment at least, on the right side of that door, sitting at an empty desk, motionless, his eyes slitted the way they get when he's seething inside.

Back in the corner at a desk somewhat more imposing than the other two, since it seemed to be real walnut instead of cheap veneer like its roommates, sat a fortyish man with a receding hairline and a gold badge pinned to a khaki shirt whose buttons were being stretched to the limit. Harbottle's badge was silver, so I assumed this was Chief.

"You Mr. Henderson?" he called. "C'mon in here a minute." Then he looked over at Harbottle. "Okay, Steve," he said, and Harbottle bobbed his head and left.

I went through the gate and stopped at Marvel's chair. "Are you okay?"

He was too enraged and humiliated even to answer. I squeezed his shoulder and proceeded to Chief's desk.

"What's the idea?" I demanded.

He laced his fingers together over his khaki-clad gut as though cradling an infant. The name plate on his desk proclaimed him to be BRILEY GORDEY, CHIEF OF POLICE. "Picked this boy up about an hour ago."

"On what charge?"

"Loitering."

I looked over at Marvel. He shook his head almost imperceptibly.

"Boy was loitering around on the public street," he said. Apparently no one in San Angelo believed in articles. "Wasn't doing anything wrong, exactly, which is why we got him sitting out here and not in back there, but we decided to bring him in and talk to him a little."

"Would you have talked to him if he was white?" I said.

"Oh, come off the civil rights shit a minute, will you?" Gordey spread his hands wide like he was describing the size of a largemouth bass. "San Angelo's not exactly a tourist paradise. There's only one motel—the one you're at. We're just a quiet little pissant farming town. So when we see someone *strange*"—he leaned on the word as hard as he could so I'd know exactly what he meant—"someone we don't know, acting suspicious on the street, we take a look." He exhaled in the manner of a man who's just taken a sip of hundred-year-old brandy. "I see my job not so much as catching criminals—on account of we don't have many of them up here—but stopping trouble before it starts. So I'm gonna ask you, Mr. Henderson, what brings you to San Angelo?"

"Do I have to have a reason?"

"No, sir. It's a free country."

Marvel wriggled on his chair, and Gordey threw him a baleful look. Then he turned back to me. "Kind of unusual, middle-aged white man traveling with a young colored boy, you have to admit."

I didn't say anything. It *was* a free country, free enough for Gordey to use the expression "colored boy" if he wanted to, I suppose, no matter how offensive he knew it to be.

"Off the record, Mr. Henderson," he said mildly, but steel flashed behind his eyes, as nasty as anyone's eyes I could remember, "what's the deal here? Is he your girlfriend? Suck your dick for you? You give it to him up the ass?" His lip curled back to reveal long horsey teeth. "Or is it the other way round?"

My breakfast was threatening to make a return appearance. Marvel didn't have to hear filth like this—not after the things he'd been through before I met him. My heart hurt for him.

And I've never been closer to killing anyone with my bare hands in my life.

I pulled a small Spiral notebook out of my hip pocket. "Mind if I use your pen, Chief?" I said, and took it off his desk without waiting for his permission. I had my own pen, but somehow using his was important to me, as though it was some kind of a psychic victory.

"What's that?" he said as I scribbled.

"I want to make sure I remember this conversation as clearly as possible. And that I remember your name." My hand was shaking so badly I could hardly write.

He snorted through his nose, and whatever it had gleaned him he swallowed. "That's interesting," he wheezed. "Well, write this down too. Write down that I asked how come, if your name is Henderson, that we run the license plate on your car and come to find out it belongs to somebody named Saxon from down in Venice." He paused and then added, "Where all the other dickie-lickers live." He stood up, reached across the desk, and snatched his pen away from me. "You want to explain that for me, Mr. Henderson? Or is it Mr. Saxon? I'm confused here." He waited.

"It's Saxon," I admitted.

"Don't you know you're not s'posed to register in a hotel under a false name? That's against the law."

"Then half the people in the world would be in jail."

"You're the one I'm asking, though." He put the pen back in its faux marble pedestal. "Wanta tell me why?"

I sighed, took out my wallet, and showed him my license. I figured he was going to ask for some sort of identification anyway, and the business cards were all I had that said I was Ed Henderson. "I'm a private investigator, up here on a missing persons case. Marvel there is my son."

His eyes flicked to Marvel, then back to me. "Yeah, I see a def'nite family resemblance," he said. "Who's this missing person?"

"I'm not at liberty to tell you that, Chief."

"Not at liberty." He returned the license and sat back in his chair, grunting in that way overweight men have. "Now that's a funny thing, liberty, i'dn it? Precious, don't you agree?"

He didn't really expect an answer so I saved my breath.

"I could deprive you of your liberty right now, Mr. Saxon. For using an alias at your hotel. And I could deprive the colored boy of his liberty too, because loitering's just as against the law as robbing a bank."

"He wasn't loitering and you know it."

"Maybe not enough to make it stick in a courtroom— even though I do happen to know the judge pretty well. But I stand ready and willing to offer you and the boy the hospitality of our facilities in the back room there neverthe- less. Maybe just for a night, maybe more. At least till we can get the court convened—and don't give me any crap about due process. This is a small town; we don't have a resident judge, so no telling how long it'd take till he got here. I'm within my rights to do that as a sworn officer of the law, and no jailhouse kike lawyer can tell you different."

Colored boys, dickie-lickers, and kikes. I felt as though I was in a time warp watching old Bull Connor, the sheriff of Selma, Alabama, leering at me on a black-and-white TV screen from behind his mirrored sunglasses. "Go ahead and book us then, Chief Gordey," I said. "And then let us have our phone calls."

"Now, now," he said, holding up a hand. "That might not be necessary at all. I'd like to avoid that if I could. I should think you would too. Save the taxpayers some money and save the two of you some sorrow. Maybe we can deal a little here. Whyn't you sit down a minute and we can talk."

I sat in the chair next to his desk while he opened the top drawer and scrabbled around in it for a second, then came up with a pack of Marlboros that had obviously been in there for a while. "I been tryin' to cut down," he explained. He took one out, tapped it on the desk, and stuck it between his teeth. If he was trying to look rakish, he had a long way to go. "I don't like things goin' on in my town I don't know about," he said. "Makes me nervous. When I'm nervous, I get irritable. I hate that."

He pulled a match from a matchbook bearing the logo of a Holiday Inn and lit the Marlboro. Taking a deep drag, he exhaled so the smoke went right into my face. "I'm thinking that if you were a little bit more cooperative and told me why you're here, then maybe I could cooperate with you some and forget about these—infractions."

"I told you: I'm looking for a missing person."

"Name!" he barked, so sharply that I sensed Marvel flinch in his chair behind me. "I want a goddamn name! I'm tired of playing games with you."

The cords in my neck were stretched like too-small rubber bands wrapped around a bulky package. Ordinarily I don't respond well to threats. If it had been just me, I would have sat in his damn jail until the autumn equinox. But Marvel was another story. He'd suffered too much in his life, been abused too often for me to even think about letting it happen again.

"Her name is Doll Kane," I said.

"What the hell kind of name is Doll?"

"It's her name."

"Why do you want her so bad?"

"I've been employed by her husband to find her. Simple runaway wife case."

"And what makes you think she's in San Angelo?"

I shrugged. "We traced her movements up to this area."

He raised his eyebrows. "No kidding. Traced her movements. Well, I know just about everything that goes on in town, and I can't remember hearing anything about anyone by that name. But maybe I've seen her around. What's she look like?"

I set my jaw stubbornly, and he grinned like a little kid and dangled the keys to the lockup in front of my nose. "The boy there won't have a very pleasant evening in an eight-by-eight cage," he reminded me.

There was no point in being a hard case here. As long as Marvel was with me, Briley Gordey held all the cards, and he knew it. I leaned back in my chair and capitulated. "She's about twenty-three, five foot two, and Chinese."

He stuck out his lower lip and nodded, his eyebrows raised. "Chinese, eh? Ah so," he said.

Chief was a riot.

"We'll leave this afternoon," I said. "We won't even spend the night."

"Whatever," Marvel mumbled, almost in a whisper. He was lying on his bed, his hands behind his head, staring at a two-foot crack in the motel room ceiling. His eyes were glittering, the veins in his forehead were almost popping out, and he fairly quivered with indignation.

What can you say to a kid who's caught every bad break imaginable, who's managed to claw his way out of all the shit life's thrown at him to the point where he can hold his head up, who was just starting to feel good about himself and the world around him, and then gets busted by a sitcom Barney Fife for the crime of being an African American on the streets of a grass-roots small town?

I wanted to tell him anything to make the hurt and humiliation go away. I wanted to tell him not to feel bad and not to worry because it wasn't really like this, that most people were of good heart, kind and loving, that he had now blossomed into manhood and was ready to take his rightful place in the world and that the chances of anything like this ever happening again were one in fifty thousand.

But I've never lied to Marvel and I wasn't going to start now. Oh, the out-and-out racists, the Lester Maddoxes and their ilk, had either died off or gone back into their dirty closets; Chief Briley Gordey was a walking anachronism. But I couldn't write it off to small-town ignorance—there are loads of good people in small towns and plenty of bigots in big ones. I had to ascribe it to a kind of global stupidity.

It's not cool to don hoods and sheets and shout "Nigger!" anymore—thank God we've come that far—but there would always be the little subtleties that a sharp guy like Marvel would catch: being called by his first name by someone who addresses whites as mister. Condescension so finely honed that a written transcript would read like good manners. The well-meaning liberals who'd hasten to tell him how they never miss Arsenio. Standing on a street corner waiting for a traffic light to change and watching drivers stopped at the intersection glance worriedly at him and then at their door locks.

I sat on the edge of the bed. "People are stupid sometimes. All people. Even me. It stinks, but that's just how it is. Don't let them get to you. Just remember who you are and be goddamn proud of that—and as long as you keep that center, anybody who doesn't like it can go piss up a rope."

He didn't say anything.

"I don't have answers, Marvel. If I did I'd be smarter than everybody else, because they don't have answers either. Maybe I've been wrong trying to keep shit like this out of your life, but I figured you'd already had your share and I was leaving some for the next guy. The world can be a great place or it can be a sewer; what your particular world will be depends a lot on how you handle things like today."

He turned his head toward me without moving anything else; his eyes were dark, and cold as a tomb. "Like bein' a colored boy?"

"If an asshole like that can make you feel like a colored boy, Marvel, that's what you're going to be. If you feel like a man—like the strong, decent, funny, bright man I know— then you are one."

"Simple, huh?"

"No," I said, "it isn't. It's very complicated, and you'd laugh at me if I said different. But you're a rational, thinking human being, and you have choices. Ever since you've been with me I've tried to make you know you're a pretty great kid. If you're going to believe Chief Gordey instead of me, then maybe I haven't done as good a job as I think."

His eyes went to the ceiling again. "If you say so," he said.

We had a quiet lunch at the San Angelo Café, which was perhaps a step above EAT but not much more than that. I don't even remember what we ate; I was feeling pretty lousy about what had happened and worried that an invisible but tangible wedge had been driven between my son and me. After he'd been living with me for a few months, after I'd decided to go through the legalities of adopting him as my own, I never stopped to think about his race. Maybe my being color-blind had done him a disservice. Maybe we should have talked more about blackness and whiteness. It had seemed to me at the time that Marvel had a lot of pain and guilt and self-loathing to work through, a savage childhood and adolescence that had nothing to do with his being an African American, and that's what I had focused on.

Maybe I'd just been a lousy father.

After lunch I sent him back to the motel to repack and load the car and walked down San Angelo Avenue, trying to confine my thoughts to the problem at hand, which was to find Doll Kane. Nappy, I was certain, didn't give a damn about my own personal problems or Marvel's—or fatherhood or racism or the National League pennant race, for that matter. He wanted his Doll and was paying me good money to find her for him.

There were two cars parked in a gravel lot behind the Far East Massage, and I thought about scared little Leng and the big smelly guy in the overalls. I guessed that when Asian Nights wasn't able to marry off the young women smiling prettily in those brochure photographs, they got put to work in a massage parlor somewhere, whether they liked it or not—not unlike the old credit-ticket system they'd used to import the workers to build the railroad at slave wages.

I went into the building next door and climbed the stairs to Rustin Imports. The top half of the door was inset with frosted glass, and behind it I could see the cold glow of fluorescent lights.

I went in, right on time for my three o'clock appointment. Helen Ng was posed in front of her husband's desk, looking as angry as I'd seen her the last time. And I smelled Earthquake McGoon before I saw him, standing just to the side of the door.

"Nice try, Mr. Saxon," Helen Ng said.

I didn't see the punch coming, so I could neither block nor duck it. The big fist hit me flush on the mouth and snapped my head back, setting off a light show behind my eyes. As the force of the blow drove me back, the heel of my shoe caught on the top step, throwing me off balance. I fell backward down the flight of linoleum-covered steps.

I didn't stop rolling until I hit the very bottom.

10

MARVEL WAS WAITING for me when I came out of the San Angelo Hospital emergency room, his handsome, coffee brown face twisted into a worried grimace. But he brightened a little when he saw that I was ambulatory and not permanently disfigured.

It wasn't as bad as it might have been. The harried ER doctor had taken five neat stitches in the inside of my mouth where my teeth had been driven clean through my lower lip; two incisors were loosened but still gamely hanging in there. I sported a couple of gigantic bruises, one on the right side of my back just above the belt and one on the front of my thigh from bouncing down the flight of uncarpeted steps. One elbow and both knees were skinned, though not seriously, and my neck and shoulders felt as if I'd been hanged.

Nothing was broken.

It was a clear case of assault, of course, but it never occurred to me to report it to the local authorities, the local authorities being Chief Gordey and Officer Harbottle. I was pretty sure they would have found some way to blame it all on me. Trespassing, perhaps, or more likely felony mopery, and I would have wound up in their lockup. Marvel too, just for being there and not having the right color skin.

So I just picked myself up and limped over to the emergency room, where they stitched me up without comment and with damn few questions. "I fell down the stairs," I told them, and that seemed to satisfy the nurse on duty, although no trained medical person would have failed to recognize the classic symptoms of a punch in the mouth.

"This was a great vacation," Marvel said as he guided me out the hospital door and onto the burning street. "Where we goin' next week? Baghdad?"

"Don't make me laugh," I begged, feeling the new stitches pull. At least he had regained a measure of his sense of humor. People are a lot more resilient when they're young, in mind and body. Marvel was still stinging from the police station incident, I knew, but he always had the knack of keeping his priorities in order, even when he'd been much younger, and his concern for my physical well-being overrode any bitterness he might have been feeling.

He insisted on driving home, for which I was grateful. I was too stiff and achy to do a very good job of it; besides, I needed to think, and at the wheel of a car on a California interstate is not the place to do that.

Having a designated driver, though, allowed me to do my thinking aloud, even though talking through my sore and swollen mouth was a chore.

"At least I was right," I said. We'd driven back to Sacramento and were headed south on the freeway, and I was sprawled all over the passenger seat trying to find a position of relative comfort. "Doll Kane is up there in San Angelo—or if she's not there, Ash Rustin knows where she is. And that cop Gordey is in on it too."

"I can believe it, that potbellied sack of shit!" Marvel said fervently, his eyes on the road.

"I know they're all involved somehow. Just before I got blindsided, Helen Ng called me by my real name. I'd told the Rustins I was Ed Henderson; the only one who knew my name is Saxon was Chief Gordey. And he was the only one who knew we were in San Angelo to find Doll Kane in the first place. So he must have tipped them off." I glanced over at him and winked. "Unless it was you."

He maneuvered the car slickly around a slow-moving produce truck driven by a dark-skinned Latino in a wide-brimmed straw hat. "But if that's so, if they know where Mrs. Kane is, wasn't it kinda dumb to show their hand like that?"

"It was. But Helen Ng's got a temper like a puff adder; she shoots her mouth off first and thinks about it later. She really lost it in the massage parlor when I started asking questions."

The muscles along his jaw jumped as he gritted his teeth. He knew all about forced prostitution. "So what we gonna do about it?"

"We? Haven't you had enough?"

"I'm just gettin' started," he said.

I frowned, staring out the window at the irrigated farm-land rushing past us. I wanted Marvel out of this, as far out as I could get him, but there was no point in debating it with him on the interstate. Besides, I hurt too much to argue.

The sun dipped behind the low-lying mountains and disappeared just about the time we reached Fresno. We drove on for a little while longer and stopped for dinner in Kingsburg, a quaint Swedish community out in the middle of nowhere next to Highway 99. I'm a great admirer of smorgasbord—of any ethnic food, actually, except for Korean—but my mouth hurt too much to eat. I got a kick watching Marvel, though. He thrived on pizza and junk food as much as any kid, but I'd taught him to enjoy the good stuff too, and he practically inhaled the aromatic meatballs and the salmon with dill the restaurant had set out on their buffet table.

"Seems to me like we're stuck," he said between bites. "We can't prove they got her against her will, we can't sic the cops on 'em. And we sure can't go back up there ourselves. That police chief'll lock us up and forget where he left us."

"Yes, he will," I said. The stitches in my mouth were making me sound like the Elephant Man. "But the ball is in the client's court at this point."

He stopped chewing. "Say what?"

"I'm pretty sure we've located Nappy Kane's wife. That's what he paid me to do. As far as I'm concerned, I earned my money." I put a tentative hand up to my lower lip, gently touching the swelling with my fingertips. "And then some."

He just stared at me for a minute. "You mean you're lettin' those clowns get away with messin' you up like this?"

"Legally there isn't much I can do about it, Marvel. In this business you can't afford to take things personally."

He pushed his plate away in disgust.

"What?" I asked.

"You bein' a wuss, an' shit." Marvel frequently reverts to street patois when he's stressed, and from the expression on his face and the disgust in his voice, his current mood more than qualified.

"You want me to lose my license? I can't go barging in there and drag her home by the hair if she doesn't want to be dragged. And as for the San Angelo cops, they've got badges and the law behind them. Write it off, for God's sake."

"Easy for you to say. You didn't get arrested."

"No, I just got knocked down a flight of stairs."

He clenched his fists in frustration. "*Damn.* Can't we do *anything?*"

"Welcome to adulthood," I said.

When we got back into the car I could tell he was ripping. I couldn't much blame him, and I couldn't help him either. It was something he was just going to have to work out for himself. When you're young, everything is possible. It's only after you've got a few miles on your odometer that you come to the unpleasant realization that there are just some lousy situations you can't do a damn thing to control. Part of the growing-up process.

Night had dropped an inky curtain over the San Joaquin Valley, and the traffic had thinned out considerably before Highway 99 merged with Interstate 5. Despite his anger, which many drivers are wont to vent when they get behind the wheel, Marvel held the speed at about seventy, five miles over the posted limit but on the highways of California, a permissible gimme. He seemed to have everything under control, and my lip was throbbing and my lower jaw ached badly, so I leaned back and closed my eyes as we passed the collection of gas stations and family restaurants that was the town of Grapevine and headed up into the mountains toward the Tejon Pass.

I awoke with my ears popping. We had just about reached the summit and the change in altitude was doing a number on the inside of my head. I yawned as vigorously as my stitches would permit and swallowed several times to clear the pressure. The digital clock on the dashboard showed a few minutes past ten.

142

Marvel flicked a glance over at me, then looked back out at the road ahead. "How you feel?"

"Brand new. You?"

"I'm cool."

"You aren't falling asleep, are you?"

He didn't answer me but shook his head.

"Want to turn the radio on to help you stay awake?"

"Whatever."

I wasn't used to prolonged periods of silence with Marvel, and it was making me nervous. I turned the knob on the radio and the car filled up with the sounds of Hammer. "There you go," I said. I couldn't stand the music myself, but he liked it, and at the moment I preferred keeping him relatively content.

At that altitude after sundown there's no need for artificial cooling, so I rolled down my window a crack and let the wind circulate through the car's interior. The airflow also masked the noise from the radio, which was a blessing; Hammer is only okay when you can see him move. I stared sleepily out at the big rigs in the right-hand lane plodding down the steep grade in low gear as we whizzed by them, glad I wasn't in one. I'm not fond of long-distance driving, and thinking of the truckers, ever alert for speed traps and struggling against white-line fever, I didn't envy them their lonely existence.

And then it struck me that we were whizzing a little too fast. The posted limit up on the Grapevine is fifty-five miles an hour, and we had to be doing eighty on one of the steepest downhill grades in the state. I don't like to nag when other people are driving, but I gave Marvel a parental "Watch your speed." When he didn't answer me I turned my head to look at him, the crick in my neck sending a knife of pain down my backbone. His teeth were clenched and the knuckles on his hands bulged as he gripped the wheel.

"Somethin' wrong with the brakes," he said tightly.

He sure knows how to get my attention.

"Pump them."

I watched his foot go all the way to the floor against no resistance whatsoever. "Gone," he announced.

We were in the center lane of a three-lane highway, where we were supposed to be. To our right were the mammoth trucks, going about thirty-five, and even had the inside lane been clear, there was no shoulder, just a sheer rock face where the road had been hacked out of the mountain, so trying to pull off the highway was out of the question. On our left was another wall of rock. Ahead of us was the rest of eternity.

The wind coming through the open window of the Corsica roared in my ears and thundered around inside my chest as the car sucked up the highway like a strand of spaghetti. Marvel flicked on his high beams and his hazard flashers and leaned on the horn for all he was worth, steering through the light traffic with one hand, and the automotive Red Sea ahead of us parted to allow our frantic passage. A few drivers flipped us off, but most seemed to sense there was something wrong. No one in their right mind goes down the Grapevine that fast if he can help it.

The red taillights of the other cars were a fast-action photograph exposed at slow speed, blurring by us as in a nightmare. The tires squealed a protest as we careened around a curve near the exit to the Templin Highway, and through the open window I smelled the rubber burning. Marvel pumped the brakes for all he was worth, but it was an impotent gesture; they were gone, never to return.

Ahead, the twinkling lights of the little mountain town of Castaic rushed toward us like the lights of a carnival midway from the downside of a roller coaster. The rap music on the radio lent a certain grotesque quality to the ride.

We were doing about ninety-five now, and the big square van conversion ahead of us was moving at half that speed, seeming blissfully unaware of what was screaming down on it from the rear, despite the horn and the high-beam head-lights. Marvel took his hand from the horn and steadied the wheel, moving deftly into the left lane and missing the rear corner of the van by about two inches. The Corsica bucked from the wind resistance and came dangerously close to the rock face on our left. He gritted his teeth and eased away from the side and back into the center lane, fighting the steering like an ancient mariner in a typhoon. His face glistened with sweat now, and a drop hung from his nose for a moment before plopping into his lap. I knew how he felt—my own shirt was drenched, my heart was beating somewhere in the vicinity of my Adam's apple, and I was uncomfortably cognizant of the smell of my own fear.

A red Dodge Shadow got the hell out of our way in a hurry, cutting in ahead of an enormous green Peterbilt in the slow lane, and if we hadn't put so much distance between us so quickly I'm sure I would have heard the sound of squealing brakes and curses.

The Lake Hughes Road exit was about three miles down the hill, but it wasn't going to do us any good; most freeway off-ramps in California are cloverleafs, and at the rate we were traveling not even Mario Andretti could have kept the wheels on the road through one of those. We'd go sailing off into space to smash against the huge boulders on either side of the road, and there wouldn't be enough left of us to pick up with a dustpan and a whisk broom.

The white reflecting letters of a big green sign at the roadside caught my eye as we rushed by it: RUNAWAY TRUCK RAMP, 1 MILE. I glanced over at Marvel and he nodded wordlessly.

The heavyweight trucks were spaced about forty feet apart in the right-hand lane, which at warp speed effectively created a solid wall of vehicles. Marvel tensed his shoulders and gulped in about a gallon of air. Several things could happen, most of them bad: he could miss the ramp and slam into the rock face at the side of the road, which would undoubtedly be fatal. He could clip one of the big rigs on the way over and take the truck driver out along with us. Or he could just plumb not be able to manage it and we'd continue careening down the road until the law of averages caught up with us and we wiped out. If we were to survive intact, the timing would have to be split-second.

Leaning on the horn again, he had the presence of mind to flick on his right turn signal. The kid had a head on his shoulders, all right, and I was proud of him even through my paralyzing fear. I was hoping we'd get out of this for his sake more than my own.

The lit escape ramp was coming up on our right, a mixture of soft sand and gravel that went for about fifty yards and then rose up at a forty-five-degree angle into a pile of sandbags and gravel about twelve feet high. Marvel beat a tattoo on the horn and the driver of the big white refrigerator truck on our right was able to figure it out. He hit his brakes hard—too hard; the back end of his Mack fishtailed out into our lane like a bullwhip. Marvel twisted the wheel to the left, barely getting out of the way of several tons of steel, then

146

jerked it the other way, cutting in front of the big guy with only centimeters to spare, and hit the gravelly sand of the emergency ramp.

We both flopped forward like those plastic dummies you see in the car safety commercials as our speed was cut nearly in half, and the shoulder belt cut hard into my chest. As I saw the wall of sand looming up in front of us a yell involuntarily burst from my throat. I braced myself for the impact.

It was every bit as bad as I thought it would be. Every muscle in my body twisted and pulled, and a Fourth of July fireworks show kicked off behind my eyes as I heard the sickening crunch of stressed metal.

And I learned something I'd always wondered about.

Air bags really work.

11

"SOMEBODY DOESN'T LIKE you, Mr. Saxon."

California Highway Patrol sergeant Jim Gelarden had a talent for understatement. He was sitting with Marvel and me in the comfortable lobby of Marymount Hospital in Castaic, where Marvel and I had spent the night under observation. Both of us had suffered whiplash, and Marvel's nose had been bloodied, but other than some pretty sore muscles we had survived more or less intact. Marvel had been fitted with a temporary cervical collar that made him look like a strong safety for the Raiders.

I was seriously considering writing a guidebook to the emergency rooms of California.

We'd put on quite a show on the Grapevine for passing motorists the night before. The flashing strobe lights atop the CHP cruisers and the support vehicles, the blinding glare of the floodlights they set up to facilitate removing the wounded car provided a sort of impromptu spectacle for looky-loos. It's only human nature to slow down and rubberneck an accident on the highway. Part of it is simple—if ghoulish—curiosity, I guess, and another part is that it's a break from the monotony of the road at night, but mostly it provides the spectators with a feeling of relief—that it's happening to someone else and not them.

Gelarden had just come from the CHP impound garage where what was left of my Corsica had been hauled for inspection. "It's pretty obvious when you take a look," he went on. "The brake line was cut—very neatly. Not all the way through, which is why you were able to get as far as you did without driving into a ditch. But when you started downhill and made the brakes work harder, it just went." He nodded over at Marvel. "Neat piece of driving, young fella."

"The brakes were deliberately sabotaged? Are you sure, Sergeant?"

"There's not much question about it, sir."

Whoever had done it must have known we'd be heading back to Los Angeles and that the terrain between Sacramento and Tejon Pass is almost surreally flat and straight. By the time the brake line parted we were two hundred miles from San Angelo.

"How long would it take someone to fix a car's brakes like that?"

"No more than two minutes, for anyone who knows what they're doing. It's nothing you wouldn't learn in high school, in auto shop." Gelarden ran his hands through his thinning hair. "Old Chief Gordey runs an interesting town up there."

It must have happened while we were at lunch, before I walked up the stairs and into Earthquake McGoon's fist. I had really played this one dumb, right from the moment we arrived in San Angelo, and I'd paid for it. The trouble was, Marvel had too, and I was pretty mad at myself about that.

In my own defense, I'd never really figured it for anything more than a simple domestic case: young, foreign wife married to older husband feels trapped and isolated and runs away. To my discredit, I hadn't factored in Nappy Kane's signing over all his assets to her. That's what turned a simple domestic case into a hot potato.

But the folks in the black hats hadn't exactly racked up genius points with the National Honor Society, either. Helen Ng had really blown it in the massage parlor, reacting way out of proportion when I'd started asking Leng questions about Asian Nights. And when she had her bouncer bounce me later that afternoon, it really tipped their hand. I suppose that's why she thought she'd be happier if my brakes suddenly stopped functioning while I was heading down the Grapevine. There were more facets to Rustin Imports and Asian Nights, more secrets to keep than simply a crude rub-and-tickle joint, of which the local constabulary was undoubtedly aware and probably had a hand in.

It takes a pretty compelling reason to try and kill two people you don't even know.

"Any idea who might have done this, Mr. Saxon?"

"Damn right!" Marvel put in.

"But," I said quickly, "we have no proof, and I'm not willing to risk a lawsuit by naming any names."

Marvel grunted in disgust and shifted his weight so that he was facing slightly away from us. He could say more with body language than an old-time politician could with a forty-five-minute stem-winder on the floor of the Senate.

Gelarden lowered his voice, looking around the hospital lobby as though terrorists lurked behind the potted palms. "When we removed the personal effects from your car, we found the weapon in your briefcase," he said.

"It's perfectly legal," I told him. "It wasn't loaded."

"I know that, and we're returning it to you." He scratched his bald spot. "You're a private investigator, right? You know the law pretty well."

"Well enough."

"Then I have to caution you in the strongest possible terms not to do anything stupid. Like taking that law into your own hands."

"John Wayne is dead, Sergeant."

He allowed himself a fetus of a smile. "Can I take that as a promise?"

"I'm not going to go back to San Angelo and blow anybody away—Scout's honor."

"How about you, Marvel?"

Marvel looked startled for a minute, and then his eyes twinkled; he was glad to be included. The very best thing you can do for a teenager is treat them like an adult, with no condescension and without pointing out that you're doing it. He responded as sincerely as he could. "Never even crossed my mind," he said.

"If it does . . . " Gelarden began.

"Jus' say no," Marvel finished for him.

Gelarden promised he'd be in touch, filled out some paperwork having to do with the disposal of my car, and left us in the hospital lobby watching a game show while we waited for Jo Zeidler to come and collect us. I had called her the night before and given her a quick rundown on what had happened, and after she had assured herself that Marvel was all right, she'd promised to drive up to Castaic the next morning and bring us home.

She arrived at about noon. Since Jo functions as both my surrogate mother and my Jiminy Crickett, I expected her to first scold me about consorting with criminal elements and then to really let me have it for taking Marvel with me and putting him in the path of danger. But instead she was supportive and concerned and nurturing and loving as we headed back toward the city. I figured the lecture was going to come later.

What with the twenty-four-hour gridlock on the streets and freeways of Los Angeles, it took more than three hours to get back to Venice, and seeing the condition we were in, Jo insisted on cooking dinner for us, an event to which she summoned her husband Marsh. Basketball season was over, though, and I had no idea what Marsh and Marvel would talk about.

Just so the party talk wouldn't drag, I invited a friend of my own, a guy I'd worked with before. His name is Ray Tucek, and if you're ever against the ropes, you could do a lot worse than to have Ray in your corner.

With my lacerated lip I didn't figure to eat much dinner, but Jo bustled around in the kitchen anyway, defrosting a leg of New Zealand spring lamb I'd been keeping in the freezer for a special occasion. While she was cooking, Marvel was in his room calling up all his buddies to recount his brush with death. This little episode was going to make him a pretty heavy dude at the mall for a while.

I went up to my study and got my client on my own phone line and told him I thought I'd located his wife up in San Angelo.

"So, you found her?" Nappy said eagerly. It sounded over the phone as if he was eating something.

"I think so. I'd rather give you the details in person, though."

"You can't tell me over the phone?"

"Let's get together tomorrow. Why don't we meet at the Rose Café?" It's a popular hangout on Rose Avenue, and it was midway between his place in Santa Monica and mine in Venice.

He demurred. "I wear one of those Medic Alert bracelets saying that even if I should drop dead in front of the Rose Café they won't take me inside. Everybody who hangs out in there is fourteen years old."

"You pick a place, then."

"All right," he said. "I'm eating at the Photoplayers Club tomorrow. Why don't you meet me there at, say, eleven o'clock."

"Isn't that kind of early for lunch?"

There was a short pause while he searched for a reply. "Who said anything about lunch?"

I'd forgotten Nappy's notorious penury, although as I hung up I realized that after Doll and her lawyer got through with him he'd have a reason for never picking up a check.

I fixed martinis for Jo and myself, and cracked open a mineral water for Marsh. Never much of a drinker to begin with, Marsh was being a health food nut these days, although like most of the other fads he'd flirted with, including numerology, astrology, Buddhism, biofeedback, and nudism, it didn't figure to last very long.

Just a few minutes before the leg of lamb attained that perfect medium-rare state that always makes me look at vegetarians like Marsh as though they're crazy, the doorbell chimed. I went to greet my other dinner guest.

Ray Tucek works as a stuntman, though not as often as he used to when he was younger. Now in his early forties, he's as hard and tough as when he'd spent two years of his youth in the jungles of Southeast Asia on an endless marijuana and Quaalude high. Those twenty-four months of dodging Charlie snipers and engaging in hand-to-hand combat with people clad in black pajamas whose fondest wish was for his death had left him with little inclination to suffer fools, and his temper had gotten him into more than one scrape in the industry. He had, for instance, been blackballed from the Fox lot several years before when he refused to swallow the crap being dished out on the set by the he-man star of a prime-time cop show and had busted his jaw with one short punch, causing an expensive two-week hiatus in production. Now most of his stunt work is on independent, small-budget shows, and in between he picks up drinking money laboring as a bodyguard-cum–security specialist.

In Hollywood, where the bullshit level frequently exceeds the pollution index, Ray is an unpretentious and honest breath of fresh air. I fixed him a Scotch on the rocks. I always keep a bottle of the cheap stuff on hand for Ray; he actually prefers it.

Then, leaving my guests in Marvel's capable hands, I went in and whipped up some of my justly famous secret tarragon sauce to enhance a leg of lamb my jaw was too sore to eat.

During dinner, since I didn't have to concern myself with talking while my mouth was full, I told everyone what had gone down in San Angelo. Marsh, munching on a bean sprout salad with ingredients from Mrs. Gooch's Natural Food Market, hung on every word, probably thinking whether it could be turned into a viable screenplay.

"Redneck pricks!" Ray muttered when I got to the part about Officer Harbottle picking Marvel up on the street. Since he had worked with me on the case that had brought Marvel to me in the first place, he'd always considered himself the kid's second father and had indeed gotten Marvel interested in martial arts, working with him until Marvel had progressed to the point where he needed a more skilled *sensei* to teach him.

Jo just looked worried, and it occurred to me, as it has so

many times in the course of our long friendship, how nice it was to have someone who cared enough about me to worry—even if she was somebody else's wife.

"So," Ray said, putting down his knife and fork and leaning back in his chair, "what are you going to do about it?"

I didn't look at Jo. "When we left San Angelo I wasn't going to do anything about it, except tell my client I thought his wife was up there. I figured a busted mouth was part of the expense of doing business. But after they cut my brake line, things got different."

Jo threw down her napkin. "You're not thinking of going back up there?"

I just looked at her.

"Damn it, you're going to get yourself killed one of these days! Haven't you evolved any more than that? A testosterone rush isn't worth your life! Is getting even some sort of weird macho thing with you?"

I considered my answer carefully. "Partly, I suppose. Getting even keeps things in balance."

"At least you admit it," she grumbled.

"Another part is my duty to my client. But mainly, if they get away with it with me, what's to stop them from trying it again with somebody else—someone who might not be so lucky?" I looked at Marvel and grinned. "And might not have such a good driver along to save his ass."

"Your ass is beyond saving," she said.

Ray took a pull on his Scotch, his third of the evening. "Saxon, since the last time I looked you were a raging heterosexual, can I assume that I'm here tonight because you want me involved in some way and not because I'm such a charming dinner date?"

I nodded. "My cover is blown in San Angelo, Ray, and it's such a small town there's no way I could even drive down the street without attracting the wrong kind of attention. I'd like you to go up there, keep a very low profile, and surveil Rustin Imports for me until we can get a line on Doll Kane."

"The usual rates?"

"Naturally."

"And when does this all kick in?"

"Day after tomorrow," I said.

"Where are you going to be while I'm slow-baking in a car trying to look inconspicuous?"

"I'll drive back up there too, but I'll get a motel room in Sacramento and keep out of sight as much as I can." I sipped at a glass of Chardonnay; it didn't raise hell with my stitches the way the martini had. "Ash Rustin is not only a scam artist, but I've got a good idea he's a white slaver too. After we find Mrs. Kane, I'm going to shut him down like a mom-and-pop grocery across the street from a Safeway."

Marsh Zeidler said, "How can you do that? He's obviously got the San Angelo police in his hip pocket." When Marsh constructs a story he likes to make sure all the loose ends are tied up, which I guess is a big step from several years ago, when he used to write esoteric screenplays that made the films of David Lynch seem as accessible as those of Frank Capra.

"Helen Ng and Ash Rustin are importing foreign nationals into this country for immoral purposes," I said, "as well as committing mail fraud. I think the feds would be very interested in their operation. We can bypass the San Angelo police."

"Okay," Ray said. "I'm in."

Marvel cleared his throat. "Uh, excuse me?" His tone

dripped ingenuousness. "There's a little piece missin' here that everybody seems t'be forgettin' about."

"Which is?"

"Me."

I sighed. "Marvel, you're not going up there again. You're too conspicuous, for one thing. And it's too dangerous."

"I'd like to point out," he said carefully, once more James Mason as opposed to hip-hopper, "that I'm old enough to vote for the president, old enough to fight for my country, old enough to sign a legal contract." He allowed himself a supercilious smile. "And although I hesitate to mention it, it was my driving that saved your white ass."

"You're still my responsibility."

"Not legally," he said, "not since I turned eighteen."

"Don't give me legally, counsellor. You're my son and I love you. I almost got you killed yesterday—I'm not going to let that happen again."

"Man, you talk about gettin' even! You're not the one got arrested because of his skin color."

"You think I don't feel shitty about that? But we're not going to fight the Civil War all over again just because your pride is hurt. I know how you feel—"

"Sure you do. I bet they call you 'white boy' all the time."

"Okay, maybe I don't. But I promise you Ray and I will get these guys. We won't come back until we do." He started to say something, but I cut him off. "This is not negotiable, Marvel."

He was so angry he didn't even bother rolling his eyes up to the ceiling or muttering an obscenity under his breath. He just unfolded himself quietly from his chair and left the table.

Jo started to push her chair away from the table. "Let me talk to him."

"For Christ's sake, let it go!" I said with more heat than I'd intended. "For once I'd like to say something to him without having to prepare a position paper to defend it!"

She kind of reared back, and I realized she was preparing to go into her Jewish Guilt mode, which very much resembles my own mother's Irish Guilt mode, only without the sarcasm. "The least you could do is explain to him—"

"Jo, I said it's nonnegotiable."

She raised her eyebrows. "What's that supposed to be, Holy Writ?"

I thought of several responses but choked them off. I was too tired and had too much on my mind. "Let's not make a *tsimmes* out of this, okay?" Most of the Yiddish phrases I know I learned from Jo, and it pleases me when I get the chance to toss one back at her. "We've got a lot to do in the next few days, and we need to talk about it now."

She crossed her arms and sulked. Ray looked on bemused, while Marsh pretended that he was eating dinner somewhere else.

I tried to take control of the meeting. "I'm seeing Nappy Kane in the morning. Ray, come by the office sometime tomorrow and pick up copies of the file and a picture of Doll Kane. Then we'll leave for up north Thursday morning. Jo, first thing tomorrow I'd like you to go down to the hall of records and . . . "

I looked at the stubborn thrust of Jo's jaw. "Never mind," I said, and got up and went into the hallway and rapped on my son's closed bedroom door.

"Hey, Marvel!" I called through the unforgiving wood. "How'd you like to go down to the hall of records tomorrow and play detective?"

12

THE PHOTOPLAYERS CLUB has been a Hollywood entity since the days of silent pictures. It was founded by three day players, guys who would never be stars but who always made a living, and it was designed to be a place where industry professionals, mostly actors with a sprinkling of writers and directors but *never* a producer, can go to relax, talk shop, and get inelegantly drunk away from the prying eyes of civilians and fans and the Hollywood press cadre. As private clubs go, it's fairly benign, having no agenda other than to exist. Its membership is exclusive only because damn few people in town who are not already members want to be. There is no particular cachet or prestige attached to membership, and it costs little to join. It's just a leave-me-alone-to-drink-quietly kind of refuge for the remaining survivors of the movies' golden era.

It's changed locations several times in its sixty-some-year history, including a brief sojourn in the moribund Knickerbocker Hotel right across the street from the office I had then on Ivar Avenue, and is now housed in a ponderous bungalow on a side street north of Franklin, where the Hollywood Hills begin. The walls groan beneath the weight of a thousand framed movie posters and stills from the thirties and forties, and signed photo portraits of now-forgotten matinee idols with patent leather hair and pencil-line mustaches whose careers had glowed brightly and then flamed out. The corridors and library and taproom smell like old men.

And oh yes, the Photoplayers are all male.

It should be pointed out that no woman ever lost out on a job by being excluded from the Photoplayers, mainly because the male members rarely had jobs themselves. The purpose of the club was never "networking"—oh, how I hate verbs that in more civilized times used to be nouns—but to afford its habitués a venue in which to sit around with other old cronies of a certain age, play gin rummy, drink honest whiskey, and concoct harmless little lies about their careers during the good old days when movies were movies. In the evenings they would bring their wives, or more often their women friends, to a listless meal of calf's liver or meat loaf and mashed potatoes in the inexpensive pine-paneled basement dining room, and about twice each year they'd put on an "entertainment"—little more than a talent show, really—that outsiders were urged to attend, to raise money to keep the venerable white elephant open for another few months.

About twelve years ago the Photoplayers were dragged kicking and screaming into the eighties and amended their charter to admit female members. And a few women had even considered joining—elderly ladies who had once been Goldwyn Girls or contractees at RKO or Monogram and now wore too much lipstick. But they all eventually opted to pass. Not many women want to sit around listening to a bunch of octogenarians who dye their hair lying about the time they *almost* got cast in *High Sierra* but lost out at the end to a Warners contract player named Bogart.

160

I arrived at about eleven in my rented car, a tan Geo—not my style, but it was the best the insurance company would spring for—and stopped in front of the sign that read VALET PARKING. The valet must have been at least seventy-five years old and had probably first learned his driving skills behind the wheel of a Model A. He took my car and parked it in the dusty unpaved lot behind the building, and I went inside.

Nappy Kane was part of the prelunch crowd gathered at the bar. Besides me and the bartender, he was the youngest person in the room.

He stood up as I approached, a half-finished bloody Mary clutched in his pudgy hand. "Come on," he said, "let's go over here in the corner where we can talk." We crossed the room to a small table in the corner. He didn't ask me if I wanted a drink.

Nappy stopped to say hello to three different people on the way. They all looked vaguely familiar, the ghosts of supporting actors and dress extras I had grown up watching in the Saturday afternoon dark. Everyone at the club seemed to fawn on him, inordinately pleased that he even deigned to talk to them, thrilled that he actually remembered their names. They, after all, had only been day players at their peak; Nappy, for a few bright years, had been a bona fide star.

"What happened to your mouth?" he said when we'd finally seated ourselves. My lip had puffed up to give me a Maurice Chevalier pout.

"That's one of the things I want to talk to you about." I laid out the whole story for him, quietly, because he kept looking around the room to make sure no one was listening. Protestations of love for Doll notwithstanding, I got the idea that Nappy's overpowering emotion over this whole affair was embarrassment. I gave him nearly the whole story—the trip to San Angelo, finding Asian Nights, Briley Gordey and Earthquake McGoon and the unexpected brake job that had rammed my nose into a pile of sand on the Grapevine. I didn't tell him that Rustin was running the best little whorehouse in San Angelo. Even so, he didn't sound happy.

"You mean you know she's up there and you didn't even try to see for yourself?" Nappy demanded. "What the hell kind of detective are you?"

"A pretty pissed-off one right now," I said. "I get that way when someone tries to kill me—and my son. I don't need any constructive criticism from you."

He took one of his stinky cigars from his breast pocket, peeled away the cellophane, bit off the end and then picked it off his tongue and put it in the ashtray. In the kindly amber light of the Photoplayers taproom you could barely see his makeup.

"Cut me some slack, all right? I love her." He made a big production out of striking a match. In the brief sulfur flare I saw that his eyes were wet. "All I want is the chance to get her back."

I waved the acrid smoke out of my face. "When you put all your assets in your wife's name . . ."

He smacked his lips angrily over the cigar. "I already admitted that was a dumb play, don't make me say it again!"

"Tell me exactly how that came about."

He frowned, trying to remember. "Doll had been . . . depressed for about a week, and I couldn't get her to tell me what was wrong. She didn't want to bother me with it, she said. That's how she was. She just devoted herself to making me happy. Finally I wormed it out of her. She was worried, she said, about what was going to happen to her after I was gone. She doesn't understand about complicated legal stuff and financial things like that."

Neither did Nappy, I thought, but I kept my mouth shut and nodded, encouraging him to go on.

"So I told her I had a will made out making her the major beneficiary, so she wouldn't be frightened. But she said she was afraid that the lawyers—she doesn't trust lawyers—she thought the lawyers would try to screw her out of it because she wasn't an American citizen." A fat ash fell from his cigar onto the linoleum floor. "This went on over a few days now, it wasn't all in one fell swoop. So anyway, she finally said that if everything was in her name, then if anything should happen to me, she'd be protected. I kind of balked at first, but she was so unhappy, so depressed. . . ."

He colored beneath the pancake base and looked away. "Our . . . love life had dwindled down to nothing because she was so worried about it—and that wasn't like her at all."

I took out a cigarette and lit it in self-defense. When you marry someone purely because of physical attraction, there is nothing more damaging to your peace of mind and self-esteem, and nothing more manipulative, than that person's withholding of sex.

"So you transferred everything into her name?" I prompted.

"I'd do damn near anything to make her happy." He gave a little shrug. "Call me a sentimental fool."

"How much money are we talking about?"

His back stiffened. "None of your business."

"My son and I almost died the other night, and that makes it very much my business. Now do you want me to stay on this or not? Because if not, just say the word and I walk."

He seemed to lose some confidence, along with his anger. "I already said I want you to keep at it," he muttered.

"Then answer my question—without the bullshit."

"Like I told you, John Garafalo handled all my money stuff. I'm not real sure . . . "

"You must have a general idea," I prodded. "Was it ten thousand dollars? A hundred thousand? What?"

He looked up as if he might discover a safe answer in the oaken beams that crisscrossed the ceiling of the taproom. "Well," he said tentatively, "I made some pretty big bucks when times were good. Vegas, Tahoe. Cahill and Kane did a limited Broadway run for about six weeks, plus the original cast album from that. I wrote a kind of a joke book, and then we made a couple of pictures in the late sixties, and—"

"I know your credits, Nappy. Just give me an approximate amount."

"Let's see. I own the condo. And there's an apartment in New York. Some other real estate invest—"

"I want a dollar figure."

Looking as unhappy as a man can be, he pulled out a fine-line felt-tip pen and started doodling on his bar napkin, frowning over the figures and moving his lips slightly. I caught a few words of his mumbling. "Disney stock . . . IBM . . . Laguna Beach . . ."

It took him about five minutes, scratching his nose and opening up the folded bar napkin so he had plenty of room to calculate. When he finally finished, he pushed the napkin across the table toward me. "This is just a rough estimate, mind you. I mean, I can't remember everything."

I looked at it and sucked in my breath, oblivious of the noxious cloud of blue smoke that enveloped both of us. Now

I could see why someone might think there was reason enough to kill me to keep me out of their affairs.

Nearly three million reasons.

Nappy hadn't been kidding when he said he'd made good money during the years he and Jerry Cahill had been on top. In an era when a thirty-thousand-dollar-a-week gig at a big Vegas hotel had been the norm, it didn't take too many paychecks to mount up, and Nappy had invested his money wisely—or John Garafalo had done it for him. Even now he probably made more than the average American family of four, what with the occasional TV talk show and shopping center ribbon-cuttings and one- and two-nighters in far-flung places like Tucson, and I already knew he had a frugal streak. But I'd never imagined that his net worth, which he'd blithely signed over to his wife, was anywhere near two million eight.

Not that he'd ever go hungry anyway. Celebrity in the United States is a curious thing; once you've attained it, it becomes permanent, like a tattoo in the middle of your face. People like Zsa Zsa Gabor are stars because they are. They don't have to *do* anything; their business is celebrityhood. And the citizenry falls all over itself kissing their asses because once they'd been on television or in the movies, they'd made a few records, or they knew Frank personally. So those enterprises with limited budgets and uncertain clout, who know they'd be wasting their time trying to land a Steve Martin or a Joan Rivers or some other top name to come and entertain their convention or conference or grand opening or club, book the has-beens for a fraction of what they once earned but still well above the national average. The celebs bank their honoraria and live on their memories and old kinescopes of the time Ed Sullivan had thrown a fraternal arm around their shoulders and exhorted the studio audience, "Let's really hear it, now. . . . "

I got to my office just before one o'clock. It seemed like forever since I'd seen it, but it had only been five days, the Friday past. Jo was out to lunch, and the answering machine was turned on, but sadly the light was not blinking.

I went into my little sanctum sanctorum and rescued the pink message slips impaled on a spindle. No one that I particularly desired to talk to had called in my absence. The stack of unopened mail was similarly uninspiring, and I tossed it onto the top of a filing cabinet against the wall. A couple of pieces slithered down behind it to fossilize.

I spun my Rolodex until I found Henry Liu's name. Henry is a Chinese-American actor I'd worked with on a TV movie several years before, and we'd spent several lunch hours together during the shoot, drinking Tsingtao beer and eating the walnut chicken that was the off-the-menu specialty of the house at the Lotus West, just a few blocks down Pico from the Fox studios. At this hour of the day I didn't hold out much hope of his being home, and if he was, I wasn't even sure he'd remember me. The bonds of comradeship forged by the movie business are most often temporary.

"The world's only private eye with a SAG card!" Henry Liu said cheerfully. I guess I'm more memorable than I think. "How the hell are you? God, I haven't seen you since Reagan was in Washington. What're you up to?"

I gave him my more recent acting credits and he told me his, and we chatted on for a while about the fast-pitch softball league in which he played, just as if life was a beach and nobody had cut my brake line and tried to turn me into roast beef hash two nights ago. Finally, though, we ran out of small talk and I got to the reason for my call.

"Henry," I said, "who do you know in the Chinese community who's a maven on importing?"

"Importing? You mean like antiques and fine furniture and things like that?"

"Yes, but beyond that. Paper fans, for instance. Or knick-knacks or kimonos."

"Kimonos are Japanese," he said dryly.

"I knew that. But you get the idea."

"Are you looking for an antique screen or something?"

"No. I need some information."

"About importing?"

"About an importer."

"Hmm," he said, thinking. "You might try James Yip. He's got a showroom on La Cienega south of Melrose. He's one of the biggest importers in town."

"Do you know him personally?"

"Yes, but not well," Henry said. "Why?"

"I was hoping you could call and ask if he'd see me."

"This sounds serious."

"It might be. I don't know yet."

"It'll cost you a dinner," he warned.

"You've got it. I'll take you to the best Chinese restaurant in town."

"Chinese food I get at home. We're talking Spago, buddy."

"You drive a hard bargain."

"It's in the genes," he told me.

Henry and I did several phone calls back and forth trying to make arrangements, but finally a meeting was set with James

Yip for four o'clock. When Jo got back from lunch, I dictated my notes from the conversation with Nappy that morning so she could bring the case file up to date. That sounds like "Take a letter, Miss Jones," but it isn't. Jo is more secretary of state than plain secretary, and she always stops me in mid dictation to ask questions, clarify, probe, to make sure I haven't left anything out that might prove important later on.

"Basically," I told her, "Doll cut poor old Nappy off in the sex department until he did what she wanted. She wasn't quite that up front about it—she kept telling him she was depressed and worried—but it amounted to sexual blackmail. The lady is a pretty good manipulator, I think."

Jo tapped her pencil against the spiral ring on the steno pad. "Yes," she said, "but she was only going along with the terms of the contract."

"What contract?"

"People make contracts with each other, unspoken ones. It's almost as if one person decides to be the straight man and the other one the comic, like Cahill and Kane. Or you play cards with someone every Thursday but don't get any closer than that, don't ever discuss personal things or go out to dinner. Look at you and Jay Dean over at Triangle Broadcasting. You have lunch once every three months and laugh a lot, and once in a while he'll help you out with something over at the network, but you don't ever talk seriously. You don't tell each other your deepest, darkest secrets or your innermost dreams."

"Those I tell to you," I said.

Jo turned those gray eyes on me. "Yes, you do," she said, boring down to the core of things. "That's what our contract is, that's what we do. We're best friends."

I plopped into the chair next to her desk. "Friends? I love you."

"And I love you too—but not like lovers. It's why we've never been lovers and never will be—because it would spoil our friendship by violating the terms of our contract."

I snapped my fingers in mock dismay. "I suppose that means a romantic weekend of sun, surf, and steamy sex in Aruba is out of the question."

"Be serious," she said. "Look, here's a guy, Nappy Kane. Fat, unattractive, and can't even remember his sixtieth birthday anymore. And he marries a woman who's not yet twenty-five. I can't believe she was swept off her feet by lust, can you?"

"No. But maybe she loved him for other reasons."

Jo fixed me with a stare. "You really believe that?"

"No, I'm being argumentative."

"All right then," she said, satisfied that I hadn't completely taken leave of my senses. "So the contract between them is implied. She supplies Nappy with her nubile young body in bed and a pretty trophy for him to take around on his arm and show off to his cronies at Nicky Blair's, and he supplies a one-way ticket to the United States and enough money to keep her more than comfortable. A man his age could be on a day-to-day basis, depending on his health, and she wants to make sure that if he dies the gravy train will keep running on schedule. Why does that surprise you?"

"It doesn't, necessarily. But in most marriages isn't a simple will—or a complicated one, for that matter—usually deemed sufficient?"

She grudged me an affirmative nod.

"So why the complete transfer of assets, unless she was planning to take a walk as soon as she could?" I shook my head. "That wasn't in the contract, Jo, and I think it was planned from the start."

"You think a twenty-five-year-old woman is cynical enough to figure all that out?"

"No. But I'll bet you a new hat somebody else is."

She tossed her pencil down on her desk. "A new hat?" she said, shaking her head. "Great. I'll wear it to the war bond rally."

I drove west on Melrose Avenue, enjoying the view of the ultrahip young people who bustled along its sidewalks. Melrose has become what the Sunset Strip used to be in the fifties and sixties, the home of cutting-edge fashion and a magnet for those who want to be seen. It slices through the old Orthodox Jewish neighborhood near Fairfax with barely a pause for breath and continues its socially conscious meander until it triangulates into Santa Monica Boulevard at Doheny Drive. Probably if any of its habitués, with their black leathers and metallic studs and stark makeup, had glanced over at my car and noticed my gray hair, they would have fallen on me and torn me to pieces as a spy from a generation careless enough to have been born before they were.

I don't really mind getting older, considering the alternative, but it bothers me that my gray hair—which I've had since I was in my early twenties—has automatically conferred upon me the mantle of the Establishment. I've never been in the same bag with stockbrokers and orthopedic surgeons and CEOs with M.B.A.s, but one day I looked around and there I was, flirting with forty, listening to Rosemary Clooney and Tony Bennett and other retro music, and wearing Pierre Cardin, and pretty young women in tantalizing leather microminis were calling me sir.

170

So although I didn't like Nappy Kane very much, and the whole idea of "buying" a wife was loathsome to me, I couldn't help but sympathize with him a little. Marrying a mail order child bride was his one last desperate lunge at youth, and now that she'd fleeced him and run off, he was in denial that she had conned him out of his socks because to admit it, to me or to himself, would be to completely shatter his self-image.

I turned south on La Cienega Boulevard. Here fancy art galleries and boutiques stood cheek-by-jowl with discount furniture stores and carpet and linoleum outlets with Arab proprietors. Once the city's elegant Restaurant Row, La Cienega is just one more victim of the breathtaking changes that have come over Los Angeles in the past twenty years.

The Palace of Oriental Art wasn't a palace at all but a discreet storefront I would have driven by without seeing if I hadn't had the address. I parked on the street, feeding a couple of quarters into the meter, and went inside, where I had to admit the ambience was a bit more palatial. Huge statues in bronze and jade stood against ten-foot-high wall hangings and meticulously painted rice paper screens. Ornate cabinets and lacquered furniture took up much of the floor space, which was covered with exquisite oriental rugs. The smell of incense hung in the air, and the tinkle of wind chimes was more a delicate and subtle suggestion than a sound.

James Yip was about sixty, with a full head of hair as black as a raven's breast and an open, pleasant face. He was wearing a beige linen jacket over a light blue shirt and yellow tie, the perfect outfit for a Los Angeles businessman. He already knew why I'd come—Henry Liu had called and greased the skids for me—but he was as gracious and eager

171

to help as though I'd been dropped off by the chauffeur and walked in trailing my credit cards. I liked him right away.

He led me to his office in the back, not quite as lavish as the showroom but furnished tastefully with a black teak desk and comfortable chairs. The smell of incense was even stronger here.

"How may I be of assistance to you, Mr. Saxon?" James Yip said, settling himself behind the desk. He spoke very precisely, the way people do when English is their second language, but he had no real accent. "Henry Liu mentioned you were a private detective?"

"That's right," I said, and gave him a business card—one of the real ones. "I'm wondering if you're familiar with a firm up north in San Angelo, called Rustin Imports."

His eyebrows shot up. "Not Ash Rustin?"

"You do know him?"

"Oh, yes, but I didn't know he'd opened his own firm. I'd heard he was up in the delta area, but that was some years ago."

"What can you tell me about him?"

"Nothing very good," he said, lacing his fingers together on the desk in front of him. "As I remember, Mr. Rustin was in the army during the unpleasantness in Southeast Asia. After the war, he moved to Taiwan for a time and made certain business arrangements with some firms over there and in Hong Kong. He dealt in the cheap junk one sees in Chinatown tourist traps—the stamped tin ashtrays, the toys and whistles, the rubber thong sandals. He'd buy them for four cents, ship them to this country, and sell them for thirty times as much. I had no idea he was calling himself an import company now. He is to the import trade what Mc-Donald's is to haute cuisine."

172

"But he was legitimate?"

Yip shrugged his shoulders. "His trinket business was. As for his other interests, one hears rumors but hesitates to repeat them unless they are confirmed."

"It'll go no further than these walls, Mr. Yip."

He took a few moments to decide. Then: "It was rumored that Rustin was bringing more than souvenirs into this country."

"Drugs?"

"So I had heard. But his career as a drug smuggler was short-lived."

"What happened?"

He unclasped his fingers and gestured with his left hand. He had small, graceful hands with tapered fingers, impeccably manicured. "Many things. In the early 1980s the use of heroin had declined measurably in this country, cocaine being the fashion then, as now. And it was my understanding—and again, this is no more than unsubstantiated gossip one hears around a lunch table—that Mr. Rustin did something to displease his customers."

"Any customers in particular?"

"You have heard of the tongs, Mr. Saxon?"

"Of course."

"Chinese gangsters. They pretty much ran the heroin trade on the West Coast at one time—and still do, what trade is left. It's too bad. They have made it very difficult for legitimate businessmen such as myself to survive. Racism in this country is not limited to that directed against the Africans and the Japanese." He sighed. "I understand that Ash Rustin was forced to leave the Los Angeles area as quickly as possible. The last I heard of him he was up in the area around Sacramento, but doing what, I have no idea."

"Do you know much about these firms that supply Asian wives to lonely American men by mail?"

His lip curled in distaste. "I've heard of them. Marriage mills. The exploitation of young women is very tragic. Marriage to a man one does not love is a big price to pay for escaping from poverty and political unrest. And that puts the best face on it. Some of the people who run such operations are no more than whoremasters, although from what I have heard, most of them are honest enough, if somewhat cynical. Is Rustin into that type of business now?"

"Yes, he is," I said. "And he's not one of the honest ones."

13

THE PARTICULAR TANTALIZING smell of spaghetti sauce wafted over me when I walked through the door of my house, and I sniffed the air, trying to sort out the ingredients. Onion and oregano and pork and fennel were the most instantly recognizable. Marvel was clanking around in the kitchen, sausage was sizzling in a cast iron frying pan, and it was fairly obvious he'd used a heavy hand with the garlic. I looked forward to a terrific dinner, sore mouth or no.

"Felt like cookin'," he said. "Hope you didn't have any plans."

"I'm all yours," I said. I went in and changed out of my sports jacket and slacks to jeans and a sweatshirt, came back out into the kitchen and got myself a John Courage.

"You make any progress today?" I asked.

"Tell you after dinner," he said. He had a smug, happy look on his face, and I had the feeling it had nothing to do with spaghetti sauce. I was glad I'd enlisted his help on the Kane case, and the sparkle in his eyes told me he had hit some sort of paydirt. It pleased him to let me hang awhile until he told me what it was, and I coaxed and wheedled for a few minutes because I knew he wanted me to. Then I settled down for what was a first-class pasta dinner; when it came to finding his way around the kitchen, I'd taught him well.

Several years ago, when it became fairly evident that because of the pressures and vagaries of my two careers I wasn't exactly every woman's idea of a dream husband, I had decided I'd better learn how to cook, if only in order to survive. Besides, eating alone out of a pot while standing over the sink is depressing when it becomes a daily ritual. Once I learned the basics I really got into it, rich sauces and exotic Chinese and Thai treats, but those I generally saved for special company. Even alone, though, I wouldn't dream of eating a peanut butter sandwich and an apple for my evening meal. I indulge myself by dining well whenever I can—because there are always those times when I'm traveling and I wind up in a grease pit like EAT.

When Marvel came to live with me after a short young lifetime of eating whatever crap happened to be cheap and handy, he was amazed to learn what could be done with food if a little effort was made and was eager to try his hand at it. He was a quick and skilled pupil. I've even given him my recipe for Chinese hot and sour soup, something I have vouchsafed unto no other living person. On occasions like this one when he surprises me and cooks something wonderful it more than pays me back. Bread on the waters and all that.

We made fools of ourselves dipping warm Italian bread into the sauce—the secret of a good tomato pasta sauce is the liberal use of wine or brandy—and I was too full for the vanilla ice cream with Heath bar chunks that Marvel had bought on the way home from the hall of records. He, on the other hand, is never too full for dessert.

Finally, after I had cleared away the dishes and scrubbed

down the counter and the range—the rule is, the one who doesn't cook has to clean up—he was ready for his news.

We sat back down at the table with coffee. With great ceremony, he took out a pocket notebook and opened it to the first page, which I could see was covered with his rather childish scribbling. "Yale Rugoff," he said. "What kind of name is Yale?"

"I guess his mother named him that in hopes that he'd go to school there."

"Lucky she didn't want him to go to the University of Pennsylvania," he said. "So what is it you wanta know about him? How many lumps of sugar he takes in his coffee? Whether he wears socks with clocks on 'em? Does he shower in the morning or at night?" He waved the notebook. "I got it all here in my little book."

"How about just what I asked you to find out?"

"Okay." He cleared his throat, ready to recite. "Yale Rugoff. Been practicin' law in the state of California for twelve years. No criminal record, not even traffic tickets."

"Okay."

"*But*—he's been sued a total of five times I could find." He grinned. "Computers are cool, aren't they? I found this stuff in about half an hour."

"Why did he get sued?"

"Once in 1986 for . . . " He squinted at the page and stumbled over the words a little bit. "Alienation of affection." He looked up at me. "What's that mean?"

"Probably that some husband sued him for screwing his wife and breaking up the marriage."

He raised his eyebrows. "They sue you for that? Whoo!" He flipped a page. "Nineteen eighty-eight he got nailed again, this time for misappropriation of funds." He looked at me again and shook his head to let me know I didn't have to explain that one. "And three times for malpractice, in 1987, '89, and '91. Which means," he explained patiently, "that he's a shitty lawyer."

"I can believe that. How did these lawsuits turn out? Did he win or lose?"

"The alienation business, the misappropriation, and one of the malpractices were withdrawn."

I shook my head. "That means we'll never know what happened."

"How come?"

"It's private business. Like you were suing me for a million dollars, and then one day we went out to lunch and I said, 'Can't we make a deal on this?' and we settled it for two hundred thousand. Nobody would ever know and it wouldn't be in the public record, because it was settled privately, out of court." I pointed to his notebook. "That's why there's nothing in your computer except a notation that the suits were dropped."

He nodded. "Seems like a big waste of time to even start the lawsuit."

"That's the legal system for you—the lawyers make money and everyone else tries to hang on by their fingernails. What about the other lawsuits?"

Marvel consulted his notebook. "The other malpractices he lost. One there was a judgment against him for twenty-six thousand dollars, one thirty-eight thousand." He took a deep breath and blew it out. "A lot of money for one little guy to have to ante up."

"He's insured," I told him. "All lawyers carry malpractice insurance. It's a necessary business expense. Most attorneys would rather go without a telephone than their insurance. Who were the plaintiffs in these lawsuits?"

"Glad you asked." He ripped a sheet out of the back of the notebook and handed it to me. Names, dates, docket numbers, judges; the whole enchilada. Marvel was turning into a pretty efficient investigator—and although I'd have broken his knees if he tried to follow in my footsteps, still I was proud as hell of him.

I scanned the list. "This is interesting."

"What?"

"The plaintiffs in each suit are individuals, and all female. No corporations or companies or groups of people."

"Could be because most of his legal work is on divorces," Marvel observed.

"You're right. Did you find out anything else on him?"

"Only that he was married once, for about nine months back in 1986."

"I'm amazed any woman could stand him even that long."

He got that big grin on his face again, the one that told me he had a goodie to lay on me. If Marvel ever tries to play poker with that open, emotional face, they'll take his skin off in strips. He waited for me to ask. He had the whole scenario laid out in his head, how he was going to tell me, and I knew that it was my move.

"Okay, Marvel, who was he married to?"

The grin widened. "Accordin' to my investigation," he announced as if he were opening an Oscar envelope, "the ex–Mrs. Yale Rugoff is a lady named Rebecca Cho."

It must have been one of those civilized divorces, devoid of animosity, else why would Rugoff have showed up at the

Blue Iris with a young woman on his arm to hear his former mate sing? And Rebecca had clearly shoved some business his way, sending her friend Doll Kane to Rugoff to obtain a divorce. It sounded innocent enough, until I thought about it for a while. Damn! What had started out as a simple job to find a runaway wife was now developing layers on its layers, and I didn't like it. I had no idea where to reach Rebecca Cho on a Wednesday evening, and I couldn't very well try to catch her at the studio the next day because Ray Tucek and I were heading back up to the Sacramento Delta. So I took what I considered to be my best shot.

Mindy Minor didn't sound happy to hear from me. She wasn't angry that I had called, or even surprised. But I think she had written our one and only date off as an idea that didn't turn out well and probably thought she was rid of me forever.

"I'm sorry about the other night," she said. "How it wound up, I mean. I get turned on fast, but I turn off even faster, and I decided I couldn't really get into what you do for a living. It's nothing personal, okay? I still think you're very attractive. But if we kept seeing each other it'd only end up in a train wreck."

"I'm sorry too. Maybe you'll think about it and change your mind."

"I don't think I will," she said, not unpleasantly. "Listen, I can't talk. I'm very heavy in tomorrow's show and I have lines to learn."

"I won't keep you long," I said, and tried not to be stung that a woman I was attracted to was brushing me off. "I just want to ask you a few things."

I could hear her breathing over the phone while she thought about it. "Look, I don't want to be involved in whatever it is you're doing," she said at last. "Rebecca and I are on the set together every day, and I've only met you twice, so it's a question of loyalties, I guess."

I admired her for that; loyalty to friends is one of the things that drives my engine. However, I persevered. "Just a couple. You don't have to answer if you don't want to."

"You got that right." I didn't like the way she said it.

Okay. Did Rebecca ever talk about her marriage?"

"Her what? I didn't even know she was married."

"Used to be. She never mentioned it?"

"Not to me."

"That was her ex-husband at the Blue Iris the other night, the one with the young Asian woman."

"The dumpy guy who's losing his hair? I thought she had better taste in men than that. I've met a couple of the guys she's gone out with, and they've all been class acts. No, I never knew there was an ex-husband."

"Did she ever tell you how she happened to come to the United States?"

"We aren't what you'd call good friends," she said, sounding exasperated. "We just work together and share a dressing room. We never talk about anything personal or heavy. Just the show, clothes, men."

"What was her comment about us being together at her club Friday night?"

"Jesus, you have a real insecurity problem, don't you?"

"Yes," I admitted, "but that isn't why I'm asking."

"She asked if I had a good time, that's all."

"She didn't want to know if I'd asked about her or anything?"

There was a long silence on her end, and some static. She must have been using a cordless phone; I could hear another conversation intruding fuzzily on the line, like two guys talking through a tissue-paper-covered comb. "I'm sorry," she said finally, "but I'm not real comfortable with this. Whatever your problem is with Bec, you're going to have to work it out without me. I'd rather not answer any more questions if you don't mind."

"I just have one more."

She sighed. "All right, what?"

"Is Christian going to really tell Quinn that Lacey isn't his baby?"

She didn't answer for about ten seconds. Then she said, "Give me a break, okay?"

The click as she broke the connection sounded as harsh in my ear as small-arms fire.

Now that Marvel was able to drive, cook, shop, and more or less take care of himself, it didn't bother me as much to leave him alone for a few days as it had when he was younger. After all, there are eighteen-year-old husbands and fathers. It wasn't any doubt about his ability to cope that worried me but what Bettyann Karpfinger had said about always leaving him on the outside looking in. I'd brought him along to San Angelo the first time and almost gotten him killed. Now I knew he wanted to come with us again, and there was no way I was going to let him.

I figured that I'd solved the problem the day before by giving him an important task to perform, looking up all the vitals on Yale Rugoff, and he'd done an outstanding job. God knows I'd told him so enough after he'd finished reporting his findings.

"I hope you understand why you can't go back up there with me," I'd said to him just before he uncoiled himself from the sofa and headed for his bedroom, and he'd just shrugged and said, "Whatever," which is what he always says when he doesn't get his way. I didn't like it, but I didn't have time to discuss it with him. We'd talk when I got back.

I suggested that if he didn't feel like cooking he could bum a dinner from Bettyann, and naturally I told Jo to keep a weather eye peeled in case he needed anything, but for the most part I had confidence that he could manage on his own for a few days without starving to death, burning the house down, or throwing a beer bust for fifty while I was gone.

Ray Tucek came by and picked me up at nine o'clock and we headed up toward Sacramento in his vintage Capri. The suspension was pretty well shot and I could feel every pebble and crack in the pavement right up into the fillings in my teeth. I had a hanging garment bag and my briefcase, and as far as I could see Ray had packed everything he'd need into a small blue gym bag with the Dodgers logo on it.

The early morning fog hung over the hills as it does three hundred mornings a year in Los Angeles, and the sun was trying to explode through it. Here and there patches of bright blue sky were visible, as if someone had poked random holes in the overcast with a pencil.

Going up into the Grapevine I got very quiet. Coming close to death does funny things to your head, and although I've been pretty near the edge several times in my life, it never gets any easier. I'm not one to waste precious moments reflecting on my own mortality, but when we passed the Lake Hughes Road ramp near Castaic, I started thinking. Mostly I got angry. Although ninety percent of my business involves doing pretty much what Marvel had done the day before at the hall of records, getting punched, shot at, or otherwise being endangered is something that occasionally happens.

To me. Not Marvel. And that's what got me mad.

Ray looked over at me, reading my thoughts. "It's like riding a horse: you have to get right back on."

"It was just so—impersonal."

"Take it that way, then. You got close—too close—to their three-million-dollar scam. They figured life would be easier if you were out of the way. To them it was a simple business proposition."

"I'm going to take them down, Ray. And their police chief buddy too."

"Let's just concentrate on finding the woman, all right?"

I thought that was a fairly curious thing to say, but I didn't want to discuss it, so we listened to the radio without talking until we'd come down out of the mountains and were on automatic pilot on the straight flat ribbon of I-5. Since Marvel wasn't with us and this was in no way a pleasure outing, Ray opted not to take the longer but more scenic route, Interstate 99.

We passed a cattle pen at the side of the road. The poor, docile cows looked at us without emotion as we passed, not knowing that within days they'd be Big Macs. The smell of manure made my eyes tear.

"So how is this going to work?" Ray said. "Lay it out for me."

"You drop me off in Sacramento, and I'll get a room. Then you go on to San Angelo—or better yet, to Isleton."

"Why Isleton?"

"San Angelo is too small; whenever anyone checks into their one motel the whole town knows it within fifteen minutes."

184

"And Isleton's a bustling metropolis?"

"Different police department, anyway."

"Then what?"

"Then," I said, "you watch Ash Rustin. You can't miss him. He's got a pink baby face and a shock of snow-white hair, and the day I met him he was wearing a bow tie and suspenders."

He grunted. "Sounds like Rustin is Orville Redenbacher's evil twin." He twisted the wheel and roared into the fast lane around a ponderous Winnebago being driven by a man who must have retired from the civil service twenty years earlier. "What am I looking for?"

"You're looking for Doll Kane. If anyone knows where she's holed up, it's Rustin. See where he goes and who he goes there with. Take lots of notes, especially if he has any contact with the local law enforcement; maybe we can nail that son of a bitch with a badge while we're at it. I owe Marvel that much."

He took his eyes off the road for a brief moment and looked at me. "You're getting soft, Saxon. You better start concentrating on that acting career of yours before you get hurt."

"How can I get hurt when I have you, Ray? You're my brawn, I'm your brains. It's a perfect marriage."

"I can't protect you from yourself," he said.

I didn't want to get into an argument with a close friend a hundred miles from nowhere in a compact car. I was damned if I'd give him the satisfaction of an answer right then anyway, but if he hadn't elaborated I'd eventually have asked him what he was talking about.

"You take things too personally these days. You have to look at yourself as no different than anyone else running a business—you've got an office and a letterhead and business cards, and you're listed in the yellow pages. You think a businessman takes it as an insult when he loses a contract or doesn't get an order? Hell no! He just shakes it off and goes on to the next thing, doing what he has to do. The only way to survive in a business like yours is to stay uninvolved. Emotionally, I mean. Be a machine, do the job, cash the check, and then forget about it and go to the movies. You used to do that, when I first met you. You were a pretty hard cookie." He glanced at his speedometer, saw he was going too fast even for the tolerant highway patrol on the interstate, and eased his foot onto the brake for a minute. "Especially about the movie business. You were the most cynical son of a bitch I ever knew."

"I know," I said, "but cynicism is tough to live with. I started not liking myself very much, so I worked on it. Besides, life changes things. I have Marvel to worry about now. I'm damn near forty years old, Ray—it's time I started thinking of someone besides myself."

"Yeah, that's all well and good. But the minute you get personally tangled up in your work, you get careless, start making mistakes. You got all moon-faced about that Mexican woman and almost got yourself killed in Tijuana a couple of years ago. Same way in Chicago when your buddy died and almost took you with him."

"Yeah, and both times I was right, wasn't I?"

He struggled getting a pack of cigarettes out of his shirt pocket and finally lit one with the car's lighter.

"Right can get you dead," he said.

14

WE GOT TO Sacramento at about five thirty. Ray wasn't much for stopping to smell the roses; we had only exited the highway once, to use the bathroom and so Ray could pick up a couple of pulpy hamburgers from one of the interchangeable fast-food franchises along the way. I hadn't really decided yet whether or not I was pissed off at him, so the bulk of the trip had been made in a somewhat uncomfortable silence, if you didn't count the twanging country tunes Ray got on the radio.

Some day I'll have to make a car trip with someone who likes the same kind of music I do.

I checked into the TraveLodge near the river, and after taking note of the telephone number there, Ray headed off across the Tower Bridge for Isleton, promising to check in with me later that night. I'd brought a few paperbacks with me and read those until it was time for the TV news. Sacramento's home baseball team is the San Francisco Giants, because they're the closest major league franchise, and the local sports guy did a lengthy feature on the team's travails. Historically, the Giants raised the June swoon to an art form.

I hadn't partaken of the side-of-the-road hamburgers with Ray, and by seven o'clock I was hungry and thinking about going out for dinner. Maybe it had something to do with Doll Kane and Rebecca Cho and Helen Ng, or maybe I was just guilty about leaving Marvel behind, but I had kind of a jones for lemon chicken myself, or perhaps a big tureen of hot and sour soup, which I don't usually order in restaurants because they never make it as tasty as I do. The closest approximation Sacramento has to a Chinatown is a big square dominated by a pagoda-style structure housing the city's Chinese association, which just happens to be at the far end of the TraveLodge's parking lot, and since I was without transportation it seemed as serviceable an idea as any.

I had just stepped out of the shower and was drying my hair with the last towel—I always use up all the towels when I'm in a hotel room, it's one of my favorite harmlessly hedonistic indulgences—and was just about to shave, when the phone on the bedside stand jangled, startling the hell out of me. I wasn't expecting Ray to call until much later, after he'd settled into his own motel and gotten the lay of the land in San Angelo.

"Are you lonesome for me already?" I said.

"In your dreams."

I scrabbled in the drawer for the ubiquitous hotel pen and notepad, finding them right next to the Gideon Bible. "Where are you? What motel?"

"I haven't gotten a room yet," he said. "I ran into a slight delay."

"What kind of delay?"

"I was passing through San Angelo on the way to Isleton and there was a bit of a traffic jam. The police were out there diverting the cars off River Road. Seems there'd been sort of an accident."

"Accident?"

"That little dinky highway was like a parking lot, and the temperature must have been a hundred in the shade and there was no shade, so I figured what the hell, I'll check it out. I parked the car on the main drag and walked down to the river to take a look. They were just fishing a body out of the water."

The hair on the backs of my hands stood up the way it always does when something ugly happens, and the shiver that ran through me had nothing to do with being naked and dripping wet in the path of an air conditioner. I threw my damp towel over my shoulders.

"It was a woman," he said. "A Chinese woman."

I held my breath. I knew Ray well enough to understand he was going to tell this in his own way, dramatically and with a maximum of suspense, but if he'd been standing in front of me I would have choked the life out of him. "Don't play games with me, Ray."

"I hung around for a while," he continued, "as long as I could without looking conspicuous, although there must've been half the county down there getting their jollies watching. I saw your police chief and his deputy too. They were running the whole show and enjoying the attention. That chief's got a General Patton complex, sunglasses and pearl-handled revolver and all. Finally when they carted the stiff away I went back into the town and had dinner at a little greasy spoon."

"EAT?"

"I just said so, didn't I?"

I let it go. "Did you find out who the woman was?"

"I saw her when they were hauling her up the bank with a boat hook. Who can identify a body when it's been in the water for a while? But I don't think it was your Doll."

"Why not?"

"I was talking to this waitress in the little café—"

"Em?"

"What do you mean, M?"

I suddenly felt as if I were trapped in a crowded stateroom with Groucho and Chico and Harpo, and that next Ray would be telling me there's no such thing as Sanity Claus. "What did she say?"

"Well, she'd been down at the river too—practically the whole town was, and—"

"Did you see anyone who looked like Ash Rustin?"

"Nope, and he was the first one I looked for. He would've been fairly easy to spot. Anyway, the waitress said she knew the dead woman, that she'd lived in town. Told me her name. I couldn't quite catch it without being obvious and asking her to repeat it, but it sounded like the noise you make when you get punched in the stomach."

"Ng? Helen Ng?"

"That's it."

"She's Rustin's partner—and wife. She's the one who sicced her little playmate on me and had me knocked down the stairs. They dragged her out of the river?"

"Right at the near edge of San Angelo, where it takes a slight bend to the east, yeah."

I thought for a minute, trying to visualize the spot. "Get yourself a motel room in Isleton, Ray, and then get back to San Angelo and keep your ears open for anything about Helen Ng's death. And try to pick up Ash Rustin—you've got his office address, and his house might be listed in the telephone book. Maybe he'll lead you to Doll Kane. In any case, I want to know where he goes and who he talks to. I'll meet you at the Grand Island Inn in Ryde tomorrow morning at ten o'clock for breakfast."

"You gonna walk there?"

"I'll rent a car."

"When your client sees the expense sheet on this case he's going to go into cardiac arrest."

"The heart has its reasons," I said.

"God, was that a pun?"

"It wasn't meant to be," I said, "but I guess it was."

I hung up, still cold and damp, pulled on a sweatshirt and jeans, and dialed the number of the California Highway Patrol in Castaic. It took me a few minutes to locate Sergeant Gelarden, and when I did, he thought I was calling about my car.

"I'm pretty sure it's fixable, Mr. Saxon, but you'll have to check with the mechanic," he said. "After we haul 'em off the highway it's out of our hands."

"That's not what I want to talk discuss with you, Sergeant. There's been a new development." I informed him of Helen Ng's fate.

He was silent for a minute. "San Angelo's a couple of hundred miles from here, out of our jurisdiction. Besides, it's in the hands of the local police. The CHP doesn't get involved with accidental drownings."

"I'll bet you a bottle of Scotch it wasn't accidental."

"Even so," he said, "it's a local matter. We can't go poking around without upsetting a lot of people, mainly your Chief Gordey."

"Gordey's dirty, Sergeant."

"Probably, but we can't pin him down just on your say-so. I just don't see what I can do about it."

I sat down on the edge of the bed, cradling the phone

191

between my shoulder and chin while I attempted to tie my running shoes. "You can do this," I told him. "Talk to your captain, or whoever, and tell him what you know—that Helen Ng's death might be tied to what happened to my car. Maybe that'll make it a CHP case."

"I doubt it," he said. "But I'll do what I can."

I hung up feeling vaguely unsatisfied and lay back on the bed, thinking. Helen Ng's death made everything different, and even more sinister.

When some sort of plan had evolved in my head, I got up and went into the bathroom to shave most of my face, leaving a day's growth of mustache on my upper lip. I've never worn a mustache, because I've been gray since my early twenties and my facial hair came in the same color, adding fifteen years to my age. But I figured that by tomorrow it would give a whole new dimension to my appearance.

Then I went out into the heat, in the opposite direction from the Chinese restaurant in the pagoda, my jones for lemon chicken forgotten. I headed toward the busy riverfront, its wooden plank sidewalks choked with tourists, in search of a drugstore in Old Sac.

I was drinking coffee at a table by the window in the art deco dining room of the Grand Island Inn in Ryde, looking out across the highway to the river, which now seemed a lot more threatening and full of portent than when Marvel and I had driven along its banks a few days before. The water was dark and the current swift under the sun's pitiless glare. Ray Tucek walked in, glanced over at me idly, then looked away, waiting for someone to seat him.

I stood up and waved. "Over here, Ray."

He looked at me again, then did a double take. It took him about fifteen seconds.

"Holy Toledo," he said, laughing, and walked over and sat down opposite me. "What happened to your hair?"

"Grecian Formula," I said. I had spent the evening bent over the sink in the TraveLodge, changing my silver-gray hair to brunette. Before I'd left that morning I'd even dabbed some on my burgeoning two-day mustache, which the package directions warn not to do, and my upper lip was beginning to itch.

"I'm embarrassed to be seen sitting with you," Ray said ruefully. "You look like an aging queen trolling West Hollywood."

"If I'm going to be anywhere near San Angelo I thought I'd better change my look," I explained, not comfortable with his characterization of my appearance. "It's such a small town, they'd spot the gray hair in two minutes flat."

"Well, you fooled me—for a second anyway." He shook his head and laughed. "Why didn't you just get those glasses with a big nose and a mustache attached?"

"Then I'd look like you," I said. "Hear anything about Helen Ng's death?"

"Your police chief didn't confide in me, surprisingly enough. But I did talk to a reporter from the Sacramento *Bee* this morning, a guy the Yolo County coroner owed a few favors. Cost me a cup of coffee, but I found out that the cause of death was water in the lungs, although there was a massive bruise on the front of her skull. They've decided that she was on a boat somewhere, fell and hit her head, went into the river and drowned, and that's going to be the official coroner's report. They also calculated that the body had been in the water for at least twenty-four hours. Maybe longer."

I did some calculating and didn't like the answer I came up with. "All right," I said. "Did you ever hook up with Ash Rustin?"

He started to answer but the waitress arrived and we ordered breakfast, eggs Benedict for him and homemade roast beef hash for me. And coffee. Lots of coffee. "This'll beat hell out of EAT," I told him.

He gave me a strange look; apparently he'd still not divined the name of the café where he'd eaten the night before. Ray acted mostly on instinct; he wasn't much of a detail man. It's what made us a good team.

He pulled out a little Spiral notebook and consulted it. "Here's what I got on Ash Rustin: He stayed in his office last night until about nine o'clock—at least, it was a guy fitting the description. When he came out, he looked like shit; very pale and nervous, with his hair flying around every which way. He looked up and down the street as if he was wanted for flashing in a playground, then he got in his car, crossed over the bridge to the western side, and drove about a mile downriver to a little marina. There's a houseboat there—there are several, but the one he boarded was a big blue jobbie called the *China Dream*."

"Subtle," I said.

"He went into the cabin, and from what I could see through the windows, which wasn't much, there were two other people inside too, but I couldn't get an idea of who they were."

"Male? Female?"

He shrugged. "There were curtains on the windows. Anyway, he stayed aboard for about an hour and then drove back toward town. He turned off on a little street called Walnut Lane and pulled into a house about a half mile east of the river. Little white stucco job. At about midnight all the lights went out, and after another half hour, I figure he had too, so I went back to my motel. I looked in the local phone book—it's about the size of *Time* magazine during a slow week—and sure enough he's listed as living on Walnut Lane. Ashford Rustin. That's a name, Ashford?"

The roast beef hash was really quite good. Homemade hash is always terrific. Canned hash, on the other hand, is probably the blue-plate special of the cafeteria in the seventh circle of Hell.

"Anyone living there with him?"

"The house was dark when he first drove up, but there was another car in the carport."

"Not a white Acura Legend?"

"Shot in the dark?"

It was nothing of the kind, and I couldn't help feeling smug that my instincts about Ash Rustin had been correct. Of course, there are a lot of white Acura Legends in the world, but I was willing to bet the farm that this one was Doll Kane's. The chances were, though, that she wasn't living at the house but aboard the boat.

"You think you could find the *China Dream* again?"

He skewered me with a look. "No problem. It's not that big a river."

I left Ray to finish his coffee and went out into the lobby to find a phone booth. I wanted to give Marvel the number of my motel in Sacramento in case of an emergency.

I wasn't getting off that easy.

"So what's goin' on up there?" he asked.

"We've got a line on Doll Kane."

"Where is she?"

"I think she's on a houseboat called the *China Dream*."

"How come you don't just go get her?"

"We can't right now."

"Why not?"

"It's a little complicated."

He sighed in exasperation. "I can prob'ly figure it out," he said. "I'm a high school graduate now."

I hesitated. I didn't want to involve him any further. Yet he'd been through a lot because of Doll Kane, and since I'd made him stay home I figured I owed him something. So I told him about Helen Ng being dragged out of the river.

He was silent for a minute. "Man, it's gettin' hairy," he finally said. "You gonna need some backup. I better come up."

"Don't even think about it," I warned him. "Nearly getting you killed once this week is about all I can handle."

I collected Ray from the dining room and we went outside, the heat hitting us like a wave from an open pizza oven. Mosquitoes and gnats hummed in our eyes and nostrils, and off in the marshy fields to the west the cicadas were tuning up for a noon concert. From somewhere upriver the drone of an outboard motor floated toward us on what little breeze was blowing. It was a Norman Rockwell summer day on a quiet country road; not the kind of morning to be thinking about dead bodies in the water, nor about runaway wives and white slavery and the cruel betrayal of love.

Ray led our caravan south. Just below Ryde we crossed over to the east bank on a rusty old steel bridge that didn't look as if it could hold the combined weight of our cars. It was only another few miles to San Angelo, and when we passed the little town on the highway I noticed a black-and-white at the side of the road with Deputy Harbottle slumped in the driver's seat, his hat brim over his eyes but watchful as a basking rattlesnake. It was a crude and obvious speed trap at best; at worst it was a place for Harbottle to goof off in an air-conditioned car without doing much work. Apparently, Helen Ng's death wasn't causing much of a disruption in the police department's schedule.

I cruised by Harbottle slowly, not wanting to give him any reason to notice me and pull me over. There was a bad moment when he looked right at my face, but he gave no sign of recognition; the itching mustache and the Grecian Formula were doing their job.

I ate Ray's exhaust for another mile, and then we reached the small marina. There were four houseboats at anchor, rocking gently in the steady current. The *China Dream* was hard to miss. It was moored at the far end of the dock and was almost twice the size of its neighbors. I saw Ray's right turn signal flashing and followed him up a graveled road lined with oak trees whose overhanging branches formed a high archway over the narrow drive. It didn't seem to go anywhere special, except away from the river, but I figured a few miles farther there would be a farmhouse or something. He pulled off to the side and parked in a shallow ditch, obviously there to accommodate the runoff from the frequent flooding that plagues the Sacramento River Delta each spring. The leaves smelled moldy and damp and were spongy under our feet.

"What's this?" I said after I'd pulled in behind him and gotten out of the car.

"This is where we park. You want to just drive down to the side of the dock in plain sight? Come on, let's go for a walk."

It was some three hundred yards through the dappled sun and shade beneath the overhanging tree branches. By the time we got to the highway we were both drenched with perspiration, and I worried that the temporary color rinse in my hair was going to start running down my face in streaks. Like two kindergartners on the first day of school we checked the highway both ways before we ran across and started down the ramp to the boat dock.

The *China Dream,* its turquoise blue fiberglass hull trimmed with white, bobbed lazily in the current. There was no deck furniture in evidence, as there was aboard the other boats. Electrical lines ran to a dockside generator, and I could hear the swamp cooler grinding away. One of the other houseboats must have had live-aboards in residence too, because there was a radio playing—country music, Ray's favorite.

We stopped behind a boat shed about fifty yards from the *Dream,* both breathing hard in the stifling humidity that was even worse here at the river's edge. Dragonflies as big as robins skimmed the water, daring the fish to come up and get them. The smell of diesel fuel was strong; I sniffed to clear my sinuses.

"Are you carrying?" Ray whispered.

"I left it in my briefcase in the car."

"Good place for it," he said, shaking his head. "What if we run into trouble?"

"That's why you're here."

We waited for about ten minutes, watching the curtained windows of the cabin and ducking around the shed out of sight every time a car passed up on the highway, leaving a wake of red dust. There seemed to be no movement aboard the boat other than the rhythmic rocking.

"I think we ought to pay a visit," I said.

"One of us should stay here and play lookout."

"You stay, then."

He snickered. "What if you run into rough stuff?"

"It's a chance I'll take."

"I think you ought to stay here and let me go aboard."

"No," I said. "You stay."

"Why?"

"Can you whistle through your teeth, like hailing a cab?"

"Sure."

"Well, I can't," I told him, "so you stay here and let me know if someone's coming. If you hear sounds of carnage, come running."

I didn't give him a chance to argue any more but stepped out from behind the boat shed and walked out onto the pier, moving along as if I belonged there. The sun was beating down on my neck as I stepped up onto the rickety gangplank and then onto the deck of the *China Dream*. I looked back at Ray, who shook his head in disgust and moved back out of sight behind the shed.

Going to the hatchway, I put my ear to the wood, but I didn't hear anything. I thought about knocking but it didn't seem like a terrific idea, so I tried the handle of the door. It turned. I pushed the hatch open and entered the air-conditioned cabin.

The main cabin was about sixteen by twelve, furnished with the kinds of chairs and tables you find in nautical stores. Off to one side was a small galley with a whistling-type tea kettle on one of the two burners of a hot plate. On the table was a teacup with orange-brown dregs in the bottom.

Beginning to feel clammy as the artificially cooled air collided with the perspiration on my body, I went below carefully and quietly. There were two staterooms; one had a double bed and a dresser and was empty, the bed made neatly. In the other one was a single bunk, and on it a young Asian woman lay fully dressed in white slacks and a red and white striped T-shirt, with one arm flung over her eyes to shield them from the sun streaming through the small port-hole.

She sensed me standing there and sat up quickly, her eyes wide with terror.

"Don't be afraid," I said. "I'm a friend, Mrs. Kane."

15

DOLL KANE WAS prettier than her pictures. Softer, even younger-looking, with a smooth bright face and large liquid eyes that seemed to plead for some sort of understanding or compassion. She cringed back against the bulkhead, frightened to death, and for a moment I felt sorry for her. But pumping up sympathy for a woman who had conned her adoring husband out of nearly three million bucks didn't come easily to me.

"I'm not going to hurt you," I said. "You understand? I'm not here to hurt you." I tried my kindest smile, but it froze on my face.

She seemed to relax just a bit, there was a lessening of tension in her neck and shoulders, but her eyes still showed fear. I couldn't much blame her. I must have seemed like some frightening apparition from the netherworld.

"My name is Saxon, and I'm a private investigator," I said. I didn't give her a business card. "Your husband hired me to find you."

"Nappy?" she said wonderingly, as if there were more than one husband to consider. Her voice was small, very young, almost musical. She wasn't wearing much makeup, and in the gloom of the cabin, with only the porthole to admit the light of the sun, she looked to be about fourteen years old. I could see how an older man might find her youth and vulnerability incredibly appealing.

"He was afraid something bad had happened to you. You never even said good-bye, Mrs. Kane."

She turned her face away from me, her frail shoulders shaking in a spasm. I guess growing up through the parochial school system in Chicago had taught me well how to lay a guilt trip on someone, and I sounded to myself like Sister Concepta, the scolding nun who had tried to teach me algebra with a flexible steel ruler. "Why didn't you tell him you were going? He's been very worried."

She didn't answer me, didn't even look at me. Her breath caught in what might have been a sob.

"I'm not going to make you do anything you don't want to," I said. "My job was to find you and tell Nappy where you are. He wants to see you, talk to you. He wants to try to work things out so you'll be happy. I can't make you come with me, and I hope you understand that. But he wants you back. He needs you."

She looked up at me. She tucked her knees under herself on the bed and tried to regain some composure. "I cannot go back," she said, blinking her eyes rapidly.

I sat down on the edge of the bed, thinking things over. My job was finished as far as my client was concerned. But someone had tried to kill me and Marvel, and Helen Ng was dead, and that made Nappy's marital and financial woes very unimportant.

"I'm sure there were problems," I said, trying to get her talking. "There are in any relationship. But you have to communicate. Maybe if you talked to him, told him some of the things that are bothering you. In America a wife can do that. She's expected to do it. A marriage is a partnership, not one person owning another one. Nappy's willing to go all the way for you. He loves you very much."

I shook my head. Just thinking about this child-woman with aging, bewigged Nappy Kane was giving me the collywobbles. Besides, the role of marriage counselor hardly suited a guy who has never been able to sustain a relationship for more than an hour and a half.

She looked woeful, tragic. "He won't want me no more," she finally said.

"I've talked to him. Believe me, he does."

"Not when he find out."

So much for Doll's speaking English better than her husband.

"Finds out what, Mrs. Kane?"

"About me," she said, looking away again. "What I do before." Twin tears rolled down her cheeks and splashed onto the front of her T-shirt.

My stomach did a little flip. I suddenly knew what was coming, and I didn't like it at all.

Shame turned her cheeks bright red. "Before I marry Nappy . . . " She covered her face with her hand. "Before, I am whore."

I didn't know what to say. I was feeling a certain amount of shame myself, for having bullied her.

"Nappy," she said, "he don't know."

Of course he didn't. Nappy might have suspected, especially after she'd bilked him out of everything he owned and left him high and dry, but with his jones for Asian women and a pretty, compliant Chinese wife young enough to be his granddaughter, he was probably deep in denial.

"He doesn't have to know," I said, hating the deception

but hating the alternative even more. "There's no need to tell him at all."

"I not tell him—*they* tell him!" she said, anger making the cords in her neck stand out.

"Who?"

"Mr. Ash. I not do what he say, he tell Nappy I was whore for him, for Mr. Ash. Then Nappy not want me no more."

"And what does Mr. Ash say to do?"

Despite the gaiety of her striped T-shirt, Doll Kane was a study in misery. "He make me leave Nappy, get divorce, come back here to him or else he tell Nappy what I am. He say I can't go back, never."

It all started clicking now; the synapses in my brain were firing like the engine of a Shelby Cobra when they wave the green flag. The whole thing had been a scam from the very beginning, engineered by Ash Rustin. He brought Doll over from Hong Kong, turned her out as a prostitute at Far East Massage, then literally sold her to Nappy Kane. After carefully orchestrating the transfer of property, he'd yanked the string, and poor Doll was caught in the middle. Either she took her husband for everything he had, or Rustin would ruin her life.

I wondered just how deep the hook went. I said, "Did you sign anything for Ash? Any sort of paper or contract?"

Her fine brows knit in perplexity, and she shook her head, confused. "Please?"

"When you first came to America, to San Angelo, did he make you sign a piece of paper, like a legal document?"

She thought about it for a long while before she answered. "I think so."

"What did it say?"

She turned both hands palms up in bewilderment. "Miss

Helen say something about money. That I owe her and Mr. Ash money. For, um . . . they sponsor me come to America."

They thought of everything, Rustin and Helen Ng. I'm no lawyer but I didn't think a contract signed under duress by a person who barely spoke the language in which it was written was going to stand up in court. Unless that court happened to be in San Angelo, California, where the document was executed. If the local police, in the persons of Gordey and Harbottle, were corrupt, it might well be that the San Angelo courts were equally dirty. Gordey had practically told me as much when I'd gone to collect Marvel.

"Do you want to stay here with Mr. Ash, Doll?"

She shook her head gravely.

"You want to come back to Los Angeles with me?"

"Nappy not want me no more."

"We'll worry about Nappy later," I said. "Just tell me if you want to come with me."

She hesitated.

"Away from here, away from Mr. Ash. You don't have to go back with Nappy if you don't want to. You can decide that later. But if you want to get away from Mr. Ash, I'll take you back with me."

"Mr. Ash not let you."

"We won't tell him," I said. "We'll just go. Right now."

Her eyes were as big as saucers, like the guardian dogs in the Andersen fairy tale about the tinderbox, and shot through with suspicion. It would be hard to convince someone who'd been used all her life that I only wanted to help.

"If you say no—if you want to stay—I'll go away and I won't bother you anymore," I said. "But I want to be your friend, Doll. I'd like for you to trust me."

Fear and suspicion warred with desperation in her brown

eyes. Finally the desperation won, and she nodded slightly.

"Good," I said. "Everything is going to work out fine. Get your things together."

She uncurled herself from the bed and stood up very slowly, as if it ached to move. Her head didn't quite come up to my chin. There were blue highlights in the dark sheen of her hair. "Everything at Mr. Ash's house."

I was about to tell her it didn't matter when a shrill whistle could just be heard outside the stuffy cabin. If you weren't listening for it, it could have been a fish hawk swooping down to capture its lunch from the river; to me it sounded exactly like someone trying to hail a taxi on Fifth Avenue in New York.

Ray.

Doll heard it too, and then the footsteps on the gangplank.

I looked around for a way out, since in the tiny cabin there sure as hell wasn't anyplace to hide.

"I'll be back for you tonight," I told her in an urgent whisper. "Late. You understand?"

She nodded, looking frightened.

"Very late. Midnight. You'll be ready?"

She hesitated, then nodded quickly.

I stepped up on the bunk and pulled the porthole open, regretting all the good meals I'd eaten in the past six months. It was going to be a tight fit.

I squirmed through the opening, head and shoulders first. When I was halfway out I felt the *China Dream* rock slightly as someone stepped onto the boat on the landward side. Only the adrenaline rush gave me the strength to squeeze the rest of myself out. There was a narrow fiberglass deck running completely around the boat, about two feet wide outside the porthole, and I hauled myself out onto it, holding a silencing finger to my lips and motioning for Doll to shut the porthole behind me. When she did I grabbed hold of the shiny railing and lowered myself over the side.

The river flowed briskly about three feet beneath me in a healthy rolling current as I clung to the railing, my feet against the bulkhead. Gnats hummed in my ears, but I couldn't loosen my grip to swat them. The boat rocked some more and I held on, feeling slightly seasick.

I heard voices coming from inside the cabin, Doll Kane's and someone else's. Both were feminine, which gave me some small comfort. They spoke in a kind of singsong, and though I couldn't discern the words I was pretty sure they weren't speaking English. When I listened for a while without hearing any baritone voice, I took a chance and pulled myself up so that I could look through the porthole.

Doll Kane was standing beside the bunk, conversing in what I assumed was Cantonese to someone I couldn't see. Finally she moved away and I was able to catch a glimpse of the other person. It was another Asian woman, small and pretty and very young, and she looked familiar. I thought for a moment she was the one I'd seen picking the mail up from the Asian Nights post office box, but that woman had been taller and a little chunkier. Then I remembered where I'd seen her before; she had been with Yale Rugoff that night I'd gone to hear Rebecca Cho sing at the Blue Iris.

I lowered myself down out of sight beside the hull again. I didn't think the other woman was carrying a gun or anything else she could hurt me with, but I didn't know whose side she was on yet, so I couldn't let her see me; I didn't want to jeopardize the rescue operation later that night. The midday sun hammered at me and sweat rolled down my forehead into my eyes. The smell of diesel fuel mingled with the fetid odor of the water, making my nose twitch.

The conversation droned on inside, and my shoulder and thigh muscles began to cramp from holding on. I wondered what Ray was up to, hiding behind the boat shed. It didn't really matter—there wasn't anything he could do to help. Dragonflies dive-bombed me, the pesky gnats tormented me, fish were jumping, and the cotton was high.

My hands were sweating along with the rest of me, and I didn't know how much longer I could stay where I was before they slipped off the rail. Besides, it was a good day to be out on the water, and it was only a matter of time before some innocent fisherman or water skier came putt-putting down the river and saw me hanging on to the side of the *China Dream* like a huge barnacle.

Finally I took my feet from the hull and let myself hang down with my toes dangling inches above the current. I let go the rail with one hand and grabbed hold of the edge of the deck, then repeated the process with the other hand, straightening my arms as much as I could. I felt the water rushing around my ankles, dragging me sideways. It wasn't exactly tepid, but it was a lot warmer than the Pacific Ocean. Thank God for small favors—it was about time I got a break.

Trying not to make a splash, I loosened my grip on the decking and slid into the Sacramento River.

I dropped vertically through the fast-moving water as though I had lead in my pockets, the river rushing up into my nose. It must have been about fourteen feet down before I hit the riverbed, and the shock of the impact traveled up my legs and spinal column to my head. Bottom mud like a living organism sucked at my shoes, pulling them off, and I pushed hard against the drag, propelling myself upward and flailing my arms to get back to where there was air.

When I breached the surface I saw that the river had carried me about twenty yards downstream of the *China Dream*. Too bad I didn't want to go that way; Ray Tucek was waiting for me upstream of the boat.

I trod water for a while, looking wildly around, trying to get my bearings. The fact is—and I'm a bit ashamed to admit it at my age—I don't swim very well. I guess it comes from all my years as an unemployed Hollywood actor: we don't go *in* the pool, we sit *beside* it, working on our tans and waiting for our agents to call.

Every moment that I wasted took me a few feet farther downstream, farther from where I wanted to be. I suddenly had an absurd vision of myself floating gently past the place where, some years ago, Humphrey the Humpbacked Whale got mired in the river and couldn't find his way out, arousing the passions of a nation. I didn't think the American public would care half as much for me if I were swept out to sea.

I put my head down and started stroking for the bank, now some forty feet away. The rushing water had carried me out where the river was its deepest. The shore, with its groves of walnut trees and occasional waterfront cabins and summer homes, seemed to zap by like a movie shot from a speedboat, and I had to duck beneath the current to avoid a jagged piece of driftwood that was hurtling downriver and would have taken my head off. I came up sputtering, like a guy in a soap commercial breaking the surface of a glittering pool. The detritus from downtown Sacramento and its nearby ship channel poured past me, and I could taste rust and silt in my mouth. I wasn't making much headway going perpendicular to the current, so I set a diagonal path. My clothes felt as though they weighed a million pounds.

I had a momentary rush of panic, that I wasn't going to reach the safety of the bank, that I was going to drown in the river and Marvel was going to have to make it the rest of the way through his life without me. I took a deep breath, swallowing water and a lot of crap I didn't even want to think about, and struck out for shore again.

The *China Dream* looked a long way off. I swam harder.

After what seemed like several days but was in reality only a few minutes, my toes scraped the bottom, and I was able to thrash my way to where I could stand up. Water poured off me as I staggered out of the river, General MacArthur wading ashore in the Philippines.

I flopped down on the bank, panting and dizzy. Dead leaves, twigs, and mud stuck to my clothes, and if the fire ants that nest on the shoreline had had a mind, they could have eaten me alive. I didn't much care at that point; I just wanted to catch my breath. After a moment I coughed violently, my stomach heaved, and a good bit of the river I'd swallowed during my swim reappeared.

I lay there, eyes shut tight to protect them from the relentless glare of the high sun. Muscles I hadn't used in years were beginning to protest, as the pain advanced into my neck and shoulders, as a truism hit me with pile-driver force—I was getting too old for this shit.

After a while I summoned the dregs of my energy and got to my feet with great effort. My soaked clothing hung on me like chain mail as I began my ascent of the fairly steep bank, grabbing on to small saplings and rocks to keep from tumbling back into the water, from whence, I was pretty sure, I wouldn't emerge again.

210

When I crested the bank Ray Tucek was waiting for me, leaning against his car with an insouciance that made me want to strangle him.

"That was quite a show you put on," he remarked, making no attempt to offer assistance.

"Thanks for your help," I gasped. I clambered up onto the berm by the side of the highway and leaned over the fender of his car, watching the dirty water that dripped from my hair onto the hood.

"After the other woman went on board, I figured you'd gone out the window, like a guy whose lover's husband just came home. Then I saw you do your little aquatic act, and I jumped in the car and drove down here to meet you." He smiled; it wasn't nice. "That's quite a swimming style you've got there, buddy. You look like a porpoise on Quaaludes."

I proposed that he perform a sexual act I knew to be anatomically impossible, which somehow made me feel a little better.

Ray took his revenge, though. He wouldn't let me back in his car until I'd stripped down to my shorts and stowed my muddy clothes in the trunk. He claimed he didn't want me ruining his upholstery.

If I hadn't felt so lousy I would have laughed. In that reprehensible old clunker of a Capri he drove, the seat covers wouldn't have been damaged if a hippopotamus had decided to use it in lieu of the nearest rest room.

As it was, it just added insult to injury.

16

WOULD MOST PEOPLE kill to protect a payday of nearly three million dollars? I don't know. It would be nice to think that most people are honest and incorruptible, but the fact is, most people would consider it, quite a few of them seriously. Some would take a life without having to think about it at all. Three million bucks is more than I make in a month.

Excluding the gang violence that has poisoned every urban center in America and the kind of senseless racial hatred, born of despair and fomented out of rage, that caused more than fifty deaths in the Los Angeles riots in the spring of 1992, an alarmingly large percentage of the homicides in this country have simple greed in one form or another as an underlying motive. It's the only reason I could come up with for the cutting of the brake line in my car: someone didn't want me getting in the way of the gravy train. The Asian Nights scam had already netted nearly three million dollars of Nappy Kane's money, and for all I knew it was being replayed in a hundred other newly broken households, with recently married Chinese or Korean or Filipino women suddenly taking off without so much as a kiss-my-ass after engineering the transfer of all the husband's worldly assets into the wife's name. Nappy found the Asian

Nights ad in the back of a magazine; it wasn't unreasonable to believe that other lonely men had as well.

The poor bastards were probably a lot like Nappy, too old or ugly or stupid to attract a lovely and pliable young woman to adore and wait on them. Even if they weren't all washed-up celebrities, they would have shelled out a considerable sum up front so Ash Rustin would provide them with a wife, only to wind up worse off than they'd been before—not only alone, but flat broke.

It was the most despicable kind of con job. The average stings are run on those looking for a fast buck, or something for nothing, and it might be argued in some criminal circles that they had coming to them whatever grief they might reap.

But to prey like a vulture on poor, sad guys already in the pits of loneliness and emotional despair seemed a particularly vicious kind of crime, even though the slobs all but bought their wives from a mail order catalogue. Should someone clean out your bank account, it can always be replenished; there's an inexhaustible supply of money in the world. But broken hearts don't ever completely mend. Broken is broken and at best can only be patched together.

And the women—like Doll and little Leng and the Chinese lady who'd suffered the crude gropings of Yale Rugoff in the Blue Iris—were even more damaged. Looking for a new life in a land that now promises a hell of a lot more than it usually delivers, and for the security of love, they were forced into prostitution or marriage to men they'd never even seen before. Their trust had been shattered, along with their hearts, while whatever financial profit was realized went to Ash Rustin.

I still couldn't understand why Helen Ng was lying in a

sliding drawer in the Yolo County morgue, though. She'd been one of them, as far as I could figure out, one of the voracious crew of Asian Nights. I couldn't get her death to make any sense.

But even though I'd had no reason to love Helen Ng, I was going to figure it out and make amends for it, just as I was going to avenge myself and Marvel for the tampered brake line. And I was resolved to close down Asian Nights tighter than a jar of last season's quince preserves.

My first priority, though, was to get Doll Kane out of San Angelo and away from Ash Rustin, and toward that end Ray Tucek and I sat in his motel room in Isleton grazing from a bucket of Kentucky Fried Chicken and made our plans. The motel was one small step above the one Marvel and I had checked into in San Angelo; the furniture wasn't quite as rump-sprung, and in a pathetic attempt at decor a bad reproduction of a seascape had been hung on the wall above the dresser.

Once I'd had a chance to put on my only remaining dry outfit, the tan chinos and black sports shirt in which we'd made the drive up from Los Angeles, we'd gone back to the side road across the highway from the marina and picked up my car. We'd decided that Doll would drive back down with Ray that night on Interstate 99 rather than the more direct and well traveled I-5, while I returned the rental car and took the first southbound flight from Sacramento in the morning.

"And then what?" Ray said, munching on an extra-crispy thigh. "What happens to the lovebirds?"

"That's up to them," I told him. "I'm going to try to convince Doll to tell him the truth before anyone else does."

"At his age that might kill him. You think he's going to

214

welcome her back with open arms knowing she used to turn tricks—after she tried to beat him out of his socks?"

"I don't know. That's not my affair. But I'm going to put Ash Rustin out of business. That I can promise you."

"You'll never be able to prove it was Rustin who sabotaged your car."

"Maybe not," I said. "But even if I don't nail him for attempted murder, I've got him for running a house of prostitution, and for using the U.S. mails to defraud. And I'm sure the immigration people are going to want to talk to him too. Any one of those will close him up. Throw enough shit at the wall, some of it's bound to stick."

"Like I said, you need proof."

"I've got Doll Kane."

Ray stood up and hook-shot the chicken bone into the wastebasket. "I love this game," he said, and went into the bathroom, where there were several bottles of Heineken chilling in a sink full of ice cubes from the motel's machine.

"You ought to be writing modern fairy tales," he called out, and I heard the hiss as he twisted off a bottle cap. "You have a vivid imagination."

He came and stood in the doorway, backlit by the fluorescent from the bathroom, a beer in either hand. "If you think a celebrity like Nappy Kane is going to let his wife stand up in open court and announce to the world that he married her through a lonely hearts ad and that before he did she used to peddle her ass, you're crazy. The papers'd have a field day."

"Nappy Kane is hardly hot news any more."

"He will be when the *Enquirer* or the *Star* gets wind that he's married to a hooker." He smiled sardonically. "Then again, it could revitalize his whole career. Nothing America loves better than a nice juicy scandal." He came back into the room, putting one of the green bottles to his lips. Ray is one of the few human beings alive who can walk and drink at the same time.

"You don't think he'll be mad enough at Rustin to let her testify?"

"Oh, he'll be mad, all right. But all you goddamn actors think with your egos, and the human ego, especially the male variety, is even stronger than the thirst for revenge." He tossed me the unopened bottle of beer, and I felt a twinge in my neck when I moved quickly enough to catch it. "Forget it, amigo, you'll never get Doll Kane into court," he said.

"They can issue a subpoena."

"On what grounds? Your word? Rustin will deny everything except running a legitimate introduction service, and since the San Angelo cops seem to be in his pocket, they'll back him up. You don't have the chance of a snowball in hell if you don't get a change of venue, and even at that it'll never get to the grand jury. Without Doll's testimony there's no case, and if you'd stop thinking with your ass and look at it logically, you'd know it. So why don't you just forget about it and drink your beer?"

"That's easy for you to say, Ray. You weren't the one who smashed into the sand hill at the end of the runaway truck ramp."

"Maybe not," he said, "but I signed on to help you locate Doll Kane and to be here for you if it got rough—not for the second Children's Crusade."

"You're getting paid," I reminded him.

"So are you. And when you deliver Doll back into the loving arms of her husband, you'll have done your job. Stop being the patron saint of lost causes, for Christ's sake, and get on with your life."

"If it had been up to Ash Rustin, I wouldn't have one."

"Deal with what is, not with what if." He sat down in the room's one comfortable chair and put his feet up on the finished-plywood coffee table. "Now, do you want to talk about tonight, or shall we switch on *Donahue* like the sensitive and enlightened males we are?"

I'll do anything to avoid the Phil Donahue afternoon love-in. "Have it your way."

"Okay, then," he said, leaning forward, his elbows on his thighs. "We'll leave your car in the same place we did this afternoon. I'll drive mine down the ramp to the marina and park nose out, so we can make a quick exit if we have to. They aren't expecting us—they don't know we're in town and they don't know we know where the woman is, so we have surprise on our side in case there's trouble. I figure all they have for firepower is the big hairy hillbilly who knocked you down the stairs. Right?"

"And Ash Rustin."

"I've seen Rustin," he said. "Even you could take him." He snorted. "You can snap his suspenders."

"What if he's carrying?"

Ray sighed with infinite patience. "He's got a piece, you've got a piece. Unless you leave it in the car again." He took a gulp of beer, and I did the same. The room had an air conditioner, which was grinding away in an opening cut into the wall under the window and dripping rusty water on the stained carpeting, but the heat and humidity of the delta was creeping into the room through the cracks. "Now, I've always been a strong advocate of planning ahead, so there's another factor in this equation that we ought to discuss. What about the local law?"

I assumed he meant Gordey and Harbottle. "I wouldn't think they'd be around in the middle of the night. They've just pulled one of the citizens out of the drink, and they have to make it look good. They've got more to do than play bodyguard for one little Chinese woman."

"You hope." He leaned back in the chair, making himself comfortable. The old chair squeaked and groaned a protest. "What if you're wrong? I don't mean to be a nattering nabob of negativity, but what if they *are* there? I don't want to get into any shootouts with the police, even if they're as corrupt as you say."

"What do you mean, if?"

He rotated the beer bottle between his palms. "According to the law, they're clean. The only thing we know they did for sure is to roust Marvel off the street because he's black. If you could make it stick, that's only a civil rights violation. A nuisance suit."

"They told Helen Ng who I was. I gave my name as Ed Henderson, but she called me Mr. Saxon, and she could only have learned that from the police."

"So when they find you trespassing on a private boat, standing over the body of a dead cop with a smoking gun, your defense is that they snitched on you?" He snickered again. "That's good, all right. You'll skate for sure."

"Let's not worry about it until it happens, okay?"

He nodded his head with mock gravity. "Good plan," he intoned. "That's thinking ahead."

Sometimes I don't like Ray very much.

* * *

When Ray had gone out to get the fried chicken, he'd stopped in a drugstore in Isleton and bought a pack of playing cards. One of us was thinking ahead.

We whiled away a few hours playing gin rummy. I'm not much of a card player, and Ray was prone to call on the fourth card, catching me with my entire hand unprotected, and at about nine o'clock the beer was all gone and I was thirty-two dollars down—which I was going to charge to Nappy Kane and call expenses—and weary of the game. We spent the next three hours watching television.

There is a very good reason why I never watch TV unless someone is doing something interesting with a ball, and those long hours in the Isleton motel room reminded me of it. Chewing gum for the brain.

When the eleven o'clock news from Sacramento mercifully wound down with a stimulating feature about an ugliest pet contest, I snapped off the set with a sense of relief and turned to Ray.

"Ready?"

"I've got nothing better to do," he sighed.

I took the Glock out of my briefcase, feeling the heft of it in my hand. I checked and loaded it, put a spare clip in my pocket, and stuck it in the waistband of my pants, on the left side so I could draw it across my body if I had to. Ray's silent nod of approval made me feel better than it should have.

We both packed our belongings; I had deposited my impossibly muddied clothes in the Dumpster across the motel courtyard, which left me with only a few toilet articles. I was charging a new wardrobe to Nappy Kane too.

Ray watched me limp over to the door like a man twice my age. "Are you feeling up to this?"

"I've been better," I admitted. In the past few days I'd

been punched in the mouth and knocked down the stairs, survived a horrendous car crash, and gone for an unintentional swim in a briskly flowing river fully dressed. My body hurt in places I didn't even know I had, and whatever pollutants contaminated the river had turned my amateur dye job a dark orange. The last thing I felt like doing was reenacting *The Abduction from the Seraglio* aboard a houseboat on the Sacramento Delta. But I didn't have much choice.

Taking a deep breath, I went outside into the night. After the sun went down, the thick, damp tule fog had drifted in and was now swirling around the parking lot in the gentle breeze off the river. It was like walking in yogurt.

"Score one for our side," Ray said. "They can't shoot us if they can't see us."

"We won't be able to see them either," I said.

He nodded grimly. "I didn't think about that."

We walked to our cars, parked side by side in front of his room, and got in. When I switched on the lights I could barely see the motel wall.

We do get some fog in Southern California, especially near the ocean, where I live. But those few days a year when fog blankets the coast, sensible people stay home, open a bottle of good wine, eat whatever is in the refrigerator, and listen to Bill Evans compact discs. They don't drive around in it and pray they won't smash into a tree or a lamppost.

We pulled out of the parking lot, Ray in the lead. His taillights were red blurs ahead of me, and I leaned forward, squinting through the mess that was accumulating on my windshield no matter how much I tried to sweep it away with the wipers. The Glock dug painfully into my ribs, and tension added to the soreness in my neck and shoulders.

The road north from Isleton was very narrow. It fell off

into a ditch on one side with the mucky, sloping bank on the other, and while not exactly twisting, it was difficult enough to drive on a sunny afternoon. In the fog it was absolutely terrifying. The last thing I wanted was to be in another car accident. I kept my eyes glued to Ray's lights about five car lengths ahead of me; if he drove off the pavement and into the river, I'd have time to stop. There are advantages to going second.

Normally it wasn't much more than a ten-minute drive to San Angelo from Isleton, but it took us almost half an hour to crawl through the fog, which grew more dense and impenetrable as we got closer to town. The thought of driving in it again after we picked up Doll was making my head pound behind my eyes.

Ray signaled for a left turn and I followed him over the old bridge, the steel grids rumbling under our tires. Beneath us the river flowed silently, but I couldn't see it, could only sense it, black and forbidding and full of unseen dread. The marina where the *China Dream* was berthed was about two miles beyond the bridge; we couldn't get there quickly enough to suit me.

Finally Ray's brake lights came on, and I slowed down behind him. There on the right was the houseboat. One small light burned inside the main cabin, and the generator outside was humming. Ray turned with care, making his way down the gravel incline to the marina. I stayed on the highway another fifty yards, peering through the fog for the unmarked side lane, turned left, and parked my car about a hundred feet in, where it couldn't be seen by anyone passing on the road. I walked back, crossed the road, and went down the ramp, where Ray had turned his car around so it faced out.

He rolled down the window, and wisps of fog drifted around inside the Capri. "You've got five minutes," he said, his voice hoarse, "and then I'll come in after you."

I nodded and patted the Glock in my waistband; knowing it was there gave me a sense of security. I walked up onto the pier, went along the gangplank that I couldn't even see beneath my feet, and boarded the gently rocking *China Dream*.

The hatch was unlocked. I rapped on it once, softly, and then pushed it open. Doll Kane was sitting in one of the canvas captain's chairs at the wooden table, dressed as she had been that afternoon. Her eyes were wide and bright, her mouth drawn tight in the light from the single lamp.

"Hi," I said, and the smile I gave her was meant to encourage her. It didn't seem to work very well.

"Are you ready?" I said. "We should get going."

She didn't answer me. She looked ready to cry.

"You'd better get your things, Mrs. Kane."

She looked up at me and then her eyes flickered to the stairs that led below. I wasn't quite quick enough to look too, so I never saw whatever it was that hit me across the back of the neck, sending me sprawling face forward over the table and into Doll Kane's lap, blinded by pain and shock.

From the feel of it, though, my guess was that it was a California redwood.

17

DOLL KANE SCREAMED as the force of the blow propelled me into her, and the two of us went down in a heap, all tangled up in the wood and canvas chair, which collapsed beneath our weight. I was dizzy from the impact, but I had some presence of mind left, and I tried to roll over on my back so I could get to the Glock. As I pulled it out of my waistband the toe of a heavy boot slammed into my wrist, and the pistol went skittering across the floor of the cabin. It had stopped sliding before I got my eyes focused.

I wished I hadn't, because what I saw was the big hairy guy from Far East Massage, Earthquake McGoon, the one I'd heard Ash Rustin refer to as Frank. He was wearing denim overalls that barely contained his enormous stomach and a dingy white T-shirt with the armpits yellowed, and he was advancing on me slowly, smiling, his fists knotted at the end of forearms that looked like Popeye's.

Still on the floor, I rolled Doll away from me so she wouldn't get hurt, which gave me some space to operate. If the big slob ever got on top of me I'd be dead meat. When he got within range I shot out both feet, catching him just below the belt line. The angle was bad so I could use neither my heels nor my toes, but the impact made him grunt, and

I heard the breath rush out of him. The kick barely slowed him down; I'm not sure a .357 Magnum would have. He was mammoth, a gap-toothed nightmare out of *Deliverance,* and like that rabbit in the battery commercials he kept on going, and going, and going . . . But I'd bought myself a few moments to scramble to my feet, where I'd have at least a slim chance.

I came up with the broken captain's chair in my grip, but the toe of his boot had so numbed my wrist that I could barely hold it, light as it was. It hardly classified as a potent weapon, but it was all I had, and I swung it at him.

It was like swatting a rhinoceros with a rolled-up newspaper—he didn't even blink as the chair leg splintered across his forehead. But it opened a deep cut over his left eye and gave him something to think about. I threw the chair at him for good measure; he batted it away, King Kong disposing of the pesky fighter planes with an irritated wave.

Wiping the blood out of his eye, he made a guttural noise deep inside his chest, an animal sound that struck even more terror in me than his truly awesome appearance. Then he came after me, an irresistible force, moving like a tank and almost as big. It occurred to me that I'd never heard him speak. I was beginning to wonder if he could.

My only chance was to stay away from him, but there wasn't much room to maneuver. I circled the table, keeping it between us, trying not to step on Doll, who had crawled into the corner of the cabin and was huddling there, whimpering quietly. The giant came implacably closer; I wished I had a slingshot and five smooth stones.

Frank kicked the heavy table out of the way with barely any effort, splitting it in two with his boot. It left him off balance for just a moment; I stepped in and flicked a left jab into his eye, already half closed to protect it from the flow of blood from the cut above it. He didn't react to the blow at all, and I cursed myself for the futility of it. This was hardly a time to get cute and remember my boxing lessons—I'd never win this fight on points.

Still, I bobbed and weaved like a welterweight, trying to keep out of his range, getting in a shot anyplace I could. I tried to banish the old prizefighting axiom, a good big man can beat a good little man, from my mind.

In contrast to my snazzy and completely useless Marquis of Queensberry style, Frank was artless as a fighter. At his size and weight he could afford to be. He aimed a round-house right at my head, and I ducked under it, feeling the wind from the blow. His forearm fell across my shoulder and drove me to my knees.

I peppered two punches into his stomach and then drove a fist into his thigh just above his knee, which evidently did some damage because it made him yelp, and he hobbled back a step or two. I managed to get my feet under me but before I could straighten up he was falling on me, literally. My arms were trapped against my sides as he locked me in a bear hug.

I tried to knee him, my knee being the only weapon I had left, but his thighs were too massive and I couldn't connect where I was aiming. The gesture only seemed to annoy him. His sheer bulk crushed me against the linoleum floor; the odor of his breath and his T-shirt made me gag, and I could smell beer on his long beard. His weight was like a truck parked on my chest, and my inability to take a deep breath was making me giddy.

I was only dimly aware of the hatch bursting open and Ray crossing the cabin in two quick strides. I didn't hear any bugler blowing a cavalry charge, but perhaps I just wasn't paying attention. Ray delivered a karate chop to the back of Frank's head, and he loosened his grip on me; a second one and he rolled off. Frantically I sucked air into my lungs to make the dizziness abate, and then I just got the hell out of the way.

Ray had to wait until Frank was on his feet—he would have been crazy to try to wrestle him. The two men squared off, and quick as a mongoose Ray was in under the flailing arms. A vicious punch to the nose buckled Frank's legs, knocking him back. He bounced off the bulkhead, and Ray hit him again on the rebound, this time in the mouth.

In the meantime I was on my hands and knees, looking for my gun, but I hadn't seen where it had gone.

Frank's face was a mess. His lips were torn and pulpy and blood poured from his nose and the gash on his forehead, matting his beard. He was breathing noisily through his mouth and shaking his head from side to side, trying to get rid of the pain. He blinked once, pushed himself away from the paneled wall, and charged like a raging Cape buffalo.

Ray timed it perfectly. He pirouetted, leapt four feet off the floor with the grace of a Baryshnikov on steroids, and connected with a hard karate kick to the hairy man's sternum. The force of it sent Frank backward, roaring in agony, and he tumbled down the five steps to the cabins below. There was a sickening clunk, which must have been his head hitting the floor down there.

Ray was about to follow him and finish him off when two figures appeared in the hatchway.

One of them had a gun, which he was aiming at the middle of Ray's chest, and a shock of white hair.

"Don't move!" Ash Rustin barked, and cocked the pistol.

Ray froze in mid stride, "it" in a dangerous game of statue maker.

Casting one last furtive look around, I finally spotted the Glock, off in the corner beyond where Doll still huddled in a fetal position. It would have been nearly impossible to climb over her and pick up the gun before Rustin blew me away.

"Bad idea," he said, following the direction of my eyes. "Real bad idea. I'd love you to try it, though. I'd like to shoot you in the stomach and watch you wiggle." He moved his gun so that it was pointing at me and came all the way into the cabin, followed by the second man, and it didn't surprise me much to note that it was Neil, the bent-nosed bouncer from the Blue Iris. Puzzle pieces started falling into place in my head, but unfortunately I wasn't in a position to do anything about it. I got to my feet slowly, holding my hands away from my sides.

"You ought to dye your hair orange all the time, Mr. Saxon," Rustin said. "It makes you look much younger." Coming from a man whose crowning glory was snow white, I would have found that amusing in other circumstances. He pushed the hatch shut to keep the heavy fog from seeping into the cabin. He'd traded in the bow tie and galluses for a white dress shirt with a tab collar buttoned at the neck under a seersucker sports jacket, but he still looked like a geek. "Go check on Frank," he said to Neil out of the corner of his mouth, like a bad actor trying to cheat toward the camera.

Ray and I exchanged disgusted looks as Neil went down the steps. "He's out, Mr. Rustin," he said when he reappeared.

Rustin glanced at Ray with what might have been admiration. "Usually you can't slow Frank down with a howitzer. I'm impressed. What did you hit him with?"

Ray didn't bother to answer. Neil walked up in front of him and drove a fist into his midsection.

Ray grunted and bent double, clutching his stomach, but he wasn't fooling me. It was all for effect. One of Ray's favorite pastimes, when he'd been nipping enough at the spirits, was to challenge any man in whatever cheap stunt-man saloon he was patronizing to punch him in the stomach. If Ray flinched, he bought the drinks; if not, the other guy did. It was one of those silly, macho guy things men do in bars, but I can't remember seeing Ray pay a bar tab. His gut is rock hard when he tenses his muscles.

From his bent-over position he made eye contact with me.

He hadn't yet figured out how to take a punch in the face, however, and I thought I'd better say something before Neil realized he'd been suckered. "Now *I'm* impressed, Mr. Rustin," I said. "Where do you hire your muscle? Punks-R-Us?"

Neil came over to me. "You got a big mouth," he said, which was not exactly a stop-the-presses news flash. He put his heel on the toe of my sneaker and ground down hard, obviously remembering our first meeting; now he had a chance to even the score, and he wasn't going to let it pass. It hurt like hell, but he'd grow old and gray before I let him know it. I sucked my breath in through my teeth.

"Not yet, Neil," Rustin admonished.

Neil looked disappointed, but he stopped, giving me one last hard grind before easing the pressure. I wasn't sure if he'd broken anything or not.

"Don't be dumb, Rustin," I said, wiggling my toes. They felt as if they were all intact, but they hurt so much I couldn't be sure. "You're in this deep enough as it is. Don't make things worse."

"You've made them worse, not me." He looked around at the broken furniture. "Worse for yourself. You're going to regret it before the night's over."

Neil walked over and picked up my gun from the corner, completely ignoring Doll, who had at least stopped whimpering but was still curled up in a ball, trying to take up the smallest amount of space possible. He looked at it, smiled, and slipped it into the pocket of his windbreaker.

"Don't fall in love with that, Neil," Rustin said. "It's going into the river."

I grimaced. I liked that Glock as well as any weapon I'd ever owned. "So now what?"

"Now we wait." He turned to Neil. "Down in the forward cabin there's a toolbox, under the bunk. Bring it up."

Neil went below. I heard him stepping over Frank's inert form.

"Rustin," I said, "you've got to be nuts if you think this is all going to go away."

Considering he'd done nothing but stand around giving orders since he'd come aboard, he was breathing very hard. "You've managed to mess up a pretty good thing, Saxon. I don't like people interfering in my business. We just have to figure out what to do about it, that's all."

Neil came back with the toolbox and set it on the floor next to Doll, who shrank from him as if he were ringing a leper's bell.

"There's a roll of duct tape in there, Neil. Take it out and make sure our friends aren't going to go anywhere."

Neil opened the box and pawed through it. He took out a roll of black tape and started for me.

"Do the other one first," Rustin said. "He's the dangerous one."

Ray gave me a look that can best be described as smug. It stung.

Rustin motioned for me to move away from Ray as Neil stripped off a length of tape and secured Ray's hands behind him, wrapping it around his wrists three or four times. Duct tape is stronger and more effective than rope.

"People know we're here," I said. "They'll come looking for us."

"They won't find you."

I thought about that for a while as Neil pushed Ray facedown on the floor and taped his feet together. Then he bent Ray's legs back and ran several strips of tape between his ankles and his hands. When he was finished, Ray was effectively hog-tied. He looked up at me, his eyes glittering.

"Now Saxon," Rustin ordered.

"Rustin, I know you're working for somebody else."

"Do you?" he said. His white eyebrows almost disappeared into his hairline. "You're smarter than I thought you were."

"Don't take a fall for some other guy."

"The only one taking a fall here is you," Rustin said. "Now shut your mouth."

Neil jerked one of my hands around behind me, holding on to my wrist. When he had stripped off another length of tape he took my little finger and bent it over on itself, squeezing as hard as he could. The pain almost lifted me out of my shoes.

I guess he was doing it because he liked it. It was bad enough they were planning to truss me up like a pig and drop me into the river, but I was damned if I was going to let them take liberties, and this one was one too many.

I jerked my elbow back into his face as hard as I could, and I felt something crunch. Not something of mine.

He howled in pain and staggered back away from me. A bullet whistled past my ear even before I heard the thunderclap of the pistol shot and lodged in the wood paneling about three feet from my head. The stink of cordite filled the cabin.

"God, but you're stupid, Saxon," Rustin said, cocking the pistol again and aiming it at my abdomen. "That's just going to make it worse for you."

The report from the gun had made my ears ring, but I heard Neil sputtering behind me and glanced over at him. He was bleeding from the mouth. I watched as he spit out one of his front teeth into the palm of his hand. He held it for a moment, looking at it with a kind of wonder, as if he'd discovered a pearl in an oyster. Then he raised his head and glared at me, letting the bloody tooth slip through his fingers to bounce onto the linoleum floor. It sounded like someone had dropped an M&M.

Tensing, I watched as he moved around in front of me. I was expecting the blow, but I didn't know how hard it was going to be. It went deep into my stomach, just about hitting my backbone—he was good at body punches. I jackknifed forward and went down, tasting the fried chicken and beer I'd had for dinner. Whatever internal muscles allowed me to breathe didn't seem to be working.

From somewhere far away I heard Ash Rustin say, "Don't let the son of a bitch get away with that, Neil. Go ahead, mess him up all you want to."

The bouncer grabbed a fistful of my hair and yanked me to my feet. Blood was trickling out of his mouth. His knuckles hurtled toward my face and there wasn't a damn thing I could do about it except turn my head slightly and take it high on the cheekbone instead of where he'd aimed it, at my nose.

A mushroom cloud of pain blossomed inside my head, and blackness rushed over me in rapid waves, alternating with bursts of whiteness that brought with them a sharp agony like the edge of broken glass. My knees turned to spaghetti al dente. The only thing that kept me from going down was his firm grip on my hair, and after the second punch even that didn't save me.

My cheek was on the floor, my head on fire from the inside, and when the colored strobe lights stopped flashing behind my eyes and I could open them, I saw Ray Tucek's face about a foot from mine.

"Stay down, you dumb bastard," he rasped.

But it wasn't to be. Hard hands dragged me off the decking and slammed me up against the bulkhead. I didn't know how much more I could take, and I was hoping the next blow would finally put me out so Neil wouldn't hit me again. He drew back his hand to punish me some more when the hatch opened, and just the whisper of a breeze blew little spider webs of the tule fog ahead of it into the cabin. Neil stopped and looked around.

"That's about enough," Yale Rugoff said.

18

I NEVER THOUGHT I'd be grateful to see Yale Rugoff. Weak as a baby, I slid down the bulkhead. It was a relief just to get off my feet. I was sitting on the floor, my head hanging between my knees, trying to figure some way of getting my eyes to focus properly. My face and head hurt so badly that I couldn't distinguish one pain from the other, old bruises from new injuries, and the muscles in my stomach and abdomen felt as though they'd been torn apart like soggy toilet paper.

Rugoff came and looked down at me with a combination of curiosity and disgust, the way you might regard a dead squirrel the neighbor's cat deposited on your front lawn. "Why do you people have to make everything so complicated, Ash?" he said over his shoulder to Rustin. "Can't you do a simple job without fucking it up?"

"He—" Ash started to say, but Rugoff cut him off with a wave of his hand.

"And I expected better of you, Neil."

Neil hung his head like the teacher's pet when he's just been caught throwing spitballs. With his tongue he was surreptitiously exploring the hole where his tooth used to be.

Rugoff stared at me. Then he allowed himself the ghost of a smile. "Having a bad hair day, Saxon?"

I was not amused.

He looked over at Ray where he lay trussed up on the floor of the cabin. "Aren't you going to introduce me to your associate?"

"No."

Ray tried to crane his neck enough to see who he was talking to. "My name's Joe DiMattia, homicide, LAPD," he managed to say.

Rugoff laughed. "I don't think so. What would Los Angeles homicide have to do with what's happening up here? And you don't look a bit Italian. You're a very bad liar, whoever you are."

"I figured you'd turn up here eventually, Rugoff," I said. It hurt to talk.

"Why is that?" he said with his supercilious lawyer's smile in place. "Did I do something wrong?"

I put my head back against the paneling, since it seemed too much of an effort to hold it up. I could feel the mouse under my eye rapidly developing into a groundhog. "It didn't take a rocket scientist to figure it out. The Asian woman you were with at the Blue Iris on Friday; I saw her here this afternoon, right on this boat. You ought to be more careful who you're seen with in public."

"Oh, Rose," Rugoff said, sitting in the chair that remained intact. "Well, like Doll's husband, I'm a great admirer of the Asian female. They're so graceful and delicate—and docile. And Rose is a particular favorite of mine, so I had her flown down to Los Angeles for the weekend. I frequently do that, with her or one of the other girls. Of course, I had no idea you'd turn up at the Iris. Or here, for that matter. I must admit, you're pretty good at what you do."

"So are you—and that's not a compliment in any league."

"Again with the lawyer jokes."

"It's not a lawyer joke," I said wearily. "It's a pimp joke."

He wrinkled his nose. "That's kind of an ugly word, isn't it?"

"You play the game so you've got the name. You bring these young women over here from Hong Kong and Taipei and Indonesia promising them jobs and husbands, and you pimp them long enough to make a profit before you marry them off to rich men for a fee. And then you blackmail them into cleaning out their husband's bank accounts, arrange for a divorce, and you take all the money and turn them out to trick again. What word would you use, Rugoff?"

"Entrepreneur," he said.

I'd have laughed if it wouldn't have hurt so much.

"Come on, Saxon, I'm living everyone's dream," he went on. "Combining my business with my hobby." He looked down at Doll almost fondly and patted her on the head like a puppy. She curled herself into an even tighter ball, as if she made herself any smaller she'd disappear.

"I thought pimping was Rustin's business."

"Shut up, you," Rustin said. There was a tiny spot of spittle on his lower lip.

"How did you get in on it, Rugoff?" I said, ignoring the white-haired man. "Or was Asian Nights your idea to begin with?"

"Oh no," Rugoff said, "Asian Nights was all Ash's idea. I simply—refined the operation."

"You started handling divorces for some of these women, steered to you by your loving ex-wife, Rebecca."

His body jerked in the chair a little on that one. He must have thought it was an inviolate secret. "You've been a busy boy," he said.

"She probably figured it was the only way she could get an alimony check out of you. You milked the poor husbands dry, because any judge in the world would cast a gimlet eye on a guy who bought himself a wife through the mail."

He gave a live-and-let-live shrug. "It is kind of shoddy when you think about it."

"But then you figured there was no reason why you shouldn't get the whole enchilada, right? That's when you moved in on Rustin here and started running the scams too, getting the women to coerce their husbands into turning over all their assets. Just for a little extra pocket money."

Rugoff crossed one ankle over the other. He was wearing Argyle socks, for God's sake. "I assure you it wasn't pocket money. It was quite profitable. Of course, nothing on the order of Nappy Kane until now, but we did quite nicely."

"What did you do, Rugoff? Invest in Asian Nights and become a partner? Or did you threaten to blow the whistle on Far East Massage?"

His mouth twisted into a self-satisfied smile. "Nothing as crude as that, I assure you."

"No? How's this, then? You knew that the tongs down in L.A. were very anxious to talk to Rustin about some—importing deals that went sour, and you convinced him that playing ball with you would keep you from talking to them."

Rugoff's eyes narrowed, and I knew I'd scored a bull's-eye. Over by the doorway Rustin moved around restlessly, his face bright red in startling contrast to his white hair.

"And how did I know that?" Rugoff said uneasily.

"I imagine from Rebecca."

Down at the bottom of the steps Frank let out a loud groan.

"How did you know we were coming tonight, Yale?" I said. "You had your whole army waiting for us."

"Doll here asked Rose to bring all her things back from Ash's house," Rugoff replied. "That made Ash a little suspicious. So he questioned her about it, and she finally told him." He smiled nastily. "Ash can be very persuasive when he wants to be. We decided it was only polite that we be here to greet you. Delta hospitality."

Doll's eyes were wide as she looked over at me. I knew the longer I kept talking, the longer I would live. But I was running out of things to say. The best I could come up with right then was "You're really puke, Rustin."

Ray croaked, "Jesus, Saxon, shut your mouth already."

Rustin moved closer to Rugoff. "Let Neil have him, Yale. He'll shut his smart mouth for him. Dirty bastard, I want to watch him crawl. I want to hear him yell."

"Don't be so bloodthirsty, Ash," Rugoff admonished him. "You should never let your emotions get in the way of business. Don't you know that?"

"But he killed my wife!" Rustin spat.

It took a few seconds for me to process the words inside my head. I could hardly believe what I'd just heard. "Killed your wife?" I echoed stupidly.

"Helen," Rustin choked. He stormed over to me, waving the pistol, and for a moment I thought he was going to shoot me right there. His chest was heaving, and his eyes were bright with tears. "You killed her to get even."

"You're crazy."

"Don't deny it, you lousy fucker," he screamed, saliva flying. "You know she had Frank fix your car and you came back and hit her over the head and dumped her in the river like so much garbage."

My face was swelling so badly that talking was a chore, but I said, "I don't suppose it'll make any difference, but I didn't kill your wife, Rustin. I was in Los Angeles when she died, and I can prove it."

Confusion creased his forehead and took some of the fire out of his eyes. He looked around the cabin as if he'd find an answer floating in the air.

"I imagine what happened," I said quickly, wanting to seize the edge, "is that your buddy here got ticked off at her for having Frank knock me down the stairs and then fix my brakes. As he said, you shouldn't let your emotions get in the way of business, and if Helen had just let it go, the chances are I would've gone away. But she was a hot-tempered lady, she overreacted, and that was going to make me start asking more questions. Rugoff decided she was too volatile, that she'd committed one indiscretion too many and had to be gotten out of the way. So he sent Neil here up to take care of it for him." I looked up at Rugoff. "Have I got it right, Yale?"

Rustin looked as if he'd been poleaxed. His gun hung loosely at his side as he turned to face Rugoff, almost like a high-fashion model pirouetting on a Parisian runway. "Yale?" he said in a little-boy voice.

"He's lying, Ash," Rugoff said, scrambling to his feet. "Trying to save his own skin."

I bored in. "Think about it, Ash. If Chief Gordey hadn't known it was Rugoff, he would have had a warrant out for me in a New York minute. But arresting me would have opened a whole can of worms, and he could never have made it stick, so he made sure the coroner came back with a verdict of accidental death because he's on Rugoff's payroll, not yours. And if I was going to bother to kill Helen, I would've come after you too, wouldn't I?"

"Yale," Rustin said again, drawing out the syllable. He was beginning to comprehend the depth and breadth of his partner's betrayal.

"Calm down, Ash," Rugoff said.

I was on a roll now, and I had to see it through to the end. What the hell, they could only kill me once. "He's some piece of work, your partner. First he takes over your operation, then he wastes your wife because she's getting in his way."

"Shut up, Saxon," Rugoff said. "Can't you see what he's trying to do, here, Ash? Divide and conquer . . ."

Rustin just stared at him, dumb with hurt. Then he said, "You did it, didn't you, Yale?" He was speaking like one of those voice-mail computers now, his tone flat, without variation or emphasis. "You told me it was him, but you were the one."

"That's not nice, Yale," I chided. "Blaming someone else for something you did. What happened to those lawyer's ethics of yours?"

Rugoff was sweating through his sports jacket, and he wiped at his forehead with his hand.

I egged Rustin on. "Sure he was the one, Ash. I had nothing to gain by killing Helen, except maybe to salve my ego, but to Rugoff she was a business liability—and nearly three million bucks is a lot more of a motive than my getting even."

Rustin wasn't even listening to me anymore; his eyes were locked on Yale Rugoff as if the gates of hell had just swung open and disgorged a demon. His face was crimson, almost purple. I thought he might be about to have a stroke. Bringing his arm up slowly so his gun was pointing at Rugoff, he put his other hand on it to steady his aim. Very Starsky and Hutch.

"Don't be a damn fool," Rugoff said.

Rustin cocked the pistol.

"Don't do it, Ash." He was whining now, perhaps the way he did in court while trying to convince a judge to send one of his client's husbands to the poorhouse.

"You bastard!" Ash Rustin growled, and then a loud roar shattered the stillness in the cabin, and a big part of Rustin's forehead disappeared in a grisly spray of blood and bone and tissue, some of which got on me. Rustin remained standing for a few seconds like a headless monster, and then he hit the floor, about eight inches from my foot. I fought hard to keep from gagging.

Neil was still bleeding from the mouth, and his hands were shaking as he lowered my Glock to his side.

The report of the gunshot was still reverberating when Doll started screaming.

"Quiet, you stupid bitch!" Rugoff snapped. Doll's face was a sickly white, but she shoved her fist against her mouth and managed to stifle the screams that were boiling up from deep inside her.

The lawyer leaned against the hatch, his chest rising and falling as he hyperventilated. His eyes were closed. He'd come pretty damn close, and he knew it.

Neil pointed the gun in my general direction and shook his head to discourage me from doing anything rash.

"It was him or you, Mr. Rugoff," Neil said, and it sounded almost like an apology. "That's what you pay me for, to protect you."

"He's right, counselor," I said. "I think he deserves a day off."

Rugoff opened his eyes. "Saxon, I hold you directly responsible for this. For all of it."

"There you go again, blaming other people."

"If it wasn't for you, none of this would have happened. You're going to die, Saxon. Hard." He took a deep breath, trying to get himself together, but his face remained ashen. He gestured to Neil. "Tape him up."

Neil picked up the roll of tape and moved toward me. "Try anything this time and I'm going to take this gun and knock your teeth out one by one," he warned. I think he would have.

Heavy footsteps pounded on the wooden dock outside, and the boat pitched as it accepted the visitors' weight. It proved to be the San Angelo Police Department, Gordey and Harbottle.

"What in hell's goin' on here?" Gordey said, his hand on his holster as he came through the hatch. "We heard a gunshot coming from—" His eyes went to what was left of Ash Rustin on the floor. "Jesus of Nazareth!"

Neil started to say something, but Rugoff cut him off. "Saxon shot Ash before Neil was able to take his gun away from him."

Yale Rugoff was one big surprise after another.

Gordey looked at me with distaste. "You're under arrest for the murder of Ash Rustin."

"I don't think that's such a good idea, Briley," Rugoff said, and whatever relief I'd felt at the prospect of being taken off the boat in one piece ebbed out of me.

"Why not?" Gordey said.

"He knows everything." He looked over at Ray, who had

managed to squirm around so he could see what was happening. "Him too."

Gordey took in the situation with a cop's practiced eye. There were a lot of us on the floor: Doll almost catatonic, quivering in the corner; Ray trussed up and immobilized on his face; me squatting against the bulkhead, too banged up to move. And Rustin.

Three of us were going to get up.

The coppery smell of blood in the small, closed-in cabin was beginning to make me a little sick, and I saw Gordey give his nose an irritated rub. "Where's Frank?"

"Below. I think he's hurt bad."

Gordey pointed to me. "He do that too?"

"Him or his buddy there."

"Saxon, I should of locked you up when I had the chance," Gordey said. He turned to his deputy. "Go down and look, Steve."

Harbottle hustled down the steps.

"This has turned into a real mare's nest here, Yale, and I'm blaming you. I'm not pleased with the way this has been handled. Not pleased at all."

"I don't give a damn if you're pleased or not," Yale snarled. "You've got no complaint."

"Not until now."

"The question is, what do we do about all this?"

Gordey cocked a cynical eyebrow. "How do you mean 'we,' Yale?"

Harbottle came up into the cabin again, looking shaken. "Frank's hurt bad, Chief. I think a bunch of ribs are busted."

I looked over at Ray. His teeth were gritted in a death's-head grimace.

The chief thought for a while. "I guess we better get him

out of here. Steve, you and Neil here go down and get him."

Harbottle paled. "He weighs more'n three hundred pounds, Chief."

The big cop sighed. "I got to do everything around here, looks like." He took my gun from Neil and handed it to Rugoff. "You think you can watch him without fucking it up? Or do you need a court order?"

Neil and the two policemen started below, but then Gordey stopped and looked down at where Ash Rustin's gun had fallen, about six feet away from me.

He shook his head, whether in disgust at being surrounded by incompetence or sadness that his cushy little bag job had turned so ugly and potentially volatile, I couldn't tell. "Jesus of Nazareth!" he said again. He picked up the weapon, uncocked it, and put it in his pocket.

I heard the three at the foot of the steps struggling to pick Frank up off the floor. Laurel and Hardy moved that piano up the hill without nearly so much grunting and groaning.

Rugoff just leaned against the hatch, the Glock pointed straight at me. There was no expression on his face, but his breathing was ragged and his eyes were as hard and cold as a dead snake's.

19

AFTER A FEW minutes of pregnant and uncomfortable silence, Neil and the policemen came lurching and stumbling up the stairs carrying Frank's enormous bulk. The big man was moaning quietly, and blood bubbled out of his mouth and nose. I was willing to bet that Ray Tucek's karate kick had shattered some of the bones in his chest and that one of the sharp ends had punctured a lung.

"Damn!" Gordey huffed, red-faced, as they paused at the top of the steps. He had grabbed Frank's legs: the lighter end. For a man so massive through the gut, chest, and shoulders, Frank had curiously slim legs and thighs. Neil and Harbottle were struggling with the greatest portion of the weight, the cords in their necks standing out with the strain.

"Let's get his sorry ass in the cruiser," the chief said, and then added to Rugoff, "I'll come back and talk to you."

They maneuvered their burden out through the hatch and I could hear swearing as they got him down the rattletrap old gangplank. I imagined them dropping him into the river and tried not to smile about it.

About a minute later the door of the police cruiser slammed, silencing for a moment the chorus of crickets in the woods. Then Gordey and Neil came back aboard the *China Dream*, having left Harbottle to watch Frank.

"Now, Yale," Gordey said patiently, "I'll be goddamned if I'm going to clean up this mess you've made here, so you're going to have to."

"All right, Briley."

"And when I say clean, I mean *clean*. No loose ends, hear me? Don't fuck this one up too, Yale."

A tick at the corner of Rugoff's eye told me he wasn't used to being spoken to in such a manner. "What did you have in mind?" he said, each word with its own frosting of ice.

Gordey scratched his head and examined his fingernails for buried treasure. "We gotta get rid of Ash, for one thing."

"How?"

"Jesus of Nazareth!" he snapped. "You got a boat here. Use it!"

Rugoff frowned.

The chief gave a weary sigh, his khaki shirt stretching over his belly as it rose. "We'll take Frank to the hospital and make up some story or other, like he fell down the stairs. It prob'ly won't wash, but who's gonna call me a liar? Meantime, you and Neil take the boat downriver—and don't use your running lights, for God's sake. When you get to the inlet, you just put Ash in the water. Weight him down good so he won't come up again, an' the current'll take him right out into the Pacific."

"People in town are going to miss him," Rugoff said. "What are you going to tell them?"

"Jus' leave that to me." Gordey looked up at the low ceiling for inspiration. "Ash lost his wife yesterday and it just unhinged him," he mused. "Too many bad memories, an' he couldn't handle it. So he just took off in the middle of the night."

"That sounds pretty suspicious to me," I piped up.

Gordey looked at me in surprise. I think he'd forgotten I was there. "Another precinct heard from," he said. "Well, sir, you're right, it does sound suspicious. But I'm the chief of police in this town, and if I accept it, others will too. Pretty soon people'll just forget about it and go on doing what they always do. Life goes on." He leered at me. "For some of us."

Rugoff wet his lips with a nervous tongue and glanced at me.

"An' to make sure Ash don't get lonely, you can put these three in along with him."

Doll wailed over in the corner.

The lawyer had been holding his breath; now he let it out with a hiss.

"Don't be a pussy, Yale," Gordey said severely. "Just as soon be hung for a sheep as a lamb, right? You let them walk away after what they've seen, we're all not only about three million bucks poorer but you're lookin' at the seat of honor in the gas chamber over at Q. I don't think you want that, do you?"

Yale didn't say anything.

"I know you don't have the stones for it, Yale, but under the circumstances you got very little other choice."

"It'll be all right, Mr. Rugoff," Neil offered. "I'll take care of everything." It was meant to sound reassuring but I don't think Rugoff was buying any.

"Good then." Gordey slapped his holster with his open palm. "Main thing is, Yale, to get out and back before the sun comes up, so nobody sees you." He checked his watch. "That's in about five hours. You got plenty of time: an hour out, an hour back. You'll probably even get home in time to get a good night's sleep."

Patting Rugoff on the back, he headed for the doorway.

Then he stopped and looked at me. "I can't say I'll be sorry to see the back of you, Mr. Saxon. But I do feel kind of guilty about one thing."

I didn't give him the satisfaction of asking.

"You're going to go to eternal damnation with orange hair." He chuckled as he went out and closed the hatch behind him. His heavy tread on the gangplank sounded like a giant's in a fairy tale. A few moments later the engine of the police cruiser coughed and I heard it drive slowly up the ramp, kicking up little bits of gravel. It turned onto the highway, where it accelerated and then faded away.

No one moved or spoke for a while, except for Doll, whose wails had subsided to shuddering sobs and whimpers. Finally Rugoff shifted his weight and threw back his shoulders, ready to take charge now that the police chief had gone.

It was about damn time.

"Neil," he said, with hope in his heart, "do you know how to run this thing?"

They weren't very well organized. In the sudden minipanic that had ensued when it was ascertained that neither one of them had ever actually piloted a water-going vessel any larger or more complicated than a rowboat, they had completely forgotten about taping me up like a hog on its way to market the way they had poor Ray—it was only at the last moment that Neil remembered he'd better undo the lines that secured the *China Dream* to the dock. I wasn't going to remind him, certainly.

Not that I posed very much of a threat. I was pretty thoroughly banged up, and my own Glock, trained at the center of my chest by a suddenly in command Yale Rugoff, was as effective a deterrent as the duct tape. As far as I could figure out, it was the only firearm aboard, Gordey having taken Rustin's gun away with him.

The diesel engine rumbled to life. Still sitting on the floor, I felt the deck vibrating beneath me, and after a thud and a lurch the boat slowly pulled out into the middle of the river. I glanced at my watch. It was just after one in the morning.

Neil was up in the wheelhouse, peering out through the fog and trying not to run the boat aground or into a rock. After pouring a couple of fingers of rye to offset the shock of nearly being shot by Rustin, Yale Rugoff had switched off the cabin lights, leaving only one dim lamp burning, and sat back down in the remaining chair to enjoy the midnight cruise in relative comfort. Doll was occupying the corner that had been hers since Frank first came aboard the boat, what seemed like decades ago, but she had stopped crying and was staring at him, wide-eyed with shock. Ray had managed to squirm around so we could look at each other. They'd dragged Ash Rustin out of the way, into another corner, leaving an unspeakable trail across the floor of the cabin.

"Things have gotten a little out of hand, haven't they, Yale?" I said. "You didn't sign on for this kind of a cruise, did you? Never figured on a bunch of dead bodies."

"Go ahead and talk all you want," he said. "It's your last chance."

"No, it's yours," I said. "Neil was the one who killed Helen Ng, and he'd have to convince a jury he did it on your orders. And he shot Rustin too. They might even make it a case of self-defense. But if you stand by while the three of us go into the river, you're finished."

"They have to prove it first. As far as anyone knows, the last time you and I saw each other was last week at the Blue Iris. And I never laid eyes on your buddy until tonight."

"My name's Ray Tucek," Ray said, twisting his head around to look at Rugoff. "You're going to dump a man in the river, you ought to know his name."

"Nice to meet you," Rugoff said coldly. Maybe he was trying to psyche himself into what he was going to do, or maybe he was what he appeared to be, a guy with no feelings or emotions.

"You're really something, aren't you, Yale?" I said.

He laughed. It came out a dry, throaty yip. "You're so damn smug. Even with an hour to live you think you're better than everybody else. Well, let me tell you something, sucker. My family was one generation removed from living over my grandfather's tailor shop on Fairfax Avenue. I was a fat, homely kid that got beat up a lot—I couldn't even get a woman into bed with me until I was twenty-two years old, and I had to pay her for it at that. She was a Korean girl, by the way—maybe that's why I've got a thing for women from the Far East. I was a lousy student in college, and I'm an even lousier lawyer, and if I didn't do something fast I was going to just disappear."

He waved the gun at me. "Ever feel like you were invisible, Saxon? You got any idea what that's like?"

"And you think killing three people is going to help you see yourself in the bathroom mirror?"

"It didn't start out to be killing! It started out to be a damn good business, and Ash and Helen let me in on it because I had some good ideas, ideas that are going to make me rich."

"Getting the husbands to sign over the property?"

"Damn right!" he said. "We cleared over three hundred grand last year. This year we're going to do ten times better than that, and I'm not going to let it all get blown away by a couple of two-bit gumshoes and a Chinese whore."

Beside me I heard Doll gasp.

"Why don't you let her go, Yale? She's got nothing to do with us."

He sighed. "I can't."

"Come on. She hasn't done anything wrong. She's cooperated with you all the way."

"Be real, Saxon. She could fry me with what she knows."

"All right," I said in a reasonable tone, "so I can't appeal to your compassionate side. I forgot you were a lawyer."

"Shut up about lawyers," he said glumly.

"Then be a good one for once in your life and look at all the different angles. Without Doll, you're screwed."

"How do you figure?"

"You need her to get your hands on Nappy Kane's property."

"That's all you know, Saxon," he said. "She signed an agreement—"

"Which is never going to stand up in court. You just haven't thought it out far enough. Being such a hotshot lawyer, you should know that California is a community property state. If she dies, her property automatically reverts back to her husband."

Some of the color left his face again, and he sucked at his glass of rye, but all it contained was a few drops of residue.

"And even if it didn't," I went on, "if no one finds her body, they can't declare her legally dead for seven years. And that means the estate is frozen." I looked over at Doll and attempted a smile of reassurance. "Alive she's worth nearly three million dollars, Yale—and with your partners gone, it's all yours; there's no one to split it with. But put her in the water and you've got nothing."

He wet his lips again. Poor Yale was having trouble with

cotton mouth. Hiring a hit was one thing; carrying one out himself was quite another.

"Face it, she was scared enough of you to tell you we were coming back for her tonight. You can probably scare her into keeping quiet about—all this." I nodded at Rustin's body. "Especially if you see to it that she gets a taste of that three mill."

Doll made a little noise. I threw a look at her, trying to caution her to keep her mouth shut.

He frowned.

"It's better than nothing, Yale."

"I'll have to think about it," he said.

We both did some thinking. Mine centered on how I could get the Glock away from him and make him eat it, but he was too far away from me, and I was in an awkward position, sitting on the floor. If I made a move toward him, he could blow me away before I got within spitting distance.

I'm not sure why I was refusing to accept the fact that they were going to kill me in less than an hour. Poor Ash Rustin in his corner was palpable proof that they had little compunction about killing.

Maybe it was sheer stupidity. But something lurks in the human soul that will not accept the mortality of its own flesh. Lincoln, Martin Luther King, and the fallen Kennedy brothers, Eleanor Roosevelt, and even Bogart, John Wayne, and Barbara Stanwyck—symbols real or fictional of that which is courageous and unconquerable in the American spirit— are all gone, but to most of us they still live, and in moments of crisis or danger we all think that we share their indomitable qualities and that we're going to live forever.

I don't think I want to hang around quite that long, but I was unready to die on that warm summer night on the

Sacramento River, so I wasn't feeling fear. I was too busy trying to come up with a way out.

Yale Rugoff was occupying himself on the dull boat ride by trying to figure out how he could get rid of Doll Kane and still get his hands on that two million eight.

Perhaps we were both in denial.

Ray and I looked at each other, and he lifted his eyebrows expectantly. Taped up as he was, he knew he'd have to count on me for salvation, and clearly he wasn't happy about it. Ray and I are good friends, but his opinion of my abilities in a tight spot are fairly low.

At that moment, staring down the barrel of the Glock, I wasn't sure I didn't agree with him.

The *China Dream* glided almost soundlessly with the current. We were in mid river, and the chances were good that no one on either shore could hear the hum of the motor, much less spot the boat through the dense fog that covered the windows like a gray curtain. They were all probably asleep, anyway. In rural areas like the delta riverfront towns there isn't much to do after the eleven o'clock news.

After a long period of silence Yale Rugoff said, "Doll? Are you awake?"

She stirred in her corner. She hadn't been asleep, I don't think, but fear and shock had rendered her immobile until the sound of her name caused her to respond.

"I am awake," she answered, uncoiling herself from her fetal ball.

"We have a little problem. You know it, don't you?"
She nodded.

He was still looking at me, still had the drop on me, because I was more likely to give him trouble than the woman was. "The safest thing for me to do is to kill you now.

I don't want to do that. I always liked you."

She stared at him.

"Do you want to live, Doll? Live to be an old lady?"

I shifted my weight; the floor was hard and cold against my butt. "You're enjoying this, aren't you, Yale? Enjoying the hell out of it."

"You be quiet," he told me. "You want to stay alive, don't you, Doll?" He didn't even wait for an answer. "Then we have to make a deal here. Otherwise I'm going to have to get rid of you tonight."

"Please," she said in a voice so small it was barely audible.

"All right then, here it is. As soon as your divorce from Nappy is final, you and I are going to get married."

Doll gasped, putting her small hand to her mouth. Maybe it was to keep from throwing up. It was probably the first marriage proposal on record where the prospective groom was staring fixedly at somebody else.

"I'm impressed, Yale," I said. "A wife can't be forced to testify in court against her husband. "Maybe you're a better lawyer than I thought you were."

"You could do worse, Doll," he said, ignoring me. "We're going to be rich—really rich. "You won't have to live in that old-fogey home anymore; we'll get a really pretty house, maybe in Pacific Palisades. And I'm a lot younger than Nappy. We'll go out a lot. You'll have the kind of fun a young girl your age should be having. I'll really do my best to make it work. I promise."

I looked at Doll. One big tear was trickling down her smooth cheek, tracing a crooked, wet path like a garden snail on a dry sidewalk.

"Say yes, Doll," he sighed. "Please. Otherwise I'm going to have to kill you."

20

"CHRIST, YALE, YOU really are a bottom feeder," I said.

He looked mildly offended. "I'm doing what you said—I'm figuring all the angles. And this way she gets to live. Isn't that what you've been bitching about?"

"I'm not sure that having to sleep with you for the rest of her life could be called living."

An angry flush spread across his face and high forehead, and his fat lips were compressed into a tight line of anger. He shuffled his feet compulsively, and for a moment I thought he was going to get up and come after me, which would at least give me a chance to get the gun away from him. But I was disappointed; he slumped back into the chair, one hand resting listlessly on his thigh.

"You're quite a moralist, aren't you?"

"Compared to you, Joseph Stalin was a moralist."

"Well, fuck you. Doll and I are going to get married and live happily ever after."

There was something very grotesque about a man talking about happily ever after while planning a double murder and holding a loaded gun on his bride-to-be.

"You don't give a damn for her happiness, Yale, and you know it. You don't give a damn for anyone except yourself."

"I object to that," he said as if he was in court. "I'm thinking of what's best for her."

Suddenly Doll uncoiled herself from her corner and got to her feet. Her soft brown eyes glittered with anger. "Not talk about me like I not here!" she said, stamping her foot, and Rugoff and I were so stunned we both shut up.

She put her little fists on her hips. "You treat me like I am just a thing! I am a person."

Rugoff moved around in the chair so that the gun was pointing somewhere between the woman and me. "Doll," I said, "take it easy."

She waved me away, glaring at Rugoff. If looks could kill, they'd be saying Kaddish for him in the morning.

"You better listen to him," Rugoff said when he'd found his voice again. "I don't want to hurt you, Doll."

"I hate you. And I no marry you for anything!"

The poor son of a bitch actually looked as if she'd hurt his feelings. "We'll talk about it later," he said.

"No, now! If you kill me, okay. But I no do anything I no want to, no more."

"You'll do what I tell you! Now go back and sit down."

"No!" she said, her small breasts rising and falling as anger pumped air in and out of her lungs. "No more!" And she advanced on him, ready to scratch his eyes out.

He stood up, throwing an arm up to protect his face when she started slapping him ineffectually with both hands. Off balance, he pushed her away.

That's when I made my move.

Unfortunately, I couldn't get much momentum going from where I was seated on the floor, and the best I could do was grab him around the middle, my head butting into his soft belly. He grunted, but as he stumbled backward he was able to bring the muzzle of the Glock down on the back of my head. It glanced off my skull, and I could feel my scalp split. It wasn't enough to knock me out, but it slowed me down enough that I loosened my grip. He stepped back and kicked me in the chest, knocking the wind out of me. By the time I was able to draw a breath he was leveling the gun at me again.

"I'll kill you both right here, I swear!" he panted.

The sound of the houseboat's diesel had changed slightly, become more muffled. Before, I was able to hear its echoes bouncing back off the riverbank on either side. Now, several miles downriver of San Angelo, we had gotten closer to the inlet, and the river had widened considerably as it prepared to spill out into the Pacific. The noise of a pistol shot or two probably wouldn't be heard at all out here; I didn't want to deal away the few minutes I had left to live. I sat back against the bulkhead, my chest throbbing along with the rest of me now, and fingered the bloody place on my head, mentally kicking myself in the ass for missing what might very well have been my last chance.

But I was damn proud of Doll Kane, and I smiled over at her and gave her a thumbs-up so she'd know it. She returned the smile with a defiant little nod, standing in her corner with her arms folded across her chest, breathing deeply in anger and fear.

"Get this through your heads, all of you!" Rugoff shouted, his voice cracking like an adolescent's. "I'm running things! Everybody has to do what I say, because I'm the one with the gun!" He sounded whiny again, even petulant. Doll's surprise rebellion had shaken him badly, and now he was desperately trying to take control again.

It suddenly occurred to me that it was a pretty hollow

threat. Yale Rugoff, sweating profusely and holding my Glock with a trembling hand, wasn't about to shoot anyone. He didn't have the guts. Guys like him never do. That's why he had Neil around, to do the wet work.

Of course, if I was reading him wrong he'd put a hole through me wide enough to sail the *China Dream* through without bumping the sides. But maybe I could use his desperation to drive a wedge in.

"You're lucky you have that gun, Yale," I said, "because without it, you're pretty pathetic."

"Shut your mouth!" He felt behind him for the chair with his free hand and sank back down into it, deflating like a punctured inner tube.

Ray decided to chime in from his position on the floor. "If someone would rather die than marry me, I'd probably wave a gun around too."

"It makes him feel like a man," I taunted. "The nicest thing about a gun is it always stays hard."

Rugoff looked from Ray to me, his face beet red and the perspiration running into his eyes. "God damn you both to hell," he screamed.

After that things went down so quickly that to this day I'm not sure exactly what happened. But the outside hatch burst open and a pair of Reebok basketball shoes came flying in, hitting Yale Rugoff square between the shoulders and knocking him forward out of his chair. The impact jarred the gun loose, and it skittered across the deck and came to rest between the dainty feet of Doll Kane.

Sometimes when you see someone you know very well out of context, in a place you've never seen them before, where they aren't supposed to be, like when you find your favorite bartender in church or your urologist at a basketball game, your brain isn't able to compute it right away. That's why it took several moments before I realized that my son, Marvel, had just made a surprise appearance in the main cabin of the *China Dream* and had taken Yale Rugoff out with one of his long-practiced but never before used karate kicks.

He stopped for only a moment to flash me a big smile, and then, as Rugoff scrambled for the gun, pivoted and swung his leg sideways, up into the lawyer's jaw. The crack was almost as loud as the pistol shots had been, and poor old Yale went down like a wooden duck at a carnival shooting gallery. Those martial arts lessons were paying off.

The door to the wheelhouse opened and Neil came charging into the cabin to help his boss, but the sight of Marvel, whom he'd never laid eyes on before, made him hesitate for a second. That gave Ray time to roll himself over once, putting him right in the bodyguard's path. Neil stumbled over him, and, waving his arms wildly, he fell flat on his nose right in front of me.

I moved fast, ignoring the aches and pains that had seemed to blend into one big one all over my body. I put a knee in the small of his back and brought my elbow down hard on the back of his neck, making him grunt. Remembering how he'd smacked me around, I did it again, mashing his nose into the floor. After the third time, Marvel took four long steps across the cabin and grabbed my arm.

"No sense in killin' the man. You made your point," he said quietly. With authority.

By this time Doll had snatched up the gun and was pointing it at Marvel. It was too large for her hands.

"Okay, you don't move!" she ordered.

I realized she'd never laid eyes on him. "No, it's all right,"

I said quickly, hoping I could stop her before she shot him dead.

Thank God she hesitated.

"It's all right, Doll," I repeated. "This is my son."

She looked from my fair, green-eyed face to Marvel's coffee brown, dark-eyed one. The gun didn't waver. "Sure," she said.

I stared up at him. Offering me his hand, he pulled me to my feet. I was feeling pretty shaky and leaned on him for support.

"You want to tell me what the hell you're doing here, Marvel?"

"Love to, ol'-timer, but I don't think it's a priority right now."

"Why?"

He shook his head sadly. "Because there's nobody driving this boat."

"Get Ray loose," I said, and hustled into the wheelhouse. The steering wheel was wavering back and forth as if a ghost were piloting the ship, and I grabbed hold to steady it, squinting out through the dense fog. With no lights, the visibility was practically zero, and the spiderweb mist was curling around the windows. Looking frantically at the unfamiliar controls in the cockpit, I managed to find the switch for the spotlight. I flipped it on, and a bright beam cut through the mist, lighting up the fog nicely, but not much else. Finally a puff of a breeze dissipated the mist in front of the bow and I was able to discern where we were. The fast-moving current had picked up the *China Dream* and was hurtling it right toward the high dark shadows of the west bank, where a row of large jagged rocks at the waterline was waiting to rip out the bottom in another twenty feet.

Where were the damn brakes on these things?

For the first time that evening I felt panic clutching my chest. My palms dripping the sweat of fear, I spun the wheel to the left. The boat gave a lurch and a groan; something scraped at the hull back in the stern, but I didn't hear anything break apart or tear. The engine coughed and stuttered for a moment, and the deck vibrated beneath my feet. Then slowly the bow swung around and we were heading straight downriver again. I held on to the wheel tightly. It was the only thing that was keeping me upright.

Ray came up behind me in the wheelhouse, rubbing his wrists and flexing his fingers. "I thought we were gonna buy the farm there for a while," he said.

"Are you all right?"

He nodded. "Except that tape pulled out every damn hair when it came off." He peered out the window. "You know what the hell you're doing up here, sailor?"

"No," I admitted.

He moved in front of me and took the wheel. "Then why don't you go aft," he said, "and I'll take this thing back to San Angelo."

I started through the door.

"Hey, Saxon," he said.

"What?" I asked, turning.

He looked over his shoulder at me. "You might think about telling the kid thanks."

I went back into the cabin. Either Doll or Marvel had finally gone below and taken a bedsheet off one of the bunks and covered Ash Rustin's body with it. Marvel was busily taping the unconscious Neil's hands behind his back with the much-depleted roll of duct tape. Doll had given him the Glock, presumably of her own free will, and he had tucked it into his white Dockers, the butt protruding over the waistband. He looked like an African-American version of Alan Ladd in *Botany Bay*.

"You'd better give me that," I said, "before you shoot off something you might need."

He gave me one of his patented looks and gazed heavenward for succor, but he took the pistol from his waistband, twirled it expertly, and handed it to me butt first as he'd seen in a million old Westerns on television.

"Don't let anybody take it away from you again, now," he scolded, his grin blunting the sharp point of the needle. "That's an expensive gun. Money doesn't grow on trees, y'know." He knelt and finished with Neil, and then he went to work on Yale. The lawyer was still unconscious, but when Marvel jerked his arms behind him he groaned.

"I think I broke his jaw," Marvel said, and it was almost an apology.

"That'll shoot down his law career for sure." I turned to Doll, who was sitting on the floor again, as far from Ash Rustin's body as she could get. "Nice going, Doll," I said.

She looked up at me and allowed herself the ghost of a smile, for the first time since I'd met her. "Nice going you too," she offered.

I watched Marvel for a minute. He was doing a thorough, professional job of wrapping up my enemies, and I suppose the swelling that seemed to be blocking my throat was a physical manifestation of pride. There were all sorts of appropriate things to say, but I couldn't think of a single one. "I guess you know I owe you one, Marvel," I finally managed.

"Owed you one for about five years," he said quietly, not looking up from his work. Then he glanced up at me and smiled. "So I s'pose if you kiss my ring every morning from now on and refer to me as Your Majesty, we can call it even." He chewed that over for a while and then said, "Or you can forget about all that and just buy me a red Corvette."

I slumped into a chair, suddenly very tired. We were making a U-turn in the middle of the river, and the motion was beginning to make me sick. "Would I seem like a total ingrate if I reminded you that I told you to stay out of this?"

"Yep," he said. He'd finished taping Yale's wrists and began working on his ankles.

"Does that mean I have no right to ask you what the hell you're doing up here when I thought you were safe at home in Venice, or how you got onto this boat?"

"No right at all."

"Would you humor me, then? As a favor?"

He straightened up, wiping his hands on his jeans, and thought it over for a minute. "Guess I could," he said magnanimously. "As a favor."

After taking a while to get his thoughts in order, he said crisply, "Okay. I called your hotel this afternoon, and they said you'd checked out. I didn't know where you were, and that got me worried. So I jumped in the car and drove up here. Man, that rental Geo is a piece of shit."

"After the other night, I didn't think you'd ever want to drive a car again."

"It's like gettin' thrown off a horse," he said. "You gotta get right back on. Anyway, when I got to Isleton, I checked every motel along the river, and nobody'd ever heard of you, but I finally found the one Ray was stayin' at, just after midnight. You guys weren't there, 'course. So I remembered your telling me about this boat, and I started drivin' around lookin' for it. When I found the marina I looked around and I saw Ray's car parked up that road a ways, and another car with an Avis sticker on it, so I just guessed you were aboard.

"I parked and walked down here just in time to see the police chief haulin' that big mother off the boat, and I figured you'd run into somethin' you couldn't handle. So I drove down the road a piece to the nearest telephone and called the highway patrol and told 'em what was goin' down. They didn't believe me at first, but I told 'em to check with Sergeant Gelarden in Castaic while I held on. They did, and said they'd be right there. So I went back to the marina to wait for 'em." He snorted. "Probably there by now."

"You better hope they are, and not Gordey and Harbottle."

He shrugged. "Then the boat started up and I figured I was gonna lose you. So I jumped aboard just as you were pullin' away, and I laid out on the deck, looking in the window. The fog was so thick nobody could see me out there. I saw the dead guy, and Ray all trussed up and you lookin' like you'd just been dragged a mile by wild horses. I knew you were in trouble, so I just waited for the right time to come in." He gave a langorous stretch. "Timing is everything."

"He had a gun," I said. "You could've been killed."

He shrugged. "That's why you paid for all those karate lessons."

"Nevertheless—"

"Chill out, okay? You'd've done the same for me, right?"

"Right—but I'm supposed to. I'm the father."

"Well, I'm the son," he said, "and I didn't want to see you turned into the Holy Ghost."

He cut off my protest with a wave of his hand. "I told you,

263

growin' up on the streets, you do what you have to do. Did you want me to just let 'em kill you?"

I sighed, my head pounding. "I guess we can talk about this later."

On the floor Neil was coming to. He wriggled around a little. "Shit," he said, the word coming out muffled through his ruined mouth.

Marvel glanced down at him, unconcerned, then back at me. "Do I get to ask a question now?"

"I guess you've earned that, sure."

He leaned in close to me. "What's the deal with the hair?" he said.

21

MARVEL WAS RIGHT; the CHP was out in force, waiting for us at the marina when we got back. The live-aboards from the other houseboats all came out in their robes and slippers and stood grumpily on their decks, their annoyance at being awakened in the middle of the night warring with the insatiable curiosity of people everywhere when the cops come out to kick some serious butt. I think they got their money's worth. I'm not sure what gave them the bigger charge—Yale and Neil disembarking in chains or Ash Rustin being off-loaded in a plastic body bag.

It was a night they could gleefully reconstruct for their grandchildren.

Despite a broken jaw that hung grotesquely to one side, making his face look like one of those rubber Halloween masks, Yale Rugoff started singing like a canary even before they took the duct tape off his wrists and replaced it with handcuffs. Hoping for a plea bargain, he incriminated everyone he'd ever met, and a few he hadn't, including Mother Teresa, the CIA, and the military-industrial complex, which will now have something new to worry about besides the Oliver Stone movie about J.F.K.

I declined a ride to the hospital; I wasn't much worse than

banged up and sore, and since I hadn't gotten any sleep at all that night, all I wanted was a hot shower to wash the blood out of my hair and cool sheets. But I'd have to spend several hours at the highway patrol headquarters in Isleton first.

With all Ray and I told them about what had happened aboard the *China Dream* and Yale Rugoff's almost compulsive *mea culpas*, the state police kicked it into high gear. Chief Briley Gordey and Officer Steve Harbottle were arrested on too many different criminal charges to enumerate and incarcerated in the California Highway Patrol lockup, which was, I'm sure, no more hospitable than their own. Yale was sent to the prison ward of the Yolo County Hospital, where they wired his jaw back together, and several days later he was indicted on three counts of attempted murder, as well as for ordering another killing by contract, kidnapping, and running a house of prostitution. His pal Neil, who was in the next room recuperating from having his face smashed into the floor of the boat's cabin, was also under heavy guard and eventually was charged with the murders of Ash Rustin and Helen Ng Rustin. Frank, who had been taken to the emergency ward by Gordey and Harbottle, would have to face an attempted murder rap for screwing with my brakes, just as soon as his punctured lungs and shattered sternum healed.

The *China Dream*, which was registered to Ashford and Helen Ng Rustin, was impounded by the state.

When it was all finished, Ray drove back to Los Angeles to compute how big a bill he was going to submit to Nappy Kane. Marvel and I went with Doll to Rustin's house to gather up her belongings and the white Acura Legend, then caravaned back to Sacramento, where we turned in the rented Geo to Avis and booked two hotel rooms, too exhausted and emotionally wrung out to even think about making the long trip back home without a good night's sleep.

I called Nappy Kane and gave him the short version of what happened.

"Is Doll going to come back to me?" he asked.

"I'm bringing her back to Los Angeles, Nappy. What happens after that is between the two of you."

He didn't say anything for a minute. Then, in a voice more suited to a small boy than a fast-talking Vegas comic, he said, "What do you think, though? Do I have a chance?"

I thought back over our boat trip. "There's always a chance," I said.

There was something I needed to do before we went back to Los Angeles. Doll and Marvel decided to take a tour of Old Sac and have breakfast in one of the many restaurants on the waterfront. When I let them out of the car, they looked like two kids on a honeymoon. They were a lot closer in age than she and her husband were, and I had a few misgivings about plopping her back into the middle of that situation. But I wasn't getting paid for making decisions about other people's lives. I'd done my job, and that was that.

I took the car over to the farming community of Woodland, the Yolo County seat, which seemed to consist of not much more than the county building, sprawling farms, and the ubiquitous shopping mall, where well-to-do farmers and ranchers stalked the corridors in bib overalls and two-hundred-dollar Stetsons. I spent an hour in the county records department, wishing that I'd brought my reading glasses, until I uncovered a piece of information that confirmed a suspicion I'd been harboring almost from the beginning.

Then I went back and picked up my two passengers and began the boring drive down I-5. I was getting so familiar with the long, straight highway that I could have done it with my eyes closed.

As we went down the Grapevine and passed the runaway truck ramp where Marvel and I had almost cashed it in, I *did* do it with my eyes closed—well, averted, anyway. It would be a long while before I'd make that drive without shuddering.

We got to Venice at about eight thirty that night. I let Marvel off at the house and headed north up Pacific Avenue to Santa Monica, where Doll and Nappy maintained their condo. The coastal fog hung about twenty feet above the ground and was turning the streetlights into fluffy dandelions, but it was nothing compared to the tule fog of the delta.

I had to struggle through the underground parking garage in the Kane's building to the elevator with all Doll's luggage. Nappy had bought her a lot of clothes during their brief marriage, and they'd all made the round trip to San Angelo and back. There was barely enough room in the elevator for the two of us by the time I was through, and the back of my shirt stuck to me like a second skin.

I rang the bell, and after a minute Nappy opened the door. He was wearing a dark blue silk lounging robe over tan slacks and a light blue shirt, and he had a drink in his hand. From the slightly vacant look in his eyes, I had the idea it wasn't his first of the evening, or even his second. Day-old stubble was poking its way through the Max Factor grease-paint.

"Saxon!" he said, slurring the *S* a little and spilling some of his drink. He stared at the swelling under my eye. "What happened, you run into a door? So come on, tell me, what's the . . . "

I stepped aside so he could see his wife, looking small and timid behind me.

"Hey, Doll," he said softly. His face was transformed into one resembling the photo of a kitten on a kitchen calendar.

I hefted three of the suitcases and edged past him into the living room, depositing them in the middle of the carpet. When I turned back, neither of the Kanes had moved. Doll was still standing out in the hall, and they were staring at one another like two beings from different solar systems.

"Are you going to invite her in, Nappy?"

He jumped as if someone had touched him with a cattle prod. "Oh, sure. I mean, I don't have to invite . . . it's her house too."

He stepped back and held out a hand. Doll picked up her remaining suitcase and allowed him to lead her into the living room. Nappy let go of her hand, and now all three of us were in the staring contest.

"Missed you, babe," Nappy said, his voice husky. The confidence and bravado of the Vegas lounge comic had suddenly deserted him, and he spoke like a postadolescent swain.

She didn't answer, but looked miserably down at her feet, her cheeks blushing an appealing pink. Somewhere in the room a clock was ticking, and the air conditioner hummed softly like Muzak in an elevator.

"Well . . ." I said.

Nappy suddenly realized I was still in the room. "Hey, Saxon, I owe you some money." He started for the den and presumably his checkbook.

"Later, Nappy. You two have some things to talk over. Why don't you call me tomorrow?"

He waved his glass at me. "Stay and have a drink, at least. Help us celebrate."

I shook my head. Now that he finally had his Doll back again, Nappy Kane was obviously terrified of being alone with her. And Doll clearly wasn't looking forward to the confession she was going to have to make. I think they both would have been glad to have me stay there and party for a week, just to postpone their moment of truth.

"Celebrate together," I suggested, and headed toward the still-open door.

"Listen," Nappy said, hurrying after me. He put his sweating hand on my arm. "I'm not real good at doing sincerity shtick, but I want you to know——"

"It's okay," I said, trying to extricate myself from his slippery grasp. I lowered my voice so Doll couldn't hear me. "Save the sincerity for your wife. Be as kind and understanding as you can, Nappy. And for once, no jokes."

He looked stricken. "No jokes?" he said, bewildered. "How in hell'm I s'posed to talk?"

I left them cocooned in one of the most dense silences I'd ever encountered. I didn't envy either of them.

It was just as well Mindy Minor wasn't working on *Love Conquers All* the next day. I hadn't made the trek all the way out to Triangle to see her anyway. The smog hanging over the Burbank hills was a brownish-yellow scrim in front of my eyes. My sinuses kicked up the minute I got out of the car, and I had to blow my nose rather violently before going into the building.

On the set in studio C, Quinn was wearing a blue suit and

arguing with an older actor I'd never seen before. The story line had something to do with shares in the company reverting to baby Lacey, but I didn't really take it in. I was giving up soap operas for the duration. I went back out into the corridor and made my way to the dressing room Rebecca Cho shared with Mindy.

Rebecca was wearing a silk kimono tied at the waist, and she didn't look happy to see me when she answered my knock. As a matter of fact, the first thing she did was threaten to call security and have me thrown out on my ass. And that's a direct quote.

"Go right ahead," I said. "I have another stop to make anyway. At the *National Enquirer.*"

That slowed her down.

"Why should that concern me?" she said, but her voice had a quiver to it that hadn't been there before. The tabloid press could strike fear into the heart of a saint, and celebrities of every rank shifted their eyes nervously and broke into a polite sweat at the thought of finding their names on the front pages.

"You want to talk about it out here in the hall where everyone can hear, or are you going to invite me in?"

"I have nothing to say to you."

"I have plenty to say to you, lady," I said with as much of a snarl as I could muster. "But I'd just as soon go to the press with it."

She sucked in a deep breath as if she hadn't had one in hours, then did a brisk about-face and walked into the room, leaving me to follow. I shut the door behind me.

She sat down on the sofa and crossed her long golden legs, the kimono falling open to mid thigh, but it wasn't meant to be sexy or enticing, and anyway I was in no mood to be vamped. I leaned against the door.

"The gravy train doesn't stop here anymore, Rebecca."

Her eyes were black marbles. She didn't ask me what I meant. She didn't have to; she'd obviously heard from Yale.

"After I turned your ex-husband and his chums over to the authorities I stopped off at the Yolo County seat and looked up the articles of incorporation for Asian Nights. And guess whose name I found right along with the Rustins and Yale Rugoff as a part owner?"

Her nostrils flared.

"I'm glad to see that unlike a lot of actors and actresses, you've made some wise investments, Rebecca."

"So what? I also own stock in Disney and AT&T. Asian Nights is a perfectly legitimate introduction service."

"Asian Nights is a perfectly illegitimate front for both a house of prostitution and a really ugly lonely hearts scam, and you know it."

She looked away from me, the muscles at the hinge of her jaw working as she ground her teeth. "I don't know anything of the sort," she said. "And you'll never prove that I do." She didn't carry it off quite as well as Bette Davis used to, but it was good enough.

"Nappy Kane told me that you and Doll had known each other in Hong Kong," I said. "But when I asked you, you said you'd run into her in the ladies' room. Somebody was lying to me, and I can't think of single reason to suspect it was Nappy."

She just looked at me.

"Maybe you lied because you were the one that recruited her for Asian Nights and you didn't want me finding out about that."

"Doll is the daughter of an old family friend," she said. "She wanted to come to America and I helped her out, that's all. It was none of your business then; it still isn't."

"A family friend," I said. "Jesus, that makes it even worse. Exploiting strangers is one thing, but a friend?"

She stood up. "I don't have to talk to you anymore, and I'm not going to," she snapped, going to the door and yanking it open. "Get out—and don't come back. If you do, I'll get a court order to make sure you stay away from me."

"I don't think you will, Rebecca."

"Why not?"

"You've got too much to lose. I've worked as an actor here at Triangle several times. I've read the standard contract. It always contains a morals clause."

Her hand went to the neck of the kimono, pulling it closed.

"I wonder how they'll feel about one of their biggest soap opera stars being a madame? Bringing young girls over here from Asia and making them work at Far East Massage in San Angelo, California?"

She stood framed in the doorway for a moment. Beyond her I could see a harried stage manager, scurrying down the corridor, one hand to his earpiece and the other clutching a clipboard. She glanced over her shoulder at him and then slammed the door shut again, leaning against it, her small breasts rising and falling beneath the silk. All at once she looked tired. And old.

"Probably about the same way they'd feel if they found out she once worked as a whore in that same massage parlor," she said in what was almost a whisper.

The English muffin and coffee I'd had for breakfast that morning turned into a hot rock in my stomach. I should have figured it out, but I'd been so intent on bringing the whole Asian Nights operation to ruin that it had never really occurred to me. I didn't say anything. She obviously wasn't finished.

She went past me to the dressing table and fumbled in a drawer for a moment, then turned back to me.

"You wouldn't happen to have a cigarette, would you?"

I took out my pack and shook one loose for her. She lit it herself, having managed to turn up a book of matches in the drawer.

"I studied English in Hong Kong until I could speak almost without an accent," she said, twin jets of smoke issuing from her nostrils. "All I ever wanted to do was come to America and be an actress. But I couldn't seem to get a visa or a work permit. One of my friends told me about Asian Nights, and I thought it wouldn't be so bad to marry an American and have some financial help while I was trying to break into television. So I signed up, and Ash Rustin brought me to San Angelo. All I knew was that it was in California, and I thought it would be close enough to Hollywood so I could work on my career. I didn't know what I was getting into until I got there."

She was reciting in a flat monotone, as if she were summarizing the plot of a script. There was no self-pity in it; Rebecca Cho was obviously way beyond that particular emotion.

"I was stuck. I owed the Rustins too much money to leave, and anyway I had nowhere to go. I figured I was better off in the massage parlor than running off to Hollywood and having to sell it on the street. So I stayed. For a while."

"Until you met Yale Rugoff," I said.

She nodded. "He used to bring me down here on weekends, just like he does with little Rose now. But there was a difference. There's nothing quite as pathetic as a wimp in love, is there? But after a while he couldn't stand the thought of me being with other men, and so he did what he had to do. He married me."

"And you moved down to Los Angeles and started making the rounds of casting directors."

"I didn't really need to, at least not like a lot of actresses who show up in L.A. and have to start pounding pavement. Yale knew people who knew people—John Garafalo, for one. So pretty soon I started getting small parts on TV. And Yale paid for my singing lessons too."

"A pretty good deal," I observed.

"Easy to say—you didn't have to fuck him. Or wake up looking at him in the morning. Fish his fallen-out hair out of the sink. Or listen to his bullshit."

"How did you get out?"

She took another deep drag on the cigarette, looking around for an ashtray. Finding none, she walked into the adjoining bathroom, where I heard the butt hiss itself out in the toilet.

"By using my head," she said, coming out into the dressing room again. "I had just landed this job. It doesn't pay as well as nighttime TV, but it's still a lot more than most people make, and my character became very popular, so I had a little financial security. I didn't need Yale to support me anymore; I had a little leverage for the first time in my life, and some time to think things over. And I figured myself out an insurance policy."

She lowered herself gracefully onto the sofa again, and I half sat on the edge of the dressing table and folded my arms across my chest, waiting.

"Ash Rustin was a low-level pimp, and Yale can barely count to twenty-one without taking off his shoes and pants. You think either of them was sharp enough to come up with the idea of marrying off the Asian Nights girls and then arranging for the complete transfer of marital property into their names? Give me a break!"

"Yale told me it was his idea," I said. "So you bartered the idea for a divorce?"

"Not exactly. I told him that if he didn't cut me in as a full partner I'd go to the state bar association and tell them how he was running a whorehouse in San Angelo. Yale is only afraid of two things—disbarment, and not being able to get it up at night. So he lost a wife and gained one hell of a partner. It was a good deal for both of us. And for Chief Gordey and his boys too." She laughed bitterly. "Everyone gets a little piece. Isn't that how it works?"

"It didn't bother you that it was a con game that broke up marriages before they even had a chance? To say nothing of being illegal."

The sound she made can only be described as a derisive snort. "Whoring is illegal too. So is slavery, and I was the victim of both. As far as that goes, just about everyone at this network does cocaine or some other drug, or has a thing for little girls or little boys or something else that could land them in jail if anyone found out. What's legal or illegal isn't even a consideration in this fucking town."

"Is what's moral or immoral a consideration in this fucking town, Rebecca?"

"Don't make me laugh," she said.

"Making people laugh is Nappy Kane's department."

Her lip curled into a snarl. "And mine is taking control of my own life."

"Taking control of your life cost the Rustins theirs," I said. "And it almost cost me mine—and my son's."

"I didn't have anything to do with that," she said, the edge suddenly off her voice. "You've got to believe me when I tell you I didn't even know about it."

"Not directly," I said. "But I wouldn't say your hands are completely clean."

"I haven't been clean since I had to spread my legs for any yahoo with fifty bucks burning a hole in his pocket—plus Yale and Gordey and his boys and that fat slob Frank." She shuddered. "You have any idea how dirty that made me feel?"

"But it doesn't bother you to force other poor girls like Doll and Rose—practically children—into doing the same thing?"

She gave a nonchalant shrug. "I do what I have to do."

"Yep," I nodded. "Me, too." I pushed myself off the edge of the dressing table and took a step toward the door.

"Wait a minute!" she ordered like someone used to command. "What do you want, Saxon? Money?"

"No, I have some of that."

"What, then?"

"You don't have anything I want, Rebecca."

"Don't be so sure," she warned. "Look, you're an actor, right? How would you like a steady gig on this show? I can fix it for you—just a word or two in the producer's ear the next time we're going to introduce a character. It's easy work, and the money is terrific." She smiled. "Then you wouldn't have to scratch around peeping through keyholes to make a living."

I smiled back. "Yeah, sometimes what I do makes me feel pretty dirty too. But I usually know how to get clean again."

"Everyone has a price," she snapped.

"I'd like to think that isn't true," I said. "But you're probably right."

Her face changed, becoming softer, warmer. Seductive. She stood up slowly, uncoiling herself from the sofa like a golden cat. "Maybe we could still negotiate." Her hands went to the tie of her kimono. It fell open. All she wore beneath it were a pair of tiny white lace bikini panties. Her body took my breath away.

"Think about it, Saxon. A lump payment now, a running part on the show that'll pay you eight or nine thousand a week—and me. Right now, and tomorrow, and whenever and however you want it." Shrugging the robe off her shoulders so that it hung from her elbows, she moved langorously toward me. Her breasts were small and perfect, her nipples hard. "And you do want it, don't you, handsome? Slow and easy at first, and then I'll do whatever you want."

When she got within reach I gently pulled the kimono up around her and tied the belt at her waist, as if I were dressing a small child.

"Rebecca," I said, "that wasn't even a good try."

And I left her there and headed up to Jay Dean's office to spill my guts.

22

WHEN I TOLD Jay Dean about Rebecca Cho's involvement in the prostitution and fraud ring in San Angelo, he almost had a heart attack. Jay's longevity at the network was due in large measure to his uncanny ability to stay out of the line of fire, and imparting this tidbit of scandal to him had put him in a rather precarious position.

"Why me, guy?" he asked tightly, and almost bit through the stem of his ever-present pipe.

Duty outweighed caution in this case, and after making me take a blood oath of *omerta,* of silence, he duly reported it to his superiors. The legal department at Triangle fudged and fussed and dithered for several weeks and finally invoked the morals clause in Rebecca's contract and relieved her of her duties on *Love Conquers All,* writing her out of the show by means of an off-screen death in a plane crash.

The two trade papers, *Variety* and the *Hollywood Reporter,* kept mum about the reason for the firing, in keeping with the tradition that the show business community's dirty linen is not for public display. "Rebecca Cho will be moving on to other areas," they said, although that has become such an overused euphemism in Hollywood that it didn't fool anyone.

But even though I kept my mouth shut, as promised, Rebecca's abrupt and unexplained departure from the program was too big a story to keep the lid on, and within two weeks of her last appearance, the lurid details were plastered all over the tabloids in big headlines for supermarket shoppers to see and cluck their tongues about. *The Los Angeles Times* picked up the story the next day and ran with it like Jim Brown on an open field.

The item caught the eye of a sleazeball movie producer named Sherwin Mandelker, with whom I'd had quite a run-in several years ago. A man who gets off on reading his own name in the paper even when the reference is a negative one and never one to miss the beat of publicity drums, Mandelker announced the next month that he had signed Rebecca Cho to a four-picture deal, the first of which was a big-budget epic about the approaching reversion of Hong Kong to the Chinese in 1997.

Rebecca was asked to sing the national anthem at the Los Angeles Raiders' home opener, and received a standing ovation for her trouble. I don't think everyone who was applauding was a patriot, either. All the world loves a scoundrel.

Yale Rugoff drew three nonconsecutive ten-to-twenty-year leases on one of the state of California's hospitality suites at San Quentin. The state bar association quietly hit the delete button on his license to practice law. Neil joined Yale at the same facility, but his sentence was for life.

Chief Briley Gordey, of San Angelo's finest, drew a five-year sentence in a minimum-security prison near San Jose, the trial judge mercifully reasoning that if he were to be incarcerated with felons convicted of more violent crimes, his lot as an ex-policeman in the general prison population would be a hard one, to put it very mildly.

Deputy Steve Harbottle served nine months of a one-year sentence in the same correctional facility. Upon his release he went to New Jersey and obtained employment as an all-night security guard at a 7-Eleven and was shot in the chest by a crazed crackhead in the course of a robbery. He received a full-disability pension and moved to Florida.

I never did find out what happened to Frank.

Nappy and Doll Kane apparently resolved their differences. They stayed married, in any case. Nappy was hired by ABC for a January replacement sitcom as the ex-vaudevillian father of three beautiful daughters, and along about the twelfth episode he managed to get me a week's work as the reluctant suitor of one of his offspring. That of course was after the orange tint finally washed out of my hair.

He was nominated for an Emmy, and his career enjoyed a sudden resurgence comparable to that of George Burns after his triumph in *The Sunshine Boys*. He signed a five-year contract for ten weeks annually at Caesar's Palace, and he worked up a comedy act similar to the one he'd had with Jerry Cahill, with another Italian boy singer, who happened to be the nephew of John Garafalo, with whom Nappy had obviously resumed his business relationship.

The old Hollywood saw, "I'll never work with that son of a bitch again unless I need him," springs to mind.

My insurance company opted to repair my car rather than declare it a total loss. It's never really run properly again, having developed a shimmy at speeds in excess of fifty miles an hour, which is a damn inconvenience because I drive faster than that sometimes.

Ray Tucek got a job as stunt coordinator on a cops-and-robbers series on CBS, which lasted about six weeks and was replaced by a "reality-based" crime show.

When the writers of *Love Conquers All* decided to take the story line in a different direction and wrote out Mindy Minor's role, she gave up show business and went back home to Minnesota, where she reenrolled in the university and eventually got a master's degree in economics.

Roger Karpfinger, the brain who walks like a man, was awarded a full four-year science scholarship at Stanford. His mother Bettyann, now freed from the full-time care and feeding of her only son, started dating an engineer, with whom she eventually moved in.

Marvel chose to continue his education at nearby El Camino College, a nearby junior college, taking an eclectic variety of courses since he still didn't know what career path he wanted to follow. Two things he was sure of after our adventure in San Angelo—he no longer had a jones for lemon chicken or anything else Chinese, and that he didn't want to be a lawyer.

Even though El Camino is a commuter school, Marvel elected to share an apartment close to the campus with three other guys, coming home only on weekends and for an occasional visit in the middle of the week—especially those evenings when I'm having a dinner party and I cook something he particularly likes. It's nice to have some privacy again.

Most men have unfinished business with their fathers—I certainly did, and I didn't resolve it until I was nearly forty years old. I'm glad the Nappy Kane case gave Marvel a chance to close a few circles with me, and to pay back a perceived debt that I wouldn't have called in in a million years.

I miss him very much.

And me? Like Ol' Man River, I just keep rolling along.